BACK TO HOPE

Deirdre Santesso

For Frank, my love, and for Aaron, Rachel, and Nathan, my inspiration.

FriesenPress

Suite 300 - 990 Fort St
Victoria, BC, Canada, V8V 3K2
www.friesenpress.com

Copyright © 2015 by Deirdre Santesso
First Edition — 2015

All rights reserved.

No part of this publication may be reproduced in any form, or by any means, electronic or mechanical, including photocopying, recording, or any information browsing, storage, or retrieval system, without permission in writing from the publisher.

All characters in this publication are fictitious and any resemblance to real persons, living or dead, is purely coincidental. Both the town of Blanchette and the village of LaPierre exist only in the author's imagination.

ISBN
978-1-4602-6506-2 (Hardcover)
978-1-4602-6507-9 (Paperback)
978-1-4602-6508-6 (eBook)

1. Fiction, Cultural Heritage

Distributed to the trade by The Ingram Book Company

PART ONE

CHAPTER ONE

The place was so far removed from the rest of the world that those few who reached it kept it forever in their memory. Some felt compelled to return, even after many years, perhaps to make sure that it was more than just a place of their imagining. Not that it was without history. There was a lake, Sturgeon Lake, large and deep and dangerous, where the native people had fished for salmon for a thousand years or more, and beside it the small town of Blanchette, once a major fur-trading centre. Beyond was nothing but dense forest and rivers and more lakes.

If you had access to a floatplane, you could fly into Blanchette and land on the water. If you were an Indian from one of the villages further up the lake, you could reach it by boat or, in winter, by sled and snowshoes. White people, apart from the few who actually lived there, most often drove the one hundred miles of unpaved highway from Prince George and entered the town by way of a wooden bridge that spanned the narrow lake head. At the end of that bridge was the sawmill, and those who arrived at night were met by the sight of the beehive burner lit up from within, spitting fiery sparks into the darkness like a mediaeval vision of hell. That was how I had remembered it, and that was the way I found it when I went back there in August of 1967, five years after my first visit. While the world around it had been undergoing radical change, Blanchette had stayed the same.

The mid-sixties were a time of upheaval everywhere, especially in the Catholic Church. Suddenly there was no more Latin, no more fish on Fridays, no more fasting before Communion, and no more Limbo—that sad, mythical region where the souls of unbaptized babies were cast adrift forever. The Church had been turned upside down, and Catholics had no choice but to go along with the changes or to drop out. Looking back now at that turbulent decade, I recall the question posed by *Time* magazine: "Is God Dead?"

I can't speak for all of Christianity, but there were many Catholics who answered with their feet. The jovial Pope John XXXIII had opened up the windows of the Church, and the not so faithful used them to exit an institution that had grown stifling and had begun to fester from within. They left in droves, priests and laity alike, taking with them a spiritual hunger that the Church had failed to satisfy. And then, liberated from the confines and restrictions of Catholicism, they looked for enlightenment elsewhere, with the Beatles leading the way in a merry, marijuana- induced cosmic dance, Maharishi Mahesh Yogi in tow, chortling into his beard.

There was a time when I had thought about joining them, but instead I went back to Blanchette. People told me I was crazy, that I was squandering my talent, wasting my life, turning my back on a promising career, but I was done with listening. I had learned that the sensible choice is not always the best choice. The safe path I had chosen had brought me to this place of uncertainty, and now I entered it willingly and hopefully. I did not know what I would find at the end of the road, but I believed that only by going back would I discover the way forward.

I set out from Vancouver on a hot day in the middle of August and left the Lower Mainland behind me at Hope, first established as a Hudson Bay Company fort and used for years as a fur brigade outpost. I liked it for its name. Hope is a good thing, and on that day I had plenty of it. After Hope came Yale, at one time the largest city west of Chicago and north of San Francisco; then Boston Bar where the highway passed through the seven tunnels built to overcome the sheer walls of the Fraser Canyon. When I reached Hell's Gate at the narrowest and deepest stretch of the river, I felt the cliffs closing in on me. Despite the glare of the sun and the brightness of the day, there was a kind of darkness to the place. It struck me as oppressive and ominous and left me wondering if it was the gateway into hell or out of it.

At Cache Creek I left the river and my dark thoughts behind, and when I reached Kamloops, I broke my journey with a brief visit to my closest friend, Renzo. I'd known him since he and his family first arrived in Canada in 1940, and we had been classmates all the way through school. He was a year older than me, but in those days immigrant kids were assigned to grade one until they got "caught up" linguistically. So Lorenzo Rosetti, at seven years old, was bigger and stronger and faster than the rest of us, which was lucky for him because most of the new kids got teased and bullied until their strangeness wore off and they became part of the group. We were all little racists in those days.

"Renzo Rosetti, eat your spaghetti."

I happily chanted it along with the rest of the six-year-old gangsters who surrounded him in the playground each day at recess. I was the only child of older parents, Charlie and Kathleen Kinsella, immigrants themselves. The year before I was born, they left County Leitrim to make their home in Canada, and seven years later they still couldn't get over their good fortune at owning their own house in the aptly named Mt. Pleasant neighbourhood of Vancouver

"Renzo Rosetti looks like spaghetti!"

But goading Renzo was a waste of time. He didn't speak a word of English when he first appeared in our class, and we soon grew tired of waiting for a reaction and started including him in our soccer games.

His parents never did become fluent in English, his mother in particular. At that time most Italians lived in the vicinity of Commercial Drive and East Hastings, close to churches, grocery stores, barbershops, and ice cream parlours where they could speak their own language. Renzo lived in a red brick house with iron railings in front of the yard and two stone lions guarding the gate. The lions impressed me until I noticed that most of his neighbours had them too, some a lot bigger than those of the Rosettis.

Renzo's dad grew figs and grapes and tomatoes and peppers, and the wine he produced in the basement gave the house an acrid, fruity aroma that mingled with the kitchen smells of roasting chicken and spaghetti sauce and espresso coffee. I was always welcome in that house and he in mine although it soon became apparent that he found Irish cuisine not at all to his taste. In those early days my father used to tease him.

"Better cook up an extra cabbage today, Kathleen. Renzo here looks like he could use a good feed." –or– "Give your parents a call like the good man you are now, Renzo. Tell them you'll be staying with us for a plateful of liver and onions."

Renzo would smile apologetically, explain that his mother had already cooked for him, and then bolt out the door and down the street. After a while Dad stopped teasing him; it wasn't worth the effort. Renzo never got flustered or fired up about things. He just stood his ground and dealt with whatever came his way, and because of that he seemed invincible.

Like most men, I don't remember how we got to be so close. Little girls seem to have a formula for acquiring new friends. It begins with a question: "Do you want to be my friend?" which leads to another question: "Will you be my *best* friend?" and still later, in times of strife and division among the ranks, to "Are you still my friend?" I have known women in their fifties who can pinpoint the exact moment, maybe at the age of six or seven, when they embarked upon a particular friendship. Boys don't discuss friendship; they just decide to be friends, almost always because of common interests or shared activities.

Both Renzo and I were athletic. In the second and third grades we won all the track and field events at Junior Sports Day. At regional meets in the intermediate grades, I would place second to his first in almost every race. In grade seven we were the best players on St Bridget's volleyball team, and in high school we were the stars of the junior, then senior basketball teams. The difference was that Renzo was a natural athlete, whereas I had to work at it.

In the summer of '52, at the end of grade eleven, Renzo's dad told him to quit the basketball team and get a weekend job if he wanted to go to university the following year. And he did. The rest of the team felt he'd let them down. So did our coach.

And so did I.

None of that made any difference to Renzo. He went out and got a job in the sports department at Eaton's Department Store and spent the whole of that summer working and saving money while I went to Ireland to attend my grandmother's funeral. That was when our friendship faltered. I was mad at him for letting the team down, certainly, but what really came between us was Molly Prendergast.

The three of us had been in the same class at Saint Bridget's. Renzo and I liked Molly because she was a tomboy and could play rough, probably because she had three brothers and was used to holding her own. Her hair was the colour of burnished chestnuts, the same shade as some of the horses I admired at the Hastings Park racetrack. What beautiful hair she had—although she wasn't in the least bit vain about it. When she was small she had worn it in two long braids tied with white ribbons, and when she got to high school, she wore it pinned up in a tortoiseshell comb. She had a sharp tongue and was quick to use it as a weapon if she thought it necessary, but she was a good sport and had a great sense of humour.

We were part of a large circle of friends, but in time we became a close-knit little group of three that lasted until grade eleven. That was when Molly stopped being a tomboy, and I started to notice the sheen of her hair and the shape of her legs and pert little breasts. I knew that Renzo noticed them too.

We never talked about it, but a quiet war waged between us with Molly as the prize. Of the two of us, Renzo was the better athlete, but I was cleverer, taller, and a lot better looking (at least according to my mother).

"You're a handsome lad," she'd say. "We'll soon have all the girls beating a path to the door. Isn't that right, Charlie?"

My dad would smirk. "And why wouldn't they? Doesn't the boy take after his old man after all?"

But in the end Molly chose Renzo, and it was a bitter pill for me to swallow when I got back from Ireland, half way through the summer, and discovered that the two of them had become an item. I felt that he had taken advantage of my absence to win her over, had not played fair, and it was that, together with his desertion of the basketball team, which drove a wedge between us.

For a while we stayed away from each other. Renzo worked long days and spent most evenings with Molly while I moped around the house reading poetry and feeling sorry for myself and driving my mother crazy.

And then one night, Renzo came over to the house and we talked, or at least *he* did.

"I know you're mad about me quitting the team, Larry. But you're still the captain, and you guys will do just fine without me. My dad's right, you know. It's time I started paying my way. Besides, I don't want to end up like him, working at Sweeney's Cooperage for the rest of my life, and if I can't pay my way through university that's exactly what'll happen. Your parents have more money than mine, so for you it's not a worry. For me it is, so I'm glad I got the job. And about the other thing. I don't know what to say about that except that Molly and I are right for each other. She's the one for me, Larry. I'm pretty sure we'll end up married one day."

After her graduation from St. Michael's, Molly studied music while Renzo got his degree in education from Simon Fraser University. They got married, just as Renzo had predicted, and moved to Kamloops where Renzo had got his first teaching job. When I dropped in on them on that hot August day in 1967, I recognized the piano in their living-room, the same piano that had dominated the small front room of the Prendergast household on East Tenth Avenue in Vancouver years before.

The curtains were drawn against the glare of the late afternoon sun, and the room was in shadow. I sat down, and while Molly bustled about making iced tea and putting out a plate of peanut butter cookies, the kids came flying in—Danny, Mirella, and four-year-old Marco—followed by their father.

Renzo had lost weight since I'd seen him a year ago. At thirty-four, he was starting to look tired and drawn. Molly poured us a couple of Kokanees, and we took them out to the porch while she started supper. There seemed to be some tension between the two of them, and I guessed that their marriage was going through a rough patch. If it was serious, I figured they'd let me know, but for now at least they were saying nothing.

"So how's life as a school principal?" I asked, hoping that Renzo would relax a bit so that we could fall into the same kind of easy banter we'd always enjoyed.

"Oh, busy as usual. Always something new going on. Great kids, great teachers, great parents. I've been lucky. I must have the greatest job in the world."

For the next few minutes he kept me entertained with anecdotes about Pineview Elementary School and life as the youngest principal in his rapidly expanding school district. Renzo had a lively sense of humour, which in itself would have made him popular with kids, but he was patient too, and a good listener. When I told him about my plan for the year ahead, he gave me his full attention, but even before I stopped talking, I could see he was appalled.

He didn't have a chance to say anything then because Molly came to call us in for dinner and the rest of the evening was given over entirely to the children and to lighthearted chat about family and friends. When I was leaving the next morning, though, he came out to the car with me, and I could tell from his expression that he had his speech prepared.

"Larry, I'm going to tell you something you won't want to hear."

"Don't say it then."

"Somebody has to, and I get to be the lucky son of a gun because I'm your friend."

"Okay, I'm listening."

"You need to do more than listen, Larry. You need to ask yourself why you're doing this, and you need to be honest with yourself. And then you need to turn the car around and get the hell back to Vancouver."

"Do you think I haven't given it plenty thought already, Renzo? This isn't some crazy whim, I promise you. I know I can do a good job for the people up there, and I'm going to give it my best shot for a year at least."

Renzo ran a hand through his still black, still thick, curly hair and rolled his eyes.

"The *people*, huh? Give me a break, Larry. If you're set on working with the Carrier Nation, then go to Fort Saint James or Dawson Creek or Kitimat. Face up to it, buddy, you're going up there for a different reason altogether, and nothing good will come of it. I'm warning you, Larry. Stay away from Blanchette."

But my mind was already made up and I think he knew it.

CHAPTER TWO

In the August of 1952, with the memory of my grandmother Philomena already fading, I got back from Ireland to find that my best friend Lorenzo Rosetti had fallen in love with the red-haired, piano-playing Molly Prendergast and had posted a "RESTRICTED ENTRY" sign in front of his life.

A rift lay between us, partly because of his desertion of the basketball team, partly because of Molly, but also—and I did not understand until much later—because he had set his sights on a future that was his alone. He had decided to go to Simon Fraser University and get his degree in Education. I wanted to study medicine at McGill in Montreal. Until that summer, I don't think I had realized that we weren't always going to be as close as when we were growing up together. The childhood friends of only children are often substitutes for the brothers and sisters they wish they had, which makes the bond of friendship doubly strong. I could be wrong about that, though. Perhaps I was just an oddball.

I loafed around at home for a few days, getting in my mom's way and on my dad's nerves. Then I went and got a job in the menswear department at Woodward's Store on Hastings Street. Shopping at Woodwards in those days was something of an event. You could get anything there: clothes, furniture, gourmet food—there was even a bank and a travel agency. Each floor was a world of its own, and when you travelled between those worlds, you rode in a stately, slow-moving elevator controlled by a uniformed operator who gave the impression that he was delighted to conduct you from floor to floor and sincerely looked forward to your return journey. It was an enormous store, taking up an entire city block, but grand as it was, it never felt overwhelming or pretentious.

I was delighted to get a job at Woodwards and even more delighted to be earning a salary for the first time in my life. The elation of being employed, however, soon evaporated and reality set in. Most of the time I had little to do but straighten the racks of dark suits, fold and re-shelve shirts, and gather up discarded hangers from the fitting-rooms. When I had finished those chores I was expected to engage in the much more difficult task of trying to look busy when there was nothing at all to do.

I found it deadly dull, and in the sombre light and musty air each hour crept by at a snail's pace. I used to wonder how the store's permanent employees could stand it. How could *anyone* spend a whole lifetime waiting to serve so few customers? But I quickly learned that my co-workers were fiercely loyal to Woodwards and considered themselves fortunate to be employed by a company that treated them like valued personnel rather than disposable units.

For me though, it was just a summer job, and knowing that I was employed by an excellent company did nothing to make time go faster. The end of each day was a beautiful, unattainable mirage hovering in the distance, lunch-break a far-off oasis which I might reach if I could only keep going. Sometimes the sales assistants outnumbered the customers—all of us hard at work trying to look as if we were fully occupied. George, who was devoted to socks and could get territorial about them, told me that the trick was not to look at the clock too often.

For a while I tried to follow George's example by developing a personal bond with the items we sold. I focused first on ties, then on shirts, but once I had picked out the ones I liked best and the ones I wouldn't be seen dead in, my interest waned and they returned to their former state of inert dullness.

At my mother's suggestion I spent the whole of my first pay cheque on new clothes for the job which seemed to impress Mr.

Bagshaw, the floor supervisor. I deeply resented spending all that money on a suit, but in those days it was *de rigueur* for sales assistants. Besides, as Mom pointed out, I'd be able to wear it for my high school prom the following spring.

During my first week at Woodwards I discovered that employees did not leave the store during the noon break. The staff lunchroom was more of a social club than a cafeteria, and it offered a good selection of well-cooked meals at a generous discount. When I first saw Benita, I had just loaded up my tray with fried chicken, potato salad and coleslaw, with strawberry jello and a hefty wedge of coconut cream pie for dessert, all of it accompanied by a bottle of Coke. I remember this only because, on that particular day, I spent a lot of time gazing intently at the contents of my tray as if it were of the greatest interest to me.

Supposedly, you could sit wherever you liked in the lunchroom, but in fact, most people sat with members of their own department and kept to the same table every day. The rest of the staff from the menswear department were all of an age that seemed to give them the right to tease me. The teasing was kindly meant though, and having been hardened by a lifetime of my dad's relentless digs, I could handle anything they dished out. Besides, it's hard to be offended by people who don't matter to you. Nice as the sales clerks were, they were not of my generation and so were of no real concern to me.

Benita was different.

The first time I saw her, she was sitting alone with her head in a book, drinking coffee. All that remained of her lunch was a single pickle. She was young, she was attractive, and she was reading— all of which combined to engage my interest and give me the courage to take my tray over to her table. She did not look up when I sat down, so I worked my way through the food in front of me and wondered how to strike up a conversation. After ten minutes or so of me chewing and her reading, she took her used dishes and cutlery over to the kitchen trolley, returned to collect her book, and walked out through the swinging doors, leaving me seated alone and feeling like a complete fool. All I had managed to learn about her was that she did not like pickles.

Mr. Bagshaw, the perpetually cheerful supervisor of the menswear department, beckoned me over to the table where he sat with the rest of his team.

"Well, Larry, it looks as if we're going to have to give you a bit of coaching. That young lady didn't seem to be too interested in you."

"I'm not interested in her either," I said. "I just wanted to see what she was reading."

There was a snicker from Harry who, at thirty, was the youngest member of the department after me.

"Sure you were, Larry. We all knew it was the book you were interested in, didn't we boys? So what was it that the young lady was reading then?"

"The poems of Mallarmé," I said, regretting it the minute the words were out of my mouth.

"Oooh, lah-di-dah!" said Harry with his nose in the air. I couldn't help rising to the bait.

"There's nothing *wrong* with poetry," I said.

"Hey, I like a good poem as much as the next guy," said Harry. "But there are plenty of good ones in our own language. How about this?" And he solemnly proceeded to quote from his repertoire:

"Half a league, half a league, half a league onward. Into the Valley of Death rode the six hundred…"

As he spoke, his gaze remained fixed on the far wall of the cafeteria. The whole table fell into a respectful silence, maybe thinking that the six hundred was a reference to Canadian troops at the D-Day landing. As soon as Harry's stentorian voice paused for breath, Mr. Bloxham—also known as the Earl of Underwear—applauded enthusiastically and everyone joined in with relief. Harry seemed relieved too, and I could tell that with "Cannons to right of them, cannons to left of them" he'd more or less run out of poem. But I was grateful to the Light Brigade for taking the spotlight away from me until the buzzer sounded the end of the lunch break and the beginning of the afternoon shift.

When I entered the lunch room the following day, she was sitting at the toiletries table. It was an all-female table just as ours was all male, and she was by far the youngest member, which, together with the French poetry text, told me that she was a student like myself. I didn't want Harry to notice that I was watching her, so I asked him to treat us all to another partial rendition of "The Charge of the Light Brigade" which got a laugh from everyone except Harry himself.

On the Friday morning I arrived early and rode straight up to the third floor where I spent the next five minutes engrossed in the many varieties of hand soap on display. As soon as I saw her get out of the elevator, I approached her before she had a chance to sign in with the floor supervisor. I had rehearsed several possible openings whilst skulking among the soaps, but in the end I went for a simple introduction.

"Hi. My name's Larry Kinsella. I have a summer job down in menswear. I was wondering if we could eat lunch together today."

Her brown eyes were empty of expression and her face blank. It seemed like an age before she replied, and then it was brief to say the least.

"Okay," she said.

Then she walked away, leaving me with nothing to do but push the button for the next elevator. The morning was busier than usual, so I gave her no further thought until I was sitting across from her in the lunchroom. This time she had with her the poetry of Lamartine.

"You must be taking French this year," I said.

Her eyes stayed focused on the clubhouse sandwich in front of her. She removed the top slice of bread, took out the pickle, and put it to the side of the plate. Her hands were square and capable. Most of the girls at school had what I thought of as noisy hands, hands that flapped and fluttered and demanded attention ceaselessly. This girl's hands were still and silent. She said nothing, and I saw the whole gang from menswear sitting back to watch the show as they ate.

"Well. *Are* you studying French?"

If I turned it into a question, I figured I might have a better chance of getting an answer.

"Yes," she said.

Once I had walked through a muddy field wearing a pair of my Uncle Jimmy's boots. They were several sizes too big for me, and the wet mud had oozed in and filled them, turning them into lead weights. Talking to Benita that day felt almost the same. It was discouraging. It was unpleasant. It was exhausting. I decided that she was unfriendly rather than shy, and that goaded me into persisting. There was also the need to save face. Without so much as a glance in the direction of the menswear table, I was still acutely aware that we had their undivided attention, so I ploughed on.

"Okay, so what school do you go to? Or maybe you're already at university?"

I heard the sharpness in my tone, but her expression did not change, and I wondered what on earth was going through her head. Then at last she spoke.

"St. Rita's Academy for Girls."

I was surprised. St. Rita's was the oldest and best known of all the Catholic high schools in Vancouver at that time. I tried to picture her in the dark green tunic and black stockings worn by senior students, but this girl had nothing of the convent schoolgirl look about her—that open, eager, anxious-to-please innocence that was as uniform as the uniform itself. Our own girls, the St. Mike's girls, lost to them consistently in field hockey and came back after each game complaining about the snootiness of the "St. Rita's Rich Girls." I used to suspect that it was just a matter of sour grapes over losing, but it struck me now that my table companion might be a snob who regarded me as her social inferior.

"If you're at St. Rita's, why would you need a summer job here?"

She smiled, and not for the first time I thought she might be part Asian. Her features were flat, her olive skin flawless, her eyes dark and steady and impossible to read.

"I don't have wealthy parents. Do you?"

We had begun a conversation. I relaxed, and as I ate my cheeseburger I told her a bit about my family, and she listened with her eyes on mine until it was time for us both to go back to work.

By the end of the summer, she knew pretty much everything there was to know about me, and I was starting to find out a little bit about her. She was no "St. Rita's Rich Girl," that was for sure. And she was not Asian. Her name was Benita Pigeon, and she was a Carrier Indian from *up north*. I did not ask her where exactly, and if I had she probably would not have told me, at least not then. She had been raised on a reservation with her brothers and sisters. Her father drank quite a bit, and sometimes her mother did too. Whenever her dad got really drunk, he beat his wife and kids, and they had learned to stay out of his way.

Benita had felt safer at the Residential School at Lejac, but because of the harsh discipline meted out by some of the teachers, she had dreaded being sent from there to the residential high school in Prince George. Shortly after her thirteenth birthday, she had run away, only to be picked up a few hours later by the police who found her wandering along the highway trying to hitch a ride home.

Back at the school, she had withdrawn into a state of silent, hostile misery. When she went home for the Christmas holidays she told her parents that she was never going back to school, that if they forced her, she would just keep running away. First her father had shouted at her, and then he had beaten her so badly that her mother had run out into the night to get help.

She returned with the priest, Father Hines, who had taken the two of them, Benita and her mother, back with him to the rectory where he made up beds for them in the spare bedroom and put cold compresses on Benita's black eye. The following morning the Indian Affairs Agent made arrangements for Benita to move in with a foster family in Vancouver, old friends of Father Hines, and that was where she had been ever since.

The O'Carrolls were good people, she told me, with six children of their own. The father, a doctor, had offered to pay for her to attend St. Rita's Academy along with his own four daughters. Of the two boys, Kevin, went to St. Dominic's in Shaughnessy, and John was in his second year at UBC.

I guessed it must have been hard for Benita to adjust to life in the city. At first she had struggled to fit in at her new school. She had nothing in common with her classmates and had hated the rain and grey skies of Vancouver. Now though, despite occasional bouts of homesickness, she no longer wanted to return to the reserve. She was a good student and had made a few friends at school. After she graduated she wanted to go to UBC and get a degree, maybe in French, maybe become a teacher, she wasn't sure.

All these things, the facts of her life, she told me calmly, without blame or bitterness or self-pity. At least that's how I remember the telling. Much later I realized that I had missed the nuances I should have picked up on: the subtle flicker of anger in the eyes, the tightening of the mouth and flare of the nostrils, the quick frown, the sudden tension in the muscles of the neck. I noticed neither the anger nor the anguish.

When I heard about her life, I was shocked. Maybe I had assumed that everyone in Canada grew up in much the same way as I had, and that any differences were based more on geography than on culture, race, or history.

Benita was the first Native person I had spoken to. There were none at St. Michael's, and she was the only one St. Rita's. The few that I saw were in the Downtown East Side, often passed out in the street outside beer parlours. It was a part of the city that I, like most Vancouverites, avoided if at all possible.

I had heard of the Capilano Band over on the North Shore, and I knew there were some big reservations out near Tswassen and in the Fraser Valley, but I had far more contact with Chinese and East Indian immigrants than I ever did with Canadian aboriginals. They were a people set apart from the rest of society, and when I first got to know Benita in 1952, they did not even have the right to vote. We never talked about those things though, and it seemed to me that she had left her Indian self in the north and had chosen to become like the rest of mainstream Canada. I admired what I saw as her strength, her stoicism, and her courage, which I already knew far exceeded mine.

CHAPTER THREE

Our summer jobs at Woodwards came to an end, and on the Saturday of the Labour Day weekend, just before we returned to school for our final year, I took Benita to the Pacific National Exhibition at Hastings Park.

Everybody loved the PNE. It had been operating as a seventeen-day annual fair since 1910 and for twenty years had been one of the largest in North America, second only to the New York City Fair. In Vancouver it was the setting for the biggest family outing of the year, and the last weekend of its run had become a ritual for students, an exuberant farewell to summer before the return to school for the autumn term.

The permanent exhibition halls had been built before I was born, and when I was small I would trail around behind my parents, dutifully admiring giant dahlias and prize-winning vegetables, handmade quilts and homemade jams and breads, none of which interested me in the least, but all part of the PNE tradition. Once that duty was done, I was released from the company of my parents, and while they stood in line to tour the prize home I got together with Renzo to watch country kids from the Fraser Valley farms collect blue ribbons for their champion hand-reared calf or piglet or goat or chicken.

I loved the atmosphere of a working farm with its barnyard smells and sounds, the cacophony of living, breathing animals, and I envied the lucky members of the 4H Club who got to compete at the PNE each year. Renzo, though, was a city kid through and through. He was repelled by farmyard smells, referred to the Fraser Valley kids as "Hicks from the Sticks," and was always looking for a way to shorten our tour of the barn.

"That's the same cow we saw when we first came in," he would say indignantly, as if I were trying to trick him into doing an extra circuit, and I would be obliged to explain.

"No, we didn't. Can't you tell the difference? This one's a Jersey heifer, and the one we saw before was a Guernsey."

I was patient with him because I could see that he felt about farm animals as I did about patchwork quilts and dahlias. He was only in the barn because he had to be—I was his friend and so he owed me his company, but I can't say it was graciously bestowed, at least not when we were eleven years old.

After the barn we would head down the hill to Bob's Lunch for a cheeseburger and chocolate shake. If the lineup at Bob's was too long, we'd move across the way to Jimmy's Lunch where we'd get a hamburger and a strawberry shake. There was no reason for the different order, it was just part of our PNE routine, and we maintained it for years, right up to the Labour Day weekend that heralded our entry into grade twelve. That was the first time Renzo and I did not go to the PNE together, because by then he was seeing Molly and I had met Benita. By that time too, the roller coasters we loved were gone, the PNE had changed, and we ourselves were on the verge of adulthood.

When we were eleven, though, it was the roller coasters that were pretty much the whole point of the PNE, and each year Renzo and I would join the throngs of people heading down the hill to Happyland where we'd watch thrill seekers round the loop and come clacking down the wooden track screaming their heads off. It would be true to say that, while we might not have given Sister Margaret our full and undivided attention when she was trying to explain the seven gifts of the Holy Ghost or teach us about the seven deadly sins, the two of us knew everything there was to know about the Giant Dipper. It was a splendid roller coaster with a sheer drop of sixty feet and cars that reached a speed of forty miles an hour. It had been a major attraction of the PNE ever since it was built in 1925, and when the Prince of Wales came to try it out one afternoon in 1927, he liked it so much that he returned the same evening for another ride. Renzo and I more than liked it, we *loved* it. For years we had had to content ourselves with watching those who were old enough to ride it, and we considered it nothing short of tragic that we only got to ride it once ourselves before it was demolished. That one time, though, gave us bragging rights on our first day back at school, and, even better, it gave us something to write about for the inevitable "What I Did In My Summer Holidays" essay.

On my first day in grade six at St. Bridget's, I wrote non-stop until the bell for recess rang and Sister Clare came around to collect our papers. I wrote about my roller coaster ride: first, the long ascent of the hill and seeing the whole fairground below me, then seeing the Port of Vancouver and beyond it to the North Shore Mountains, where the pointed ears of the Lion's Head were clearly visible behind the forested hills. I wrote about the way the sea looked, and how ribbons of bright pink lay across the mauve sky as day turned into evening. I wanted to explain how the scene spread out beneath me had jolted me into an awareness of something great and mysterious and immensely beautiful, but I couldn't find the right words, so instead I wrote about letting go of the hand bar and throwing my arms above my head and yelling, and then about the terrifying, thrilling plunge into the void. I received an A+ for that essay, and I think my mother has it still.

I would have loved to ride the Giant Dipper with Benita but by the time I met her, it, along with its smaller sister, were long gone. The Baby Dipper had been torn down in the war years to provide parking space for Canadian troops, and the Giant was demolished to make room for the new racetrack. And despite a protest launched in 1948 by the Pacific Coast Amusement Company—on the grounds that thirty-five percent of its revenue had been lost by the discontinuation of the Dippers—they could not be replaced at that time because of a ban on importing amusement devices.

My father passed the newspaper over to me one morning to show me a large photo of an unhappy fourteen-year-old called Bob sitting among the rubble of the partially demolished Dipper. He was quoted as saying, "if they want to rip things apart in this town, why don't they start in on a few schools?" Good old Bob surely voiced the thoughts of every kid in Vancouver. At school we briefly mourned the passing of the Giant Dipper, exchanged lavishly embellished accounts of rides taken on it before it succumbed to the wreckers, and then let it slide away into PNE mythology.

I met Benita at the main gate and took her straight to Jimmy's Lunch for a hamburger, followed by a scone with strawberry jam and clotted cream at Fisher's Scones. We spent the afternoon wandering around the exhibits, and she was interested in everything except the homemade preserves.

"Better stuff where I come from, I think," she said. "Just not so fancy."

Later we made our way through the fair grounds, stopping at every sideshow and trying our luck at all the games. Evening came softly, a royal-blue radiant evening at the end of a hot day. A little breeze drifted up from the harbour and cooled the air. People carried jackets, but were reluctant to put them on because wearing a jacket was a sure sign that summer was on its way out, and nobody was willing to let it go. The air shimmered and glimmered around the neon-lit fairground as a silver moon appeared high above us.

At the bottle stall, Benita smiled when I missed with my first hoop, but it turned out that I was a far better shot than she was and finally I got three in a row. I told her to choose a prize from the row of gigantic plush toys on display at the back of the booth, and she deliberated for such a long time that the stall-holder, his hooked pole poised for action, grew impatient and told her she was holding up the show.

"Okay, okay," she said. "Give me that tiger on the end of the shelf, the one next to the elephant."

"They're all the same, lady, not one bit of difference between them. Here you go."

He hooked the nearest tiger and held it out. And that's when I discovered that Benita did not back down easily.

"No," she said. "They're different. I want that sad looking guy next to the elephant."

All of us, including those waiting for their turn to throw hoops, looked up at the tiger at the end of the row and saw that she was right, its downward-drooping mouth *did* make it look sad.

The guy standing next to me said, "What's the big deal, Buddy? Just give her the one she wants. We've been standing here long enough."

So Benita ended up with the tiger she wanted and carried it around for the rest of the evening, her dark hair spilling over its striped orange head. She named him Horace, and I said I'd be sad too if I had a name like Horace, and that's when I heard Benita laugh for the first time.

After that we saw each other most weekends. At first we took the bus, she from the west side, I from the east, and met at English Bay or Lost Lagoon or the zoo in Stanley Park. Then in October, my dad taught me to drive, and when I got my licence he let me borrow his precious two year-old blue Ford sedan to take Benita to a movie at the Hollywood cinema over on West Broadway.

The O'Carroll house was huge and stately, with iron gates, mullioned windows, and a circular driveway. When I rang the bell, I was expecting to see Benita, but it was Dr. Cormac O'Carroll who came to greet me at the door and invite me in. He seemed affable enough, but I knew I was going through an inspection of sorts, especially when Mrs O'Carroll appeared on the scene and began to bombard me with questions. I understood what they were doing and was glad that they cared enough about Benita to want to scrutinize her companions, particularly her *male* companions.

I must have passed the test because when Benita finally came downstairs, Dr. O'Carroll shook me by the hand and told me he was glad to have met me. Then his wife reminded Benita not to stay out too late, and we were on our way.

We arrived at the cinema early and shared the back row of the stalls with several other couples. I can't recall a single thing about the newsreel that preceded the feature film because during it I held Benita's hand for the first time. It might seem hard to believe now, with ten-year-olds knowing everything there is to know about sex and a lot of twelve-year-olds on the pill, but those were different times. At eighteen we were still children.

If you were a nice Catholic kid in those days, not only did you not "do it", you tried your damnedest not to even *think* about it, for fear you would end up the following Saturday having to confess to entertaining impure thoughts. Masturbation, a violation of holy chastity, was considered a grave sin and had to be got rid of via a Saturday trip to the confessional so that you could receive Holy Communion at Mass the next day. If you stayed in your seat and failed to join the rest of the congregation at the altar rail on Sunday morning, it was obvious that you were not in a state of grace, and if you were an adolescent, people would have a pretty good idea of the reason why. Worst of all, your mother would be sure to ask you why you hadn't received the sacred host.

When I reached over and took Benita's hand in mine for the first time in the back row of the Hollywood movie theatre in Kitsilano, I was transfixed by the feel of her skin, the warmth of her, the nearness of her. We stared at the screen in front of us without seeing a thing, and then she wrapped her fingers around mine and squeezed, and it felt like a silent welcome. I put my face against the silky softness of her hair and touched her ear with my lips. When I whispered her name, my voice was breathy and ragged, and she turned to me and smiled and squeezed my hand again. And that was it. Our first touch. A meeting of hands, and then my mouth, her hair, my lips seeking out ear, my voice saying her name. Nothing more than that.

But I still remember every detail after all these years, and sometimes, even now, I wonder if she does too.

Once the feature film began it was suspense rather than passion that tightened the grip of our clasped hands. When it came to choosing a movie we had almost settled for Bob Hope in *The Paleface* even though I had seen it the year before when it first came to Vancouver. "Buttons and Bows," the song from the movie, had become an instant hit and was still being whistled, hummed, and sung everywhere. I could have watched that film a second time and let its frivolous inane plot wash over us and leave us laughing, but I came across the reviews of *Rope*, Alfred Hitchcock's first movie filmed in colour, and they were mixed enough to intrigue me.

In *Rope* the action takes place in real time and there is a constant display of clocks ticking down to the final discovery. Some critics had condemned it as "stagey" and contrived, but even those critics were as gripped by the plot as Benita and I were that night at the Hollywood. The film was based on the notorious Leopold and Loeb murder case.

Two students at an expensive prep school in New England had been learning about Nietzsche's vision of man as Superman. Their teacher told them that, according to Nietzsche's philosophy, powerful, gifted people need not accept a moral code which had been established for their inferiors. Feelings of guilt or "bad conscience" were a consequence of Christian morality which is based on self-deception and was designed for the weak and the scared.

The two boys, Brandon and Phillip, believed that they were superior beings and therefore had the right to rid the world of a person whose life wouldn't make a difference one way or another. Their classmate David, selected for their macabre experiment, is strangled and his body dumped in a wooden chest. The two boys are so confident that they have committed the perfect crime that they invite their philosophy teacher and the victim's father to a party, and use the chest as a buffet table.

In the movie, Brandon, Phillip, and David are university students, and Hitchcock adds a romantic twist to the story by giving the murder victim an attractive fiancee who is at first puzzled and then alarmed when David fails to show up for the party. In the end, though, it is David's father whose suspicion leads to the dénouement of the plot, and that night at the Hollywood cinema I think the entire audience held its collective breath throughout that final scene.

Benita said nothing until we were almost at her house. The whole way home she gazed blankly ahead, and when I reached for her hand she moved away.

"Maybe we should have picked a different movie, huh?"

There was no response and I was reminded of our early days at Woodwards.

"Did you find it disturbing?"

"No."

"Can we talk about it?"

But she had wrapped herself in silence as if it were a shawl, excluding me completely. I found it infuriating.

"Well, can you at least express *some* kind of opinion about the film, Benita, instead of just sitting there like a bump on a log?"

At last she reacted.

Larry, you're full of opinions about *everything*, full of your own words. Maybe you just talk too much. I prefer to think about things for a bit *before* I speak about them, okay?"

And then, suddenly, she laughed and the angry tension that had been building up inside the car—crackling and sparking in the empty space between us—slid out the window and vanished into the night, and we were easy with each other again. By the time we were at her gate, I was no longer thinking about *Rope*. I was thinking about how much I wanted to kiss her, and then about whether Mrs. O'Carroll might be waiting up for her, maybe watching out the window for the car, and I hesitated.

With her back to the window Benita faced me.

"Hey, Larry, do you think it's true, what that professor guy in the movie said, that there are different codes of behaviour for different people?"

"You mean is it okay to kill as long as the victim is inferior to you?" I said.

"What? No! Of course not! Nobody believes that, not even the teacher in the film. He was just teaching a philosophy course," she said. "The thing is that Nietzsche believed it, didn't he? We've been studying him at our school too, just like those guys."

"Well then," I said. "You also know that Nietzsche was crazy. He had a major mental breakdown right after he said that God was dead, and he never recovered."

Benita rolled her eyes at me

"Next, you'll be telling me that God was punishing him! Come on, Larry!"

"Hey, I'm only mentioning something you can read about in any account of his life. But, okay, yes. I do believe that when you eliminate God from the universe, the result is chaos, anarchy, and the absence of morality. I think old Nietzsche really wanted us to believe that some lives are of more value than others."

"And maybe that's true," she said.

I tried to figure out if she was deliberately trying to provoke me, as she sometimes did, for her own amusement.

"How can you *say* that, Benita? *Every* life is of equal worth, at least in the eyes of God. You know that."

"Do I?" Her face was expressionless, her eyes empty. "Larry, tell me something. Do you *really* believe in God? I'm not your mom or your parish priest. You can be honest with me."

I was always honest with her. Did she not know that by now?

"Do I believe in God? Absolutely. Don't you?"

"I don't know what I believe," she said. "I'm not sure about God, Jesus Christ, Our Lady, all the angels and saints, none of it. Sometimes I think it's all just a story, kind of like the stories the elders used to tell us kids on the Reserve. My grandmother told us that our people used to believe that all the plants and animals have spirits and that it was wrong to kill or harm them needlessly. She said that whatever energy you put out, whether good or bad, would come back to you, and she said that the earth contains many power spots where healers can work with supreme spiritual energy. The things she told us about aren't in the catechism, but what if they're true? How do we *know* what's true? I don't really know *what* I believe any more. I kind of wish I was as sure as you are, but I'm not."

Looking back on that night now, I wish I'd had the wisdom, the insight, and the compassion to have said nothing at all. I wish I had just taken her in my arms, touched her face, stroked her shining hair, kissed her and let silence keep her safe. But I was eighteen and arrogant and did none of those things, and when I spoke my voice must surely have been as sounding brass, and clashing symbol.

"What you're talking about, those old Indian *superstitions*, they're Pagan, not Christian. How can you *believe* that stuff and still go to Mass every Sunday? You go to a Catholic school, Benita. If you're having doubts about your Faith, maybe you should go and talk to one of the nuns or priests."

She turned away from me, opened the door of the car and got out. Then she bent down to speak. There was no anger in her voice, but her eyes were cold and hard.

"Larry, you're a real big talker, and you're a pretty smart guy. But you know what? You're a pompous asshole."

The car door slammed, the front gate clanged, and she was swallowed up by the house before I could say a word. And when I drove away, I did not feel in the least bit contrite. She had insulted me, and I was angry.

We never spoke about *Rope* again, nor about what I thought of as Benita's crisis of faith. It was God's business, not mine, I decided in the end, although by then it was much too late. I made no apologies for what I had said that night, and neither did she, so it was as if the dispute had never taken place at all. In any case, words fade fast and, unless they are recorded in some way, become blurred and smudged by time.

"*You said...*"

"*No, I didn't. I said...*"

"*But I distinctly remember hearing you say...*"

"*Wrong! What I said was...*"

Language, like memory, is not to be trusted.

CHAPTER FOUR

In early November Benita's father drowned when his fishing boat capsized during a sudden storm on Sturgeon Lake. He was thirty-six years old, and he had not seen his daughter since she was thirteen years old. Word of his death reached Benita by way of a phone call from the priest in Blanchette and when she heard the news she reeled in shock and began to shiver uncontrollably.

She slept poorly that night, and early the next morning she and Dr. O'Carroll took to the road so that she could attend her father's wake and funeral.

It is a long journey even now, and in those days, with the road still under repair from flood damage, it was daunting. But at least that year the snow came late, and they were able to reach Prince George by nightfall. They spent the night at the home of the doctor's hunting buddy, an old classmate from medical school, and when they reached the Dena'dzlie Reserve the following afternoon, Dr. O'Carroll stopped only long enough to pay his respects and then drove back to town, leaving Benita with her family.

Her father's body lay in a coffin on a trestle table in the corner of the room. There were bronze chrysanthemums in a vase at the head of the coffin, and an amber altar light flickered in the draft from the constant opening and closing of the front door. It was a grey November day, and the room was dimly lit. Smoke from the stove and cigarettes thickened the air, and Benita found it hard to breathe.

She had grown used to space and fresh air and had forgotten how cramped and stuffy the homes on the reserve were.

The room had been cleared of furniture except for the borrowed chairs that lined the walls. Seated on the chairs were the women, some of them talking quietly amongst themselves, others praying the rosary. In the kitchen, where a long table had been set up to hold the cold meats and buns, the salads, pies, and cakes that had started to arrive within hours of the death, were the men, their voices fuelled by the beer and wine they had brought with them. They stayed until the booze ran out, making occasional forays into the mourning room to stand unsteadily by the body and mutter a prayer before returning to the solidarity and safety of the kitchen where they became briefly tearful and then raucous in the telling of stories about the hunting trips or fishing expeditions they had been on with poor, dead Johnny Pigeon.

When Benita came through the door, all the seated women fell silent and the drone of the rosary ceased. Then her grandmother Florence Pigeon and her two aunts, Emma and Clara, began wailing and keening for their dead son and brother. As a child, Benita had heard the sounds of mourning many times, but now it struck her as eerie and otherworldly. She was overcome by a feeling of dread and stood rooted to the ground, unable to move until her other grandmother, her mother's mother, took her by the hand and led her to the alcove where her father waited for her in death.

She did not want to look at his face. Instead she fixed her gaze upon his hands and recognized them. These were the hands he had used to punch his wife and beat his children, hands that had ripped the clothes from her body leaving her naked and ashamed, a stranger in her own home. She remembered how she had hated and feared her father's hands, and seeing them now, lifeless and still, she was consumed by hot anger. Rage drew her eyes upward to his face, but when at last she looked at it, she saw the face of a stranger.

Had he changed so much in the four years that had passed, or was it death by drowning that had so disfigured him? She turned away from his body in disgust, and she did not pray for his soul. Instead she went and sat with her brother Paul and her sister Martina. They did not talk much beyond a solemn greeting, having nothing to say to each other any more. Benita saw that they had grown closer to each other now that they were both at the Residential School in Prince George, and that she had become a stranger to them. It struck her that for some kids, herself included, residential school felt like a prison, but perhaps for others it was a refuge, a safer and happier place than their own home.

Later that afternoon, Johnny's body was brought to the church for the funeral and then his two younger brothers, Clarence and Billy Pigeon, and two of his cousins, Nathaniel Thomas and Jericho George, carried the coffin up the hill behind the church to the graveyard where all their people were buried.

It was very cold, and the air carried the smell of snow. Above their heads, dark-winged clouds trailed silver tentacles and moved in slow procession to gather forbiddingly over the lake. Before the burial, Father Hines intoned the prayer for strength and consolation:

"Emitte lucem tuam et veritatem tuam; ipsa me deduxerunt in montem sanctum tuum et in tabernacula tua."

[Send forth thy light and thy truth; for they have led me and brought me to Thy holy hill and Thy dwelling place.]

Then the warden, Reuben Prince, said the Prayers for the Dead in the Carrier language as translated long ago by the Oblate, Father Morice:

"Ahwulyiz narhulyis perahwonin'aih, Nemutihthi, inkez itiz hweni pepa padethunat. Hwotizrel et narhulyis. Ndehoneh,"

The altar server swung the ciborium aloft, and incense drifted upward in the frigid air as the coffin was lowered into the grave. The priest bent down and scooped up a handful of earth. When it hit the coffin, Johnny's mother wailed, and his sisters began their lamentations while the men, one by one, approached the coffin and scattered earth upon it. Then the warden took a shovel and covered it completely until it vanished beneath the ground.

Benita remained at the grave with her brother and sister, her two grandmothers, her aunts and uncles and cousins until the last of the light was gone from the sky and the candles had burned out. Then they walked together down the holy hill and back across the reserve to the house where one of their uncles was waiting to take Paul and Martina back to the city. They seemed relieved to be on their way, and their goodbyes to their sister and grandmothers were brief and subdued.

CHAPTER FIVE

When Benita returned from the graveyard, the house was full of people, and the sombre hush of death had given way to noise and laughter. Clarence and Billy Pigeon were taking turns telling stories about their brother's exploits as a young man. They were drinking beer, both of them, and were already half-intoxicated. Clarence grew maudlin as he recalled the days of glory.

"Yuh, ol' Johnny he sure had a lot of guts. I can still remember that time when he shot that one big moose up near Tachie. He shot him in the chest, but that big bull, he di'n wanna die. He started to go after Johnny. Remember that, Billy?"

"Sure I remember. And ol' Johnny, he run like hell."

"Uh-uh. Johnny never run away, Billy. I seen him standing there in front of that one big moose, same way you're standing in front of me right now. Remember that Billy?"

Everybody in the room knew that Billy should back off and let his brother continue the story all the way to its heroic conclusion, but the beer had put Billy in a truculent mood.

"Uh-uh. All's I remember is that Johnny was plenty scared of that one ol' bull. I seen him run like hell. Damn near shit himself he was so scared."

Billy laughed and Clarence stepped forward.

"Our brother never run. You calling me a liar, Billy?"

"Yuh, guess that I am. You always was a liar, Clarence."

Clarence assumed a fighting stance just as everyone knew he would, a sorrowful look on his face.

"Guess I'm gonna have to hit you now then, Billy. For calling me a liar."

Their cousins and fellow-pallbearers, Nathaniel Charlie and Jericho George, had just come down from the church with Father Hines, and the three of them were able to intercept Clarence's half-hearted blow before it had a chance to land. Nathaniel turned Clarence around and led him into the kitchen.

"You sure showed him, Clarence," said Jericho. "Billy's real sorry now for what he said."

Jericho put an arm around Billy. "You stood up to him real good, Billy. Better let him go now. You don' wanna hurt him none. Remember what happened to me and Nathaniel that one time?"

Then their mother, Florence, came and gave Clarence and Billy a tongue lashing and reminded them that their brother was dead, upon which all three of them shed fresh tears and all was forgiven.

In the kitchen, somebody poured Benita a glass of wine from the gallon of Calona Red that stood in the middle of the table surrounded by plates of roast meat and smoked fish and jerky and pickles and bologna sandwiches and macaroni.

Living in Shaughnessy with the O'Carrolls, she had grown accustomed to drinking a glass of wine with the Sunday lunch, but it was never served in a tumbler, and she had never taken more than a single glass. Now she drained her glass, and her aunt Emma, who was not much older than Benita herself, sniggered and filled it up again.

"Hey, you drink pretty good for a girl who lives with white folk. They let you to drink in the big city, huh? Maybe I should go down there too, huh? What d'you think, Benny? Think I should go to Vancouver some day? Hey, drink up now. You gotta catch up with your old auntie, eh?"

She drained her glass and looked at Benita. There was an angry challenge in her eyes. Emma was a mean drunk, Benita's mother had once said, just like her brother Johnny.

Now she put her face close to Benita's. Her breath stank of booze and smoked fish.

"Whassa matter, little white girl? You too scared to drink like an Indian?"

Benita recoiled in disgust and stepped back against the table. She could think of nothing else to do but raise her glass and drain it, more out of confusion and embarrassment than competition. Emma laughed.

"You think I'm a piece of trash, huh, Benita? You don' wanna be near me no more, eh? You too damn good for us now or something? Well, you listen up, girl. You made my brother real disappointed when you took off for the city. Why'd you have to go and do that, huh? Made him feel real bad, poor Johnny, and now he's dead."

Emma's strident voice suddenly acquired a catch and a sob as she briefly succumbed to tears.

"Johnny was a good guy, and he died all alone with no wife, no kids, nothing. He had real bad luck, first with you, then with that no-good wife of his, your mother. Lucky she didn't show her face round here, I tell you. You and her belong together. We don' wan' you round here no more. Why don' you just shove off?"

Without warning, she hurled her glass at Benita. Red wine ran down her face and splashed the front of her navy-blue blouse, soaking it and turning it black. The glass shattered when it hit the floor and brought an immediate halt to the talk and laughter going on around them.

For a moment Benita stood frozen in shock and shame, and then she began to shake with with rage. She heard the sound of her own voice and did not recognize it as it rose above the silence and pierced the thick, smoky air with all the pent-up fury and grief of the past.

"You bunch of hypocrites! You know nothing! You never saw your precious Johnny when he was drunk, when he beat up on my mother, when he hit us kids for no reason at all, did you? He was a mean, vicious drunk, that's what I remember about him. He was a lousy father! I hated him and I'm glad he's dead."

The faces of the people around her faded into a blur as she struggled to hold back her tears. Then her mother's mother, Hepzibah King, appeared at her side and enfolded her in arms that were familiar and loving. She led her outside into the cold clean darkness and held her while she was violently sick. Benita wished that the wind would take her, that she could be blown away across the lake and into nowhere. That was what she told her grandmother when she was able to speak again.

"Your spirit will do that when this life is over, but first you have a job to do."

"You mean like be a nurse or something?"

"No, I mean the job of living the rest of your life. Remember what I used to tell you when you were a little girl, Benita? God is already in us when we are born. Our task while we are alive is to open ourselves to His presence in us and around us and to listen when He speaks to us."

"Well, maybe God speaks to you, Granny, but I've sure never heard Him, that's for sure."

"If you're listening for words, Benny, you'll never hear them. Words are just for the mind. God, He speaks to the spirit. We can hear His voice in the wind through the trees and in the sound of the rain. We can hear it in the call of the loon and the cry of the raven; sometimes too, a person can hear it in the silence of their own heart when it's still and at peace. That's what I call real prayer. But I guess it's not so easy for you in the big, noisy city, huh? I'm thinking that it's maybe time now for you to come back to LaPierre, Benita. Anyways, you need to go see your mother."

Hepzibah King did not waste words, and when she spoke people listened. She was tall and stately with strong features and a direct gaze. She wore her steel grey hair tied back in a heavy coil, and at sixty her skin was still smooth and unlined. Her knowledge of the medicinal properties of trees, plants, and berries was legendary among the Carrier-Sekani Nation and among the remote communities up and down the length of the lake, those far removed from doctors, clinics, and hospitals. She was the first to be consulted whenever someone fell ill. As a child, Benita had often accompanied Hepzibah in her travels, and she had grown up knowing the names of all the native plants and their power to cure most ailments. She admired and respected her grandmother more than anyone else on earth, but she was no longer the compliant child she once had been.

She had set her feet on a different path, and her mother had become a shadowy figure in her life.

"I wrote to my mother lots of times, Granny, and I never once heard back from her."

"Clara was real proud of those letters, Benny, always happy when they arrived. She let me read all of them."

"But she never answered a single one of them, not even at Christmas. I never even got a birthday card from her, only from you."

"She cares about you, Benita. She just never was one for writing letters. Besides, she's been going through a pretty rough time."

"Well, I can't go up to see her, Granny. I have to go back to the city tomorrow. I can't miss any more school. I have to keep on getting good marks because I want to go to university next year. I want to be a teacher."

"Sounds real good, Benita. I know you can do it too. Right now, though, you're gonna have to see your mother. She's not doing so great these days, and we're all pretty worried about her. You come up to LaPierre with me for a couple of days, okay?"

It was the voice of authority and was not to be denied.

CHAPTER SIX

Benita used the phone at the Sturgeon Lake Hotel to call Dr. O'Carroll and let him know that she needed a couple of extra days before she could go back to the city with him. Then she and her grandmother climbed into Jericho George's pickup truck for the journey up the lake.

There were very few vehicles in the village at that time and no real road, just a rough track through the bush that was impassable for part of the year. In the summer, people could get to Lapierre by boat. When the snow came, they travelled by sled. The rest of the time they used Jericho George and his pickup as a taxi service to and from the village, partly because of his good nature and partly because he was always sober and could be trusted to get them to Blanchette without hitting a tree or falling asleep at the wheel. If they had money, they paid him. If not, he didn't much care. Gas was cheap and his willingness to act as chauffeur made him a popular and respected figure in the community, even though he consistently refused to provide transport for those who were drunk.

Jericho George would have nothing to do with alcohol. He said it was a curse on families and had preached against it since he was twenty years old and he and his cousin Nathaniel Thomas had emptied a case of Molson's ale between them one night. In the days and weeks that followed, neither of them could remember who had thrown the first punch or who had said what to whom, but in the end

Jericho had beaten Nathaniel to a pulp. When he finally recovered consciousness, Hepzibah King gave him a concoction that relieved the pain and reduced the swelling in his face, but she could not restore vision to his left eye nor eradicate the permanent slur in his speech. When Jericho George saw the damage he had inflicted on his cousin, he vowed never to touch alcohol again and never to lay hand on another human being for as long as he lived, at least not in anger.

Hepzibah King had travelled in Jericho George's truck so many times that she no longer noticed the bumping and jouncing and tilting and swaying that were a part of every journey, but Benita, accustomed now to the paved streets of the city and the smooth suspension of newer model cars, felt every jolt of the forty mile trip. When at last they reached the little house by the lake, she climbed down from the truck as slowly and stiffly as her grandmother, and had to take a few minutes to stretch her back and relax her tight muscles before following Hepzibah through the door.

The house was exactly as she remembered it from the summers she had spent there with Hepzibah and Saul King, her kind and perpetually smiling grandfather who had died when she was twelve years old. Benita had always thought of it as a happy house, but now when she entered it again after being away for such a long time, she knew that its spirit had changed and that trouble had somehow found its way inside and made it darker.

She breathed in the familiar smoky smell and saw her mother step from the shadows and stand before her. She did not kiss her, did not put her arms around her nor greet her in any way. She just stood there in silence while her daughter took note of the fading bruises, broken nose, swollen eyes, and scarred mouth. She was not shocked. There was nothing she had not seen before.

"So he managed to get you good one last time, huh?"

"Yup. Looks like."

Clara Pigeon moved her cracked lips just enough to attempt a smile, and Benita saw that only the jagged stumps of her front teeth remained, making her once lovely face ugly.

"Ma, you need to see a dentist. You can't stay like that. You have to get new teeth."

"Maybe Jericho, he can take me to the dentist in Prince George some day, eh? But it's sure good to see you, Benny. You got real tall in Vancouver. You're taller'n me now. Sit yourself down and tell us about the big city. What's it like, living down there?"

Hepzibah put the kettle on the stove, made tea, and opened up a can of Carnation evaporated milk. There was no fridge in the little house, nor in any of the homes in Lapierre. The settlement was still without electricity which meant there was no light either, other than that from oil lamps. Heat came from the wood stove in the one room that served as kitchen, dining room and living room, and in the winter, when the temperature often dropped to forty degrees below zero, the stove burned day and night. At night smoke from every chimney in the village coiled its way up into the starlit sky and hung there paralyzed by the cold.

Nobody ever froze to death provided they stayed indoors during a cold snap, but sometimes a smouldering log would start a fire, or a lamp would get knocked over and spill hot oil, and a house would become engulfed by flames. Sometimes an old person or a baby would die from smoke inhalation. Sometimes children would suffer terrible burns. Occasionally a whole family would perish before their neighbours had a chance to douse the flames. It was a small village and remote. The only firefighters were neighbours wielding whatever apparatus they could lay their hands on.

They drank tea and ate their way through the packet of chocolate chip cookies Benita had brought with her from Vancouver, and by her second cup she was hearing about the last day of her father's life. The story her mother told was familiar enough, except for the way it ended.

Johnny Pigeon had gone into the beer parlour of the Sturgeon Lake Hotel when it opened its doors at eleven in the morning and would have stayed there until closing time if he had not run out of money.

Johnny was not and never had been a habitual drinker. When he was sober he was a skilled hunter, fisherman and trapper, often going into the bush for days at a time to tend his trap lines or spending long hours setting his nets and retrieving salmon, a staple of the Carrier diet. When he was sober, he was a good companion in the bush, trustworthy, reliable, good-tempered and generous.

Clara King had not been able to resist him when he had first come up to LaPierre to hunt with his cousins. He was nineteen years old with a reputation for being wild. She was seventeen and didn't care. All she knew was that he treated her like a princess, he was handsome, and she loved him. She had never been with a man before, and her parents would not let them marry until they had known each other for a year and he had convinced them that he would be a good husband to their daughter.

On their wedding night he was patient with her, a gentle and tender lover, and it was not until they had moved down to live on the reserve in Blanchette that Clara saw the other side of him. The first time Johnny came home drunk, she had refused to sleep with him. His response had been to hit her in the face and then to force himself upon her. There was no tenderness then, only violence and pain.

She did not sleep at all that night but lay rigidly beside him, terrified that he would move toward her and hurt her again. But he did not wake until morning. and then, when he opened his eyes and saw the bloodied sheets and the bruises on his wife's face, he wept in shame and disgust at what he had done. He'd begged her to forgive him and swore it would never happen again.

Clara believed him. Besides, it turned out that she was pregnant and she chose to banish the incident from her memory. Maybe it hadn't been as bad as it had seemed at the time. He had never come home drunk before. Perhaps if she had been more understanding, more tolerant, he never would have forced himself upon her. In a way she was to blame for his outburst. It would never happen again.

But it did.

Johnny Pigeon did not drink for pleasure. He drank to get drunk. He was a solitary drinker who would sit in a corner of the beer parlour and down one half-pint after another until he could barely stand up to make it to the door. But he never caused trouble in public, never raised his voice, never got into a fight. He was not one of those Indians who had his police photo pasted on the wall behind the bar, forbidden entry because of a history of disruptive behaviour.

Only once had he ever been thrown out of the bar, and that was the time he had put his head down on the table and fallen asleep in a puddle of beer. Johnny Pigeon was a quiet drunk, a polite one even. It was only within the confines of his own home that he turned mean and destructive. That was when he became a threat to others, and those others were always his wife and children.

So when he stumbled out the door of the beer parlour on the day he died, he was greatly relieved to see Marvin Henry's truck parked right in front of him. Unlike Jericho George, Marvin Henry had no qualms about providing transportation to drunks. For a price, he would also make runs to the liquor store and deliver booze right to the doorstep, a service which made him unpopular with most of the women on the reserve. He made lots of money, but spent little of it. He had never married, and the house he lived in was a dilapidated shack guarded by his two vicious mixed-breed dogs. Not that there was much there to guard, or any real danger of theft on the Reserve.

People tended to share what they had and were not territorial about property. Money, if you were able to earn it through a trap line or by logging or fishing, was to be spent, not hoarded. Families were large, and the line between who was a blood relative and who wasn't was blurred to the point that every kid grew up surrounded by aunts, uncles, and cousins, some of whom were official and many more who weren't. In short, Marvin Henry, close-faced, taciturn, and grasping, was a misfit and people steered clear of him and his vicious dogs, except for when they needed his services.

When they reached the house, Johnny Pigeon told Marvin Henry to wait for him. He came through the front door and found Clara at the stove stirring a pot of soup. He stood before her swaying on his feet, reeking of beer and cigarette smoke.

"You're drunk, Johnny. You need to go and lie down a while."

"I just had a couple beer, Clara. I got no more money. All's I need is a few bucks."

"What for?" So's you can guzzle more beer?"

"No, so's I can pay Marvin Henry for the ride home."

"Okay, you go and sleep it off, Johnny. I'll pay Marvin Henry."

"Just give me the money, Clara. Goddamn it, I earned it."

"No, Johnny. You're plenty drunk already. I got no money for beer."

"Shut your face and do what you're told."

He was a mean drunk when he was at home, always had been. Clara looked at her husband and knew what would happen next. She grabbed her coat from the hook behind the door and ran outside not stopping to change her moccasins for boots. She told Marvin Henry not to wait any longer, that she'd pay him later, and then she made her way to Joanne Isaac's place at the end of the street.

She spent the next hour chatting and drinking tea with her neighbour, and when she returned to the house she was confident that she would find her husband sprawled out asleep on the chesterfield. She was wrong. As she came through the door she saw that he had torn the place apart in his frantic search for money. Evidently he had not discovered the tobacco tin underneath the galvanized bathtub where she kept her stash of bills, her "safe" money. It would have been better for Clara if he had, because then he would have been gone.

As it was, he was waiting for her.

He had taken off his belt and was swinging it. The room was small and there was nowhere for her to go. Johnny did not have to move at all. With the first swing, the buckle caught her across the mouth and opened up her lip. The metallic taste of blood shocked her but she stayed silent, knowing that any sound she made would only fuel his rage. The second time he swung the belt it caught her eye and she could not stop herself from crying out, although she knew it would not help her.

"Enough, Johnny. For God's sake, that's enough!"

"Quit your yelping, Bitch. You need to learn a lesson. Should'a given me my money when I asked you the first time."

He dropped the belt and went at her with his bare fists, beating her until she passed out. When she came to again, the house was dark and cold and she was alone. She was bleeding from the mouth and nose, and her damaged eye was swollen shut. She dragged herself to her feet and managed to light the lamp. She gazed at the battleground she had occupied for the past eighteen years and knew that it was no longer her home.

The only thing she felt was relief that her children had not had to witness their father's attack on her, that she had been the one to take the beating and not one of them, especially not Benita, the only one who had ever tried to stand up to him. Thank God that Benita had escaped. Thank God that Paul and Martina were happy with the nuns who taught them. Now it was her turn to leave.

CHAPTER SEVEN

By the time the police arrived at the house with the news of her husband's death, Clara was already on her way to LaPierre in Jericho George's pickup truck.

She brought with her nothing but her money tin and as many items of clothing as she could carry. When he saw the state she was in, Jericho had made no comment, just helped her up into the passenger seat and put her two bags next to her. They travelled the entire distance in silence, partly because it caused her pain to speak and partly because there was nothing to say. It was dark when they reached the village. Jericho brought her to her mother's house and waited for Hepzibah to open the door before he drove away. When Clara offered him payment for the ride, he waved it away.

"Keep your money, Clara. Johnny did a real bad thing this time. He's a good man, but the booze makes him crazy. I always tell him not to drink no more, but he never listens. He'll be sorry he did this to you. I think he's gonna be real ashamed of himself. I sure feel bad he hurt you."

Hepzibah washed Clara's eye with alumroot and made a poultice out of crushed teaberry leaves for her battered face. She brewed a tea that eased her pain and then put her to bed where sleep came quickly and lasted until late the next day. She woke to the sound of voices in the kitchen, her mother's and that of a stranger, a white man for sure. Her mother came into the bedroom and helped her out of bed and into the kitchen where the police constable was waiting to notify her that her husband had drowned. As he delivered his message he took note of her bruised and battered face, her swollen eye, her body hunched over in pain.

"Did Johnny do this to you, Clara?"

She said nothing, did not look at him, just stared at the ground.

"Had he been drinking? We're trying to find out what happened to him. He knew the lake, knew when not to trust it, knew how fast the wind could come up. It just doesn't make sense that he took the boat out when he did. Can you help us at all, Clara?"

Clara swayed on her feet, and Hepzibah reached out to support her. "My daughter's hurting pretty bad right now, Officer. She needs to lie down. Maybe when she's feeling better, she can answer your questions, but not now."

She led Clara back into the bedroom and the constable drove back to Blanchette where the official verdict was "death by misadventure." In a brief report in the local newspaper, inclement weather was given as the cause of the drowning of the well-known and experienced fisherman, Johnny Pigeon.

They had come to the end of the story, the end of her father's life, and Clara had nothing more to say. She stood up stiffly and crossed the floor to the stove, lifted the lid of the pot and stirred the contents with a wooden spoon, her back to her mother and her daughter. Hepzibah looked over at Benita and then spoke into the silence.

"Seems like Johnny was running away from himself maybe. Could be he didn't like himself too much. Maybe he was so full of shame he didn't know where to go, what to do, except get in his boat and push out onto the water"

She stood and put a hand on Benita's head, and she kept it there until at last the tears came.

"I'm not crying for him, Granny. I'm only crying for the waste of a life," she said when she was able to get the words out.

"He was your father, Benny. You are crying for the loss of your father. It's good that you can cry now. Your mother, she can't cry."

Hepzibah went to help Clara set out three bowls for the stew that had been simmering on the stove. Benita had eaten nothing all day, and the rich blend of familiar tastes and textures warmed and comforted her. Her mother, silent and withdrawn, ate almost nothing, and Hepzibah fetched a mug of warm water and added salt to it so that Clara could rinse her swollen mouth at the kitchen sink.

"Your mother's mouth is pretty sore. She can't brush her teeth yet; it still makes her bleed real bad. The salt water helps to stop infection. Remember all the stuff I taught you when you were a little girl, Benny?"

"Most of it, I guess. Ma, did he hurt your back, too? It looks like it's hard for you to straighten up."

"Uh-huh, he got a few good kicks in, that's for sure. Still hurts pretty bad."

Benita turned to her grandmother. "Maybe you should give her juniper berries, eh, Granny? In case of kidney damage. I remember you told me those berries are anti-inflammatory and help to wash out infection in the kidneys."

But Hepzibah had turned away, her attention seemingly caught by something else, and Benita hoped she had not offended her by questioning her choice of treatment.

While her grandmother helped her mother prepare for the night, Benita boiled water to wash the dishes. When she had cleared the table and tidied up the kitchen, she washed her face and borrowed Clara's toothbrush to clean her own teeth. She said goodnight to her grandmother and got into bed beside her mother who was already asleep. She closed her eyes and prayed to the God she said she did not believe in for the rapid healing of her mother's broken body, her broken spirit. Then she said a prayer for her father, Johnny Pigeon, that his troubled soul would find its way to a happier place and that God would judge him more kindly than his own daughter had been able to do.

CHAPTER EIGHT

By the time Benita woke the next morning, her mother was up and sitting at the kitchen table cautiously sipping tea. Clara was thirty-eight years old, but seeing her now, her battered face and hunched over body, it struck Benita that she looked older than Hepzibah. She poured herself a mug of strong tea, added some milk from the can on the table and stirred in three heaping spoons full of sugar.

"How's the pain today, Ma? Any better?"

"Some, I guess. Your granny's been giving me stuff that helps. At least I can sleep okay now. She's gone out looking for teaberry leaves. She's used up pretty much her whole supply."

"Which way did she go? Maybe I should go and help her, eh?"

Clara smiled her broken smile. "You always were the best little berry picker out of all of the kids. Remember when we used to bring you to the summer camp to gather stuff for the winter?"

Benita thought back to her visits to the *keyoh* and smiled.

"How could I forget? I loved being taken out of school to go berry picking. It was just the women and us kids and we always had fun."

"So listen, Benny, do you think you could get me some juniper berries before you leave for the city again? I can't move around so good yet. I'm pretty sure Granny has a whole bunch put by in the cold house. You know what they look like. Go get me some of those, okay?"

"For your back? But how come Granny hasn't given them to you already, Ma? She knows they're the best thing for kidney troubles. I wouldn't want to take them without her knowing. She's got the knowledge, not me. I'll go see if I can find her and ask her. You go lie down again for a while, okay? I'll be back as soon as I can."

The coat she had brought with her was fine for Vancouver where it never got too cold, but up here it offered little protection against the weather, and she wrapped herself in an old plaid blanket before stepping outside. It was a frigid, silent morning. The sky was a uniform grey and the air was still. Smoke curling from the chimneys of neighbouring houses had nowhere to go and just hung around adding to the greyness of everything. The trees stood motionless, and Benita felt the bite of the cold on her face, caught the unmistakable smell of snow on its way.

She did not have to go far to find her grandmother. Hepzibah was in her cold house sorting out the bulbs and roots she used to make infusions for every kind of ailment. Benita recognized lady's slipper and remembered that the root could be ground up and used to treat insomnia. She saw that her grandmother was well supplied with cedar branches which she burned in combination with sage and sweet grass and used in smudging. It was believed that their smoke could heal and purify those who were sick. When she was young, Benita had accompanied Hepzibah to the home of a dying woman and had seen how the smoke helped her breathe more easily and made her calm. Sometimes too, if she could find it, she used Indian pipe for smudging, but mostly she used it for treatment of inflammation of the eye.

The cold house was just steps away from her grandmother's house, but for Benita it was like stepping into the past. There was a big wooden table in the middle of the room where Hepzibah did all of the cutting, grinding, pounding, crushing, and mixing. The walls were lined with shelves where everything was stored in plastic containers and labelled alphabetically, and one big window set into the back wall let in all the light that was needed. Nothing had changed about the place since she was a child. The fragrant, tangy smell of branches and berries, the spotless orderliness of it, the tranquil workspace, and most of all the sight of her grandmother surrounded by all that she had gathered from the forest, the source of her treasure and her wealth, all of it was just as she remembered.

Hepzibah did not stop what she was doing, and Benita spent a few minutes re-acquainting herself with her grandmother's stock. Soapberries were the most familiar to her. She snapped open the lid of the container, took out a handful of the wrinkled dark red berries and held them to her nose. The smell alone was enough to transport her back to her childhood when she had been part of the large multi-generational group wandering the campgrounds for days at a time in search of berries. She remembered running free with the other kids, their clothes and mouths stained red with the juice of wild raspberries. They were allowed to eat all they wanted of the ripe fruit because the raspberries were too seedy to preserve for the winter.

Hepzibah always ignored the raspberries, but whenever she found a stand of soapberries she would stop and spread a blanket beneath the bush and tap the branches one by one. The ripe berries would fall into a blanket to be funnelled into her waiting wicker basket. Then she would take her knife and cut off branches still laden with unripe yellow berries. When she got them home, she would soak them overnight to soften them and then steep them in boiling water along with the branches. The resulting infusion she left for up to two weeks in a glass jug and then used it to treat digestive ailments. The ripe berries she spread out on a tray to dry in the sun before storing them in airtight containers.

If the summer had been particularly hot and there was an overabundance of soapberries, the kids got a special treat. Hepzibah would crush some of the ripe berries and mix the juice with water and sugar and a bit of lard. Then she would use a wire whisk to whip it all up until it formed a stiff pink froth and turned into what they called Indian ice cream. Thinking about it now, Benita recalled that it looked a lot better than it tasted because the berries were tart and tangy. If they were lucky, her grandmother would add salal berries to sweeten the mix which made it delicious. If not, after they had eaten a few mouthfuls they would start throwing it at each other and that had been a lot more fun than eating the stuff.

The next container was full of the purple-red sumac berries that Benita remembered for the lemonade they produced. As a little girl, she and all the kids had learned that they could pick only the red berries and were warned never to touch the white ones because they were poisonous. She remembered too the time when one of the girls from the village had come to her grandmother's house at night asking for sumac berries. Hepzibah had sent Benita away while she talked to the girl for a long time, and Benita, watching from the bedroom, saw that when the girl left she was in tears.

The teaberries nestled in their tub like little round red jewels, tiny and perfect. These were what her mother had been taking for pain, but Hepzibah also crushed their leaves to make poultices.

Benita searched the shelves until she found what she had come for. She snapped off the lid and removed a single juniper berry. It sat in the palm of her hand, its natural blue sheen dulled to a purplish black by the drying process. Then she felt, rather than heard, Hepzibah come up behind her. She was light on her feet and moved quietly, although she was not a small woman.

"Benita, juniper is not what your mother needs right now. Her kidney might be bruised from the kicking, but it's not ruptured. If it was, she'd be running a fever and throwing up. These berries are good for cystitis, but they're too harsh for her condition, might even cause real serious damage."

"Then why did she send me out to get berries for her?"

"Because she wants them for something else. Did she tell you she's pregnant?"

Benita recoiled. "Pregnant? How can she be pregnant? Oh my God! Did he rape her when he was drunk? Don't tell me her raped her too!"

"Benita, shhh. Calm down, child. Your mother is nearly three months pregnant already, but not with your father's child."

Benita put her hands to her face as if to ward off a blow, as if her grandmother's words could wound her.

Hepzibah made no move toward her, just carried on talking quietly.

"Ever since she came back here, she's been saying that she doesn't want this baby, can't go through with the pregnancy. Taking juniper berries can cause contractions and bring on menstruation. You were too young for that knowledge before, just a little girl. Now you are a woman, and you need to understand."

The quiet voice and even tone of her grandmother calmed and steadied Benita. For a minute, maybe longer, she stayed silent and then she said,

"In that case, I'm also old enough to know who the father is."

"Clara won't say. I'm sorry to be the one to be telling you all this, child, but sooner or later you'd have found out. Better it comes from me than from somebody you hardly know, or from one of your aunts down in Blanchette. Right now your mom is in real bad shape, Benita. She's still in shock from Johnny's death, and she's blaming herself for causing it. She's not too strong, you know."

"Not strong enough to go through with this pregnancy you mean? Okay, I get the picture now. The only thing I don't understand is why she wants juniper berries. I always thought it was sumac that caused miscarriage, not juniper. I still remember that girl who came in the night that one time when I was staying up here with you. She was pregnant too, wasn't she?"

"That was a pretty sad story. You weren't supposed to be around for that. That's why I sent you away. She was four months gone when the boy took off. I'm not mentioning any names here, okay? She ended up going to a woman up the lake at LaGlace and she gave her bark of slippery elm, told her it would bring on a miscarriage. Instead it gave her a bad infection that spread all through her body. Eventually that poor girl died. She was only seventeen years old. Slippery elm is bad stuff. The forest is full of good medicine, Benita. That's what I was teaching you those times you came with me when you were small. We need to use what is good and leave the bad stuff alone."

Benita looked at Hepzibah and saw the grandmother she had loved and admired for the whole of her life. This was the first time she had ever felt the need to question her judgment.

"Granny, if you had given her those sumac berries that one time, would they have worked?"

"They would have brought about contractions and she would have lost her baby, yes."

"Would she have gotten the same infection if she had eaten the berries?"

"No. She got the infection because slippery elm bark is not swallowed, it's inserted into the cervix as an irritant. But it's not clean. That's why it can be dangerous."

"So, Granny, that means you could have saved the life of that poor girl. Why didn't you? Why didn't you just give her those damn berries? It would have been so easy!"

"Benita, my job is to heal, not to destroy the life of an innocent child. What kind of healing would that be?"

"But you didn't heal her, did you? You let that girl die!"

"It was her choice to take bad medicine, Benita. She could have kept that one baby. I tried to tell her that night that it wouldn't have been such a terrible thing to let that child be born."

"But she wasn't ready to be a mother. She was only seventeen, Granny, the same age as me! I know you were young when you had your children and so was my mother, but this girl got pregnant by accident. She didn't *want* that baby".

For the first time since they had started talking, Hepzibah frowned and her mouth tightened in anger.

"Even a dog on the reserve, if it's not wanted, is given away to someone else. Some women might think it's okay to destroy their babies, but not me. That girl's family could have raised the child for her, and if not them, then some other family would have been happy to take it. You know there are couples that want kids but can't have them. That child would have been loved, no matter who raised it. Our people always take care of each other's kids. Have you forgotten that?"

Benita had never given much thought to abortion. In the sheltered world she lived in now, the subject was almost taboo. Of course she and some of her friends in Vancouver had heard horror stories about illegal abortions performed by untrained practitioners using primitive surgical methods. It was said that sometimes they injected poisonous solutions or inserted objects into the womb in order to dislodge the foetus. They often worked in an unhygienic environment and always in secrecy because abortion was illegal. And of course, she had been taught that human life was sacred, that the artificial termination of a pregnancy was in violation of the sixth commandment, that an embryo was a living being, part of God's creation, and as such had the right to be born and to live. But she was thinking about the girl who had died, how scared she must have been, and how desperate, to have gone through with such an invasive procedure. She thought too about the pain, and about the sickness and fever she must have suffered as the infection spread through her body. Then she thought about her mother, Clara.

"Granny, in another week, maybe less, Ma will be well enough to get what she needs herself. You know you won't be able to stop her if she's made up her mind."

"I always keep this place locked up, Benita, and I keep the key with me. Otherwise people could come in and help themselves to whatever they think they need. If you don't have the knowledge, most of this stuff can be dangerous."

"If you lock her out, she'll just go somewhere else."

"Maybe, maybe not. I'm thinking she'll be too ashamed to do that. There's not a person around here who doesn't know Clara, and anyway we still have some talking to do, her and me. You can't let yourself worry about her, Benita. Right now she's still in shock. She needs time to get over that first."

But Benita was imagining her mother crossing the lake to LaGlace. She'd have to go before freeze-up; otherwise it would mean a long trek on snowshoes, and she wasn't fit enough for that. She had visions of her mother collapsing in the snow, maybe dying of hypothermia. And even if she got there safely and was treated with slippery elm bark, she could die of infection like the girl that Hepzibah had turned away, and if her mother died, then she, Benita, would surely be to blame.

She snapped the lid closed and picked up the container. Then she marched across the floor and grabbed the tub of sumac berries. "I'm sorry, Granny, and I mean no disrespect, but I'm going to give her these and you can't stop me."

She spoke defiantly and felt ashamed when she saw the wounded look in her grandmother's eyes.

"No. I can't stop you," Hepzibah said. "You are making a choice. Just be certain that you can live with it is all I'm going to say. Okay, we're pretty much done talking here."

CHAPTER NINE

Together they walked the short distance to the house where Clara was still sitting at the table, her gaze fixed on nothing. Benita saw from the clock on the wall that only fifteen minutes had passed since she had left her mother, and yet it felt as if she had travelled to some far place and back again. She felt different, older in some way, no longer a daughter or granddaughter but like someone in charge, someone who knew what to do.

She placed the two containers on the table and sat down facing her mother, anger and pity at war within her.

"Ma, are you sure this is what you want to happen? It's probably going to hurt a lot."

"You think I don't know pain already? Just look at me, girl." Her mother's broken teeth showed briefly in a wry smile. "I know your Granny is against it and I'm sorry I gotta ask you to help me, Benita, but I can't wait no longer. I'm nearly three months gone already, and pretty soon it'll be too late. I've thought about it plenty, and I'm real sure."

"Who's the father of the child, Ma?" Benita had to ask the question and already dreaded the answer. She needn't have worried.

"Doesn't matter."

"Did my father know about it when he beat you up?" The question was out of her mouth almost before she had thought to ask it.

"He knew. That was why he went out and got drunk. It wasn't really about the money when he came at me that one last time. He said he was gonna to kick the child right out of me. Too bad he didn't succeed, huh? It would've saved you all of this bother." Clara laughed, a harsh and bitter sound.

Hepzibah had been standing in the background. Now she stepped forward to make her final plea.

"Listen, Clara, don't get rid of your child because of guilt or anger or hatred. Those are just feelings. Right now I know it's hard for you, but in time you'll be able to deal with all of that. But this little baby has done nothing wrong. Let it be born, and then you can give it to me. I'm not too old to raise another child. If you destroy it, you will be destroying my grandchild and Benita's brother or sister—Paul and Martina's too. Think about that."

Clara shook her head, looked away, then looked back at her mother.

"There's no more thinking to be done. I can't keep it. I'm sorry."

She opened the container in front of her and took out a handful of the deep blue berries and crammed them into her mouth, barely chewing before she swallowed and reached for a second handful and then a third. She looked set upon consuming every berry in the tub but Hepzibah reached out to prevent her.

"Stop. Enough. Now you need to wait for the bleeding to start."

"What if it doesn't?" Clara turned to her daughter, not her mother, to ask the question.

"Then you'll take the sumac berries. Don't worry, Ma, I'll stay with you until it happens."

The morning passed, long and dreary. The little house felt like a cage, and Benita paced it restlessly. Here there were none of the diversions available to city dwellers, no radio, no television, no books, no music—*nothing* to help while away the time. She peered through the window and saw only the grey gloom of November. There was nobody around, no sound or movement anywhere.

"Where is everyone?" she asked her grandmother. "This place is like a graveyard."

She wished she could have caught the word before it reached her mother's ears, but it floated in the air and hung there like bad smoke while Hepzibah answered the question.

"The men are hunting for moose. They've been gone for a few days now and won't be back till they have something to bring home."

"How do they stand the cold at night? Where do they sleep?"

"Looks like city life has chased away your memories, girl! Don't you remember how your grandfather used to go out in the fall with his brothers, your father too after he married your mother? A whole bunch of guys would set up camp at the keyoh, sleep there nights, and in the daylight track down the moose. They were good hunters, all of those guys, used to haul out four or five moose every year, sometimes a couple of caribou too. Saul and Johnny would bring three good ones up here to the village and then take a couple more to Johnny's mother down in Blanchette."

"I was never here for that. What did you do with all that meat?"

"First we skinned and stripped it. Then we hung it to drain the blood. Some of the meat we roasted right away and shared it with everyone who wanted to eat. Saul and me, we made a feast. Pretty much everyone came. What they didn't eat, they took home with them. The rest of the meat we dried for pemmican. And then all of us women would set to work on the hides. We'd tan them and make shoes, moccasins, mukluks, sometimes maybe a jacket or something. That's what me and Clara will be doing next week when the men get back, right Clara?"

But Clara didn't answer, seemed not to have heard a single word that had been spoken and Hepzibah went back to waiting patiently, getting up only to add wood to the fire or to make more tea which she urged Clara to keep drinking as the hours crept by.

At some point in the afternoon Clara stood up suddenly and moved to the window. "The pain is coming now," she said. "I think maybe it's starting."

"Yes," said Hepzibah. "Pain starting and life ending."

CHAPTER TEN

Benita seemed like a different person when she got back to Vancouver after her father's funeral. For one thing, she was a lot more talkative. When we first met, I had been the one who had done most of the talking, but now she was the talker and I the listener. It took her a long time to tell her story but from the gaps in the narrative I figured that there were parts she was withholding from me. She told me very little about her mother for example, and next to nothing about her side-trip to LaPierre. I suppose it shocked me to hear her say she had hated her father, but I could understand her rage—although everything about her past life was so far removed from my own that it was hard to believe that the two of us had grown up in the same country. I felt sorry for her, but she made it clear that she did not want my pity, and I learned soon enough never to show it.

Benita had changed in other ways too. She was harder, edgier. She started to smoke and kept a pack of Craven A cigarettes at my house because the O'Carrolls abhorred tobacco and would not allow it in their home. In this they were unusual. Pretty much everybody smoked back in those days, every man at least. Women who smoked were seen as *common* or *fast*.

There were a couple of times, too, when we met downtown that she arrived flushed and voluble, and I could smell alcohol on her breath. I asked her once if she had been drinking, and she told me defiantly that the O'Carrolls didn't mind if she helped herself to a drink or two on a Saturday evening. They had plenty, she said, and would never miss it anyway—which told me that her foster parents were unaware of her drinking.

I was uneasy about it, not the drinking itself, but the fact that she was deceiving them. I said nothing though, not wanting to sound like a sanctimonious prig by voicing my concern. Besides, I often had a beer with my dad, and neither of us thought twice about it. My mother, though, with the exception of a genteel glass of sweet sherry on Christmas Day, did not drink at all, and I had been brought up to believe that nice women didn't. Perhaps that was why it troubled me now to know that Benita obviously did.

During the Christmas holidays, she met my parents for the first time.

Doctor O'Carroll drove her over to our house and came in himself for a cup of tea and a slice of cake. He put my mother at ease right away with his big smile and old-fashioned courtesy, but I could see from Dad's bluff, almost belligerent manner that he was determined to hold his own against the doctor's social prestige and superior education. After an uncomfortable ten minutes of unwanted tea and polite conversation, Benita and I made our escape from what my mother referred to as the "Front Room." Our house was much like all the other houses on Winchester Avenue and a lot smaller and shabbier than the O'Carroll's posh home on the other side of town, but Benita seemed to like it well enough.

"Your house is sure nice and comfortable, Larry. Smaller than where I'm staying, but way bigger than the house I grew up in."

There was a wood and coal fireplace in the dining room and on top of the bookcase beside it was the radio. On the rare occasion that my parents and I wanted to listen to the same programme, they would sit in the armchairs on either side of the fireplace and I would sit at the dining table. Now, while Benita scrutinized the row of framed photos on the mantelpiece, I added a log to the fire and and we listened to "The Tennessee Waltz" and then Nat King Cole singing "Mona Lisa." Benita was wearing a red dress that night, and when the little room grew warm from the fire, she removed her dark blue cardigan.

Her arms were bare and I found myself wanting to touch them, to stroke her smooth skin. I reached over and slid my hand down the length of her arm and then back up along the inside where it lay against her breast. Her skin felt as soft as sun-warmed rose petals. I stroked the velvety softness of her inner arm and felt her breast through the silky fabric of her wine-red dress. She did not move. Her expression was unfathomable, her eyes fixed on the blue flame spiralling and curling around the cedar log burning sweetly on the Christmas fire. When I touched her nipple she sighed and stirred and turned towards me.

"Larry," she said. "*Larry.*"

And then, unmistakably, I heard the creak and groan of the chairs in the front room and the sound of footsteps in the hallway. In a panic I withdrew my hand and leapt to my feet just as the dining-room door opened and Dr. O'Carroll poked his head into the room.

"Benita, Larry's parents would like you to stay over for dinner. How about I pick you up after Midnight Mass? Margaret and I and the rest of the kids are going to morning Mass, so I am at your service tonight, young lady."

For as long as I could remember, my mother had cooked bacon and cabbage and potato cakes on Christmas Eve. I wondered what Benita would think of such traditional Irish fare, but she tucked in as eagerly as I did which earned her a big smile of approval from my mother.

"I've always liked a girl who's not afraid to eat."

She scooped up our used dishes and went to fetch the traditional Christmas Eve dessert, a lavish, sherry-soaked, whipped-cream-topped trifle. Dad was quiet during the meal, very much on his best behaviour. I noticed that he did not attempt to tease Benita as he did the rest of my friends, but then I had never brought a girlfriend home before, and he was unaccustomed to feminine company other than that of my mother—who did not count.

After the meal, Benita offered to help with the dishes, but Mom would not hear of it.

"Not on Christmas Eve, and certainly not on your first visit to us, Benita, but thanks all the same, love. Now why don't the two of you go and sit by the fire and listen to the wireless while Dad and I clean up? I'll give you a call when it's time to get ready for Mass. We'll have to leave early or we'll never get a seat."

So we sat and listened to Perry Como and Lauren Hutton singing "A Bushel and a Peck" and Eileen Barton singing "If I Knew You Were Coming I'd Have Baked a Cake" followed by a medley of Christmas carols, and when the table was cleared and my parents busy washing dishes in the kitchen, I closed the door and we exchanged Christmas gifts. Benita gave me the collected poems of Gerard Manley Hopkins and a tie that my dad later described later as *gaudy*, and I gave her the lambs wool sweater I had chosen for her right at the beginning of December.

As soon as the famous window displays had been installed at street level and the entire store decorated for Christmas, I had visited the Ladies Wear department at Woodwards. One of the sales assistants who had worked with Benita brought out three sweaters that she thought would compliment her dark skin and eyes. Two of them were different shades of red, and the third, which I chose without a moment's hesitation, was moss green. I saw that I had made the right choice on Christmas Eve when Benita took it out of its tissue wrapping and put it on over her red dress. It was perfect, and in the soft glow of the firelight, so was she.

"It suits you, Benita."

"Hah, you sure I don't look like one big Christmas ornament?" she said with an embarrassed little laugh. But she left the sweater on and wore it to Midnight Mass, and I was glad that my gift had made her happy. I learned that night that a man can make a woman happy by giving her something beautiful. Over the years I have used that knowledge when I counsel men who come to me in despair because their wives are restless and unhappy and have fallen out of love with them. Of course a gift cannot heal a broken marriage, but it can be a step in the right direction, or at least a starting point.

On Christmas Day, it was just the three of us as usual, and my mother cooked a goose as she had done for each Christmas of my life. She cooked a goose because my father claimed that turkey meat was dry and tasteless, and because, for both of them, it brought back memories of Ireland. It had become a family tradition and was, therefore, sacred. The goose being such a large bird and with only the three of us to eat it, my father made his usual comment before he began to carve.

"You know, this seems like a terrible waste of good food. We have enough here for twenty people at least. There must be plenty poor souls in this city who'd be happy to be eating this goose with us. Kathleen, did you never think to invite them? Isn't Christmas a time to share with those less fortunate than ourselves? Isn't that what our religion's supposed to be about, for God's sake?"

My mother responded irritably, as she always did. "Why do you wait till we're sitting down to eat, Charlie, to bring up the subject of those in need? If you feel so strongly about it, go out yourself into the highways and byways and gather up a few hungry people, invite them in off the street why don't you? And if you're not going to do that, then would you hold your tongue and let Larry and I enjoy our dinner in peace."

By the time the goose was carved Dad's self-righteous wrath had subsided. He bestowed lavish compliments on my mother's cooking, uncorked the wine, and the three of us tucked into our Christmas dinner.

It was true, though, that in those days three was an uncommonly small number for a family, certainly for an Irish Catholic family. When I was little, I had begged my parents for a brother to play with in much the same way that I begged for a train set and later a bike.

"If I'm really good this year, do you think Santa would bring me a little brother?"

"Ah now, Larry, I'm afraid Santa doesn't deliver babies," my mother told me.

"How come?"

"Because babies come from God, not from Santa."

"So should I ask God then, Mommy?"

"You can indeed, son, but just remember that He might say no. Your daddy and I have been praying for a baby for a long time now."

"Then why hasn't he given you one?"

"We don't know, Larry. We just have to trust Him and accept that He knows best when it comes to giving out babies."

Instead of a baby brother, when I was seven years old, I got a puppy for my birthday, a little West Highland White Terrier that I christened Rice because when we went to Burnaby to pick him out of the litter my dad said, "Hey, Larry, look at that little guy. He's no bigger than a grain of rice."

He was small and feisty and he looked as if he was smiling, so he was the one who went home with us. Dad had already bought a little dog basket, and my mother had cut up an old blanket so he'd have a cozy place to sleep, but on his very first night with us, the minute my bedtime arrived he launched himself out of the basket and scuttled up the stairs behind me. For maybe a week, my dad waged war with him over his sleeping quarters, but we all knew who would win the battle, and every night until I left home, Rice slept in a ball at the foot of my bed.

My parents went on praying for another child, or at least my mother did. Dad was never much given to prayer. He told me once that he regarded it as women's work, along with the cooking and the cleaning, and that I'd be foolish to spend too much of my life on my knees, but that was much later. In any case, there were no further pregnancies, and I became reconciled to being an only child. I had plenty of friends, I had a *best* friend in Renzo Rosetti, and I had my dog, Rice.

When Renzo's parents told him he could not have a puppy of his own, I offered him half shares in mine, and as proof that I meant it we conducted a joint naming ceremony in which Rice became Rice-a-Roni. That seemed to make everyone happy, my mother in particular. She liked the idea of an Irish-Italian-Scottish dog and liked even more the fact that I was willing to share my possessions with others. But I was relieved that I was not expected to let Rice-a-Roni sleep at Renzo's house because my generosity did not extend that far.

Besides, Renzo's mother would not permit the dog in his bedroom, let alone on the bed, so it never became an issue.

On Christmas Day, I waited for my parents to say something about Benita, but it wasn't until after the goose had been eaten and the Christmas pudding served that Dad let his views be known.

"So why did you never tell us you were dating a native, Larry?"

The word, once uttered, seemed to hover in the space around his mouth, the sound of it lingering long after it was spoken. I watched my father's lips opening to receive another forkful of the dense, dark, fruit-filled pudding, and it struck me for the first time just how repulsive the act of eating can be.

"Why should I have told you? Is it important?"

"Damn right it is," said my father.

My mother looked at me and then at her husband.

"Will you take a little more wine, Charlie?" She filled his glass and looked across the table at me. "She seems like a really nice girl, Larry. We're so glad you brought her home to meet us."

I ignored her.

"Why does it matter, Dad?"

"Why does it matter that my son has an Indian for a girlfriend? Well, how about this for a start? How about because no matter how good her marks are in school, no matter how pretty she might look when she's all dressed up, no matter how hard the O'Carrolls have worked to take the savage out of her, that's what she is. Give her a couple of years and I guarantee she'll be back on the reserve living on government handouts and drunk every weekend like all the rest of them."

Suddenly the sight of the half-eaten food on my plate disgusted me, and there was a bad taste in my mouth.

"You can guarantee that, can you, Dad?"

"Oh, I can indeed. Doctor O'Carroll told us some of her story. I admire the man for taking in a girl like that, but I tell you, Larry, she's nothing but trouble, and I'm telling you for your own good, son. Get rid of her, and get yourself a decent girlfriend before this one goes bush on you."

With a nervous clatter my mother swept up knives, forks, and spoons from the table and piled up the used plates beside her.

"Ah now, Charlie, you should pity the poor little girl, the hard life she's had. It must have been terrible for her having to leave home like that and move in with a strange family in a big city, start at a new school and everything. I'd say she must be a great girl altogether, sure she must."

I hardly heard her. I pushed my chair back and stood up abruptly.

"You know nothing at all about Benita, Dad. You call her a savage; that was the word you used, wasn't it? Aren't you forgetting that her people have been in this country a lot longer than you have yourself? With an ignorant attitude like yours, I'd say that it's you who are the second-class citizen here, not Benita. Don't worry, though. You won't need to spend any more time with her. I'll make sure you never have to see her again."

I wanted to hurl every plate, glass, knife, fork, and spoon at the wall, to hear the crash of things breaking. Instead I hurled words. They shattered as they hit the air and fell into shards that would never be swept away completely. I did not know that then, but maybe my father did. Certainly my mother knew.

"Please, Larry," she said. "Please. This is a holy season, and there should be no angry words spoken. Can we just pretend that this conversation never took place and have peace in our home on Christmas Day?"

She began to cry, and that shocked me as much as anything my father had said. My mother always projected happiness in a determined, even resolute way, and she regarded tears as foolish and self-indulgent.

My father got up from the table and put his arms around her.

"Now, Kathleen, this is no more than a little family squabble, isn't that right, son?" He didn't look at me as he spoke. And I answered, without looking at him.

"Sure, Dad. Sorry for upsetting you, Mom."

I cleared the table, helped with the dishes, and took Rice for a stately stroll around the park. At the distinguished age of ten, he had grown stiff in the joints, but when I let him off the leash he would still scoot off into the trees to explore new scents. Today though, he didn't budge. He stood at my feet wagging his stumpy tail hopefully and looking up at me questioningly. He could always tell when I was upset over something.

"It's okay, Rice-a-Roni, go off and play now."

But he wasn't interested. Instead he ambled along beside me and gave me the gift of his company until I was able to rid myself of anger and it was time to go home again.

CHAPTER ELEVEN

For the remainder of the Christmas holidays and well into the New Year, my father and I maintained a wary truce. We avoided each other as much as possible, and whenever we were forced into each other's company, we were as polite and distant as two strangers. Once the new term began, I would hang around with friends after school, and by the time I got home he would already have left to join his buddies at the local beer parlour, or gone to watch a hockey game, or even to attend a Knights of Columbus meeting. On those occasions my mother could hardly complain about his absence from home, knowing that he was in the company of good Catholic men and under the sheltering wing of Holy Mother Church.

In January the weather grew bleak, and for three days Vancouver disappeared in a heavy grey fog which came slithering down from the mountains and swallowed up the entire city. Outdoors it was damp and dismal, the air chill and dead. Downtown streets looked drab and dispirited and instead of the daily clatter and grind of the port, the only sound to be heard was the mournful lament of foghorns as cargo ships came and went in the becalmed and ghostly harbour. With the North Shore out of sight and the Lion's Head lost from view, Vancouver lost its identity and became anonymous, a city full of nameless streets and dull buildings. I hated the fog, and when the rain arrived, I was glad to see it. Rain felt normal. We were familiar with the rhythmic splash and clatter of it, with sidewalks full of umbrellas manoeuvring to pass and overtake, with dripping trees, overflowing drains and gutters, the smell of wet wool and wet dog. And just when the whole world seemed hopelessly waterlogged, the wind came sweeping down from the north and dried up the wet and weary city, dispersing heavy purple rain clouds, driving them out to sea and out of sight.

Growing up in Vancouver I had always watched clouds. As a child I used to wonder where they had gone when the sky grew clear again. I asked my mother once and she answered the same way she answered most of my questions.

"I don't know. Sorry Pet. You'd better ask your father."

There was never a chance of an "I don't know" from my father. He had an answer for everything, no matter how fanciful, and I was confident that he would know all there was to know about clouds. He did, of course.

"Where do the clouds go? They go straight over to Japan."

"Where's Japan?" I wanted to know.

"Over on the other side of the ocean."

"What do they do when they get to Japan?"

"They lay around and rest for a while, and then they blow right back again to Vancouver".

After that I kept a watchful eye on the clouds as they travelled to and from Japan. Even now, fully informed as I am about the West Coast climate and meteorological conditions, I find them fascinating, far more interesting than a clear blue sky which has little appeal to the eye and none whatsoever to the imagination.

"What's so great about a blue sky except for being blue?"

That was what I had asked Renzo once, back when the two of us were still in primary school. He pondered briefly, then rolled his eyes.

"Larry," he said, "that has to be the dumbest question anyone has ever asked."

Years later though, Benita agreed with me that clouds were more interesting than a clear blue sky, and I felt vindicated at last.

When I returned to school after the Christmas holidays, I found that classes which before had held my interest now seemed dull and interminable. As a result I acquired a lackadaisical approach to homework, and that led to a sharp decline in my marks. But it wasn't until I began to show up late for school each morning that I received a summons to stand before the High Priest in the office known to both staff and students as the Holy of Holies. Father Howard Martindale had been Principal of St. Michael's Catholic High School for ten years. He was a big, beefy man with fleshy features and little beady eyes that gazed upon those called into his presence and held them captive until they succumbed to his iron will. Despite his bulk, he reminded me of a Border Collie trained to establish eye contact with a hapless sheep that has foolishly chosen to detach itself from the flock. At the sheepdog trials in Dublin one summer I saw those watchful dogs quell delinquent sheep with an unblinking, relentless glare that sent them scrambling to re-join their brethren. Of course Father Martindale would not have seen himself as a dog at all, but rather as a good shepherd whose duty it was to go in search of a sheep gone astray and to lead it home to safety.

"Come in, come in, Larry. Sit down. Good lad. So tell me now, how're things?"

"Fine, Father, thank you.'"

"Parents well, I hope? Good, good."

With the niceties out of the way, he cut to the chase.

"Now, Larry, Father Garnet tells me you've been late for class a few times lately. Why is that?"

It mattered not a whit that I was almost an adult, that I could drive a car, that I had proven myself capable of holding down a responsible job with a reputable company, or that I had a girlfriend. I might just as well have been seven years old again.

"I'm sorry, Father. I overslept. I'll try not to let it happen again."

I spoke apologetically and allowed myself to risk a quick glance at the door. This was a mistake.

"Oh, don't be in a rush to leave now, my boy. We're not finished here yet. Have you been staying up too late at night? Is that the problem?"

"Uh, yes, Father. I guess that must be it."

His hard little eyes of indeterminate colour bore into mine.

"You guess. I see. Well, would you permit me to hazard a guess of my own?"

I nodded as if I had a choice in the matter.

"Well, my guess is that the reason for the late nights is not your dedication to the academic courses you are taking this term, nor to your upcoming mid-term exams, which, as you know I am sure, will affect not just your future but also the reputation of this school. Of course, you might prefer to call that an educated guess since I'm basing it on information given to me by your teachers. Your homework seems to have fallen by the wayside recently, has it not, Larry?"

"Well, perhaps a bit, Father."

"A bit. Uh-huh. Well, let's see now. Here's what we have to date. An essay on Wordsworth handed in three days late at a cost of a thirty percent reduction in the final mark. A French translation not handed in at all. Two math assignments not completed. Ditto biology. You failed your last chemistry test and scored miserably on the one before that. All in all, I'd say that your academic performance is slipping more than 'a bit'. Would you agree with me there?"

"I suppose so, Father."

"You suppose so. That's a definite improvement over a mere guess, so I'd say we're making some headway now. Allow me to formulate another supposition then. Just suppose that you continue to arrive late for class and continue to neglect your studies, what do you suppose the outcome might be?"

"That I won't do too well in my final exams, Father."

"Ah, now we're finally getting somewhere, my boy, because that's exactly what I suppose, too. In fact, I'd even go a step further. I'd say there's a pretty good chance of you failing your exams altogether which would mean you wouldn't get into McGill University, if that's what you're still intending to do."

"Yes, Father."

"Alright. Enough supposing. What's troubling you, Larry? Anything you'd like to talk about?"

"I don't think so, Father".

There was no 'think' about it. I doubt that there was a single student at St. Mike's who wouldn't have preferred to talk to a grizzly bear than to Father Martindale.

"Is it girlfriend trouble?"

"No, Father."

"Trouble at home?"

"Not really, Father."

He pounced, and I knew I had made a tactical error.

"Ah, so that's it, is it? Tell me, Larry, how's your spiritual life these days?"

"Uh, alright, I think. I'm not sure how to answer that. I mean, I'm not sure what the question means, Father."

"Well, Larry, I couldn't help noticing that you didn't receive Holy Communion at Mass last Sunday. That's usually a good indication that something's not right."

And there it was. The hard eye, the unwavering stare forcing me to hold its searching gaze, pinning me in place, trapping me. But I was not some woolly-brained sheep ready to submit to the power of a higher-ranked animal. Besides, what right did he have to nose into my life outside of school?

"Ah, now don't look at me like that, son. I know exactly what's going through your mind. You're thinking, 'Why does this old fool think he can intrude on my inner life when only Jesus Christ Himself has the right to do that?' Don't bother to deny it, Larry. I can see that's what you're thinking, or close enough anyway."

I almost believed him. I almost believed that those gleaming little eyes of his could peer into my mind and read my thoughts. I said nothing and we sat in silence for a minute or two while I briefly contemplated making a run for the door. Then he surprised me.

"And you're absolutely right, of course. I have no right to invade your inner sanctum. The problem is this. As head of this school, since it is a Catholic school, I am as much responsible for your moral and spiritual welfare as I am for your academic progress, and of course those three things are inextricably related. I understand your reluctance to talk to me. I probably wouldn't much want to talk to me either. I'm not the most approachable of people. But if there is something worrying you, Larry, it's best to get it out in the open and deal with it. It might not be a bad idea to go to confession, you know. It is the most liberating of all the sacraments. You go into that dark, stuffy little box weighed down by guilt and anxiety. You mumble and stumble your way through an account of all that is burdening you. On the other side of the grille some tired priest who has heard it all before listens, and with the power invested in him by God absolves you of guilt and anxiety. You resolve to try to avoid re-occurrences of the behaviours you have just confessed. The priest asks you to say some prayers as penance for any wrongdoing, and then you leave, lighter of heart and clearer of conscience. A wonderful sacrament! No wonder people line up to take advantage of it! How about it, Larry? Think you might want to give it another try?"

Father Martindale's glowing account of what Catholics have recently come to call the sacrament of Reconciliation was a far cry from the way I would have described it then. My mother, the spiritual adviser of the family, had always prescribed monthly confession whether I needed it or not, a view supported by the schools I attended, but not by my father who argued that unless he were guilty of murder or grand larceny he would simply be wasting the priest's valuable time on a monthly list of minor infractions. Had I not been an only child, I think he might have backed me up when I began my own feeble protest at the age of twelve, but, as it was, he rebuked me sharply and reminded me that when it came to matters of religion I was to follow my mother's example, not his. Perhaps his own father had told him the same thing if he had had the temerity to question the monthly visit to the confessional. I asked him about it one Saturday afternoon.

"I did what my mother told me, Larry. Make sure you do the same." Then he slid out the door to go to the racetrack, and I was left to accompany my mother to church.

So by the time I was in my teens, monthly confession had become as much a habit as Sunday Mass. Most of the kids I knew went as regularly as I did, and it became, if not exactly a social event, then at least a shared experience. Going to confession was part of the Catholic way of life at that time, and classmates who did not conform found themselves in a small and uncomfortable minority. For the rest of us, it was a matter of routine. It was not that we didn't take it seriously or treat it with respect, but we were also experts, highly skilled at presenting an acceptable list of venial sins interspersed at carefully timed intervals with "the big ones," promiscuity, masturbation, lying, cheating, and stealing, the ones we all tried to slide past the priest without him noticing.

We never succeeded. Still, though, we went on trying to lessen the shame of having to admit that we were less than pure, less than holy, less than good. And yet, in spite of all that, as I saw Father Martindale glance at his watch and close the file before him, I believed him. I believed that he did have my welfare at heart and I knew he had given me good advice. When he stood up to dismiss me and I thanked him for his time, I meant it sincerely.

The following Saturday, when I saw Father McGowan's name above the confessional, my heart sank. He was the most junior of the three priests who served our large Irish-Italian parish, and also the most popular. Despite his degrees in history and philosophy, he never condescended to his working-class parishioners, many of whom had not graduated from high school. He was athletic and sports-loving which endeared him to the men, and his sense of humour and sympathetic, easy-going manner won him the approval of the women. All the girls considered him good-looking, and many of them had a crush on him. His only problem as a priest was that nobody below the age of twenty-five wanted to confess their sins to him.

"I would plain *die* of embarrassment if I had to go to him," said red-haired Molly Prendergast shortly after Frank McGowan's arrival in our parish. Her opinion was shared, if not voiced, by the rest of us, so when I got to the church on the Saturday following my session with Father Martindale, I was hoping to find everybody's favourite on duty. Father Vanelli needed no sign to announce his presence other than the thick haze of tobacco smoke that permeated the airless confessional whenever he occupied it. It was rumoured that, over the years, he had acquired the skill of being able to doze off to the drone of the human voice and to come instantly awake again just in time to administer the penance, confer absolution, and hear the final act of contrition. The other great thing about him was that, friendly as he always was whenever we ran into him at school or in the neighbourhood, he never remembered our names and would simply smile benevolently and continue on his way. If you were ever to rob a bank say, or hold up a train, he'd be your man for sure. He'd say nothing and forget everything, and it was the opinion of many that every parish should be blessed with at least one priest like him. But it was not Father Vanelli that day, it was Father McGowan.

"Bless me, Father, for I have sinned. It has been three weeks since my last confession..."

I rattled through the formalities and got down to the painful business of my Christmas confrontation with my father. I was completely truthful and left out nothing. When I reached the end of the account I tacked on the rest of my usual monthly list that included laziness, bad language, masturbation, selfishness, impatience. As always, I was thankful for the grille between us and the welcome darkness which assured me of privacy and anonymity—at least that's what I fervently hoped.

Father McGowan sat for a few moments in silence, and I could hear the sound of his quiet, steady breathing. Had it been Father Vanelli I might have coughed discreetly to wake him up and prompt a response. As it was, I sat back and relaxed, knowing that my part in this exchange was more or less over. Finally he spoke.

"You are angry with your father because you think he spoke unfairly. You believe he let you down, and you are disappointed in him."

Exactly, I thought

I said nothing, though, because he had not asked for a response. I was expecting him to launch into a sermon, or at least to tell me that whether or not I agreed with my father I still owed him respect, was still obliged to honour him, but he did neither.

"I don't blame you," he said. "I'd feel the same way myself. Well, your father will have to come to terms with his own conscience, and it is not for us to judge him. What you have to do now is much harder. Are you able to forgive him and let go of your anger? This might be no help at all, but I'm certain that in speaking the way he did on Christmas Day he was motivated solely by his concern for you rather than by a poor opinion of your friend and her people. Sometimes children have to be wiser than their parents, which doesn't seem fair, does it? I'm sure, though, that without forgiveness there will be no real peace in your family."

As a counsellor, Father McGowan was a natural. More to the point, as a priest, he absolved me from the outrage and anger that had consumed me ever since my father had revealed himself as a racist and a bigot. And he was right about the connection between forgiveness and peace. I went home after confession that day lighter of heart and fully prepared to forgive my father. Of course he himself saw no need to apologize and had no intention of ever doing so, that much was clear. So in the end, for the sake of peace in the family, I gritted my teeth and said my piece.

"Sorry, Dad, for my anger and lack of respect."

"Just try to remember *why* I said what I did, Larry," he said. "You are our only son. All our hopes rest in you."

He made no further reference to the quarrel, but the next morning I heard him whistling while he shaved, and that evening instead of meeting his friends at the beer parlour, he stayed home with my mother and listened to the radio. On the surface all was well again, but I knew that my relationship with my father had changed in a way I did not like. What I wanted was to be seventeen and carefree again, but what I felt was eighteen and sad.

CHAPTER TWELVE

Of course I said nothing to Benita about the aftermath of her Christmas Eve visit, not wanting to spoil the memory of it for her. Besides, she had problems of her own to deal with. Not long after the new term began, she asked if she could come over to the house on Saturday afternoon so that I could help her with an essay. I came up with a plausible excuse for the weekend and suggested instead, a weeknight when I knew my father would be out. We got through the assignment and had a brief chat about school, but the whole time she was there I was uneasy, worried that Dad might decide to come home early that night, and I was vastly relieved when she said she had to be on her way so as to make her nine o'clock curfew.

"Is that something new, Benita, the curfew?" Mom asked her as she saw her to the door.

"Yeah. I guess I'm not doing too well at school these days, so I'm not supposed to stay out late,"

I was not the only one whose marks were dropping. Benita had failed three of her recent tests and had started to skip classes and hang around downtown with a couple of older girls she described as "pretty wild." Dr. O'Carroll had already been summoned twice to St. Rita's to discuss her altered attitude and the alarming decline in her marks, and it had been Benita herself who had suggested the curfew, more because she felt sorry for him than because she felt it would make any difference to her performance. She could not, or would not, explain her sudden lack of interest in school, but she begged him not to go to the trouble of hiring a tutor for her.

"Larry can help me more than any tutor," she had assured him, which was why he was willing to let her come over to our house on school nights. She explained all of this to my mother whose expression registered first sympathy and then alarm.

"Well, I don't know that Larry would be the best one to help you, love. He's having enough trouble getting his own homework done these days."

But I could tell that she too was more concerned about Dad coming home and finding Benita in the house than she was about about my performance at school—and was every bit as relieved as I was to see her leave.

Rain was falling in sheets when I walked her to the tram stop at the end of the road, and even though she clutched my arm tightly and tried to match her step to mine, we did not quite fit together under the sheltering dome of my mother's red umbrella. In the end, I held it over her and let the rain fall upon me, happy to get wet if it meant that she stayed dry. With her face hidden from view, I watched our feet hit the wet sidewalk with a splash and finally establish a rhythm that kept us locked together and moving as one person.

The wind blew in from the sea in fitful gusts, and the red umbrella fought with me as I tried to rein it in and prevent it from launching itself into the night sky. Each time I tightened my hold on the wooden handle, I felt Benita tighten her grip on my arm, as if I too might be snatched away and go floating off into the darkness. In the end, though, she was the one who came adrift, and I was the one who let go.

We didn't talk until we reached the tram stop. Then she asked, "How come you're not doing your homework, Larry?"

"I don't really know," I said. "I just can't seem to concentrate on it any more."

"Me either."

"Neither" I said, automatically.

"What?"

"It's 'me neither', not 'me either'."

She rolled her eyes. "It might be correct, Mr. Professor, but it sounds fake, and it's not my way of speaking. I want to ask you about something else though, so let's forget about my grammar for now, okay?"

"Okay. What do you want to know?"

"I want to know if your mom likes me or not."

"Of course she does."

"How about your dad?"

I looked into the distance, hoping to spot the tram on its way down Main Street but saw only needles of rain illuminated by the blur of passing headlights.

"Yes," I said. "He likes you, too."

"You sure about that? So how come he's never at home when I'm at your house? Seems to me you only ask me over when you're sure he won't be there."

"No, it's not like that, Benita. It's just that we're not on the best of terms right now, my dad and I."

"Because of me?"

"No! It's because we had a bit of a falling out on Christmas Day and I guess we're still pretty mad at each other."

"Uh-huh. So what did you fight about?"

"We didn't exactly fight, we just had an argument."

"Do you and your dad argue a lot, Larry?"

"No, I'd say this was probably our first major disagreement."

"So it was pretty serious then, huh?"

"I guess so," I said, and then the tram arrived. Just before Benita stepped aboard she looked at me and shook her head.

"Know what, Larry? You're a real bad liar. But that's okay. People don't always want to hear the truth."

There was no time for me to reply. Clinging to the rail, she leaned out precariously and spoke into the rain-swept darkness.

"So why don't you come over to the O'Carroll's instead? How about Saturday? We can work on our weekend homework."

The overhead wires hissed and clanked as the tram slid away into the rain-washed night. I stepped out from the shelter, unfurled the red umbrella, and set out for home.

Soon after that, things began to change. At least for me they did. First there was my session with Father Martindale. Then I went to confession. Finally I apologized to my father which made my mother happy and restored peace at home. I started doing my homework again, stopped getting to school late in the morning, and found I was able to concentrate in class again. In short I returned to being the good student I had always been, a role that seemed to suit me better than being a rebel and also made life a whole lot easier. But something else changed too, and that was my relationship with Benita.

For a while I continued to tutor her, but it soon became evident that I was wasting my time because she simply didn't care. Sometimes I'd be explaining something to her or working out a math problem on paper, and I'd look up and catch her gazing at me with a half-smile on her face. I'd ask her if she understood the example and she'd yawn and say something like, "Sure, Larry. You're a great teacher. Want to go to a party tonight?"

But the one party I went to with her was in a squalid basement suite on East Cordova where everyone got drunk and a fight broke out because one guy tried to grope another guy's girl. It might have turned nasty if one of the antagonists hadn't passed out first, but Benita found it funny. Of course by that time she was drunk too.

"Come on, Larry, loosen up a bit, will you? Let's have some fun!"

But if there was any fun to be had that night, I wasn't able to find it, and when Shirley-Ann, one of Benita's new friends, threw up all over my shoes, I almost got sick myself which made her laugh even harder. At that point all I wanted to do was to walk out the door and keep walking until my lungs were full of the cold, clean air of winter and I could breathe freely again.

"Let's go, Benita. These people are disgusting."

She stopped laughing, and when she spoke her voice was harsh and strident, far different from her normal soft, even tone.

"What did you just say? Are you calling my friends disgusting? You think you're better the rest of us, huh? Well, let me tell you something, Larry. You're not…"

Her eyes grew unfocussed and she lost the drift of what she was saying. She swayed toward me and grabbed my arm.

"Better take me home now, Larry. I don' wanna stay here no more. I just gotta get my coat, okay?"

We had left our jackets in the bedroom, and when I went to get them, I found two people lying on top of them, half-dressed, half-drunk, making out in a half-hearted way. They weren't too keen to move and swore at me when I tugged at the mound of coats to find Benita's. But even their cursing was half-hearted, and I yanked extra hard, hoping that they would tumble right off the bed.

When I went back to find Benita, she was locked in the tight embrace of a tall, skinny guy with greasy hair and serious acne. I don't think she even knew his name. He let go of her right away when he saw me coming and even helped me to put her arms through the sleeves of her jacket.

"Goo' night, then" he said, and lurched away into the crowd, beer spilling from the open bottle in his hand.

Shirley-Ann, cleaned up and almost sober, came over and put one arm around Benita's waist and between us we got her as far as the door although it soon became clear to both of us that she was incapable of going further, and I knew I had no hope of getting her on the tram to take her home.

"Poor kid," said Shirley-Ann. "She hasn't learned to hold her liquor yet, eh?"

Other than walking out on her, I could think of only one thing to do, and it was something I hated the very thought of. I left Benita with Shirley-Ann and went in search of the phone. When I asked my father if he would come and pick us up, he asked no questions, just told me he'd be there in fifteen minutes and to be waiting for him outside the house.

Another girl was standing where I had left Benita, and when she saw me she said, "Are you Larry? Hey, Benita wasn't feeling too good. Shirley-Ann took her to the washroom."

Kids today have a way of expressing an unpleasant experience. "It was a total nightmare," they'll say, and you get the picture right away. Too bad the expression didn't exist when I was young because, for me, that whole evening was a complete nightmare.

By the time Dad arrived we were standing in the street outside the party house, and Benita had sobered up considerably. She was deathly pale, and when I saw her shiver in the cold wind, I took off my jacket and wrapped it around her. Neither of us spoke. There was really nothing to say, and my father, to his credit, said nothing either except for, "Okay, guys, hop in."

Once in the car, Benita closed her eyes, and I concentrated on giving directions. It was late and the streets were almost empty, but still it took us quite a while to get to Shaughnessy. My father sat in the car and waited while I took Benita to the door and handed her over to the O'Carrolls', mumbling something about Benita not feeling too well.

"Please thank your father for bringing her home," Dr. O'Carroll said, courteous as always. "And thank you for taking care of her. You're a good kid, Larry. Okay, Benita, you go on up to bed now. We'll talk in the morning."

I said goodnight to the three of them, walked up the driveway and got into the car. All the way home I waited for my father to ask for an account of what had happened, but he did not. My mother was waiting up for us. The kettle was boiling, and when I looked around the kitchen, I felt the warmth and the welcome of it. I sat down with my parents and drank a cup of tea that nobody really wanted. The only thing they wanted, I realized then, was just for me to be there with them, safe at home again. Nothing was said about the party, nor about Benita, and I felt the tension slip away and release me from its grip. Just before I went to bed I turned to my father.

"Thanks, Dad."

"Any time, Son. Good night now."

She was hard to love, I see that even now. And I was eighteen, too young and too naive to deal with the complications of another life when I found my own confusing enough. I tried hard to understand her and blamed myself when I could not. Her problems became my failure.

"You can't save her, Larry," my mother said once when she was in the middle of cooking the evening meal, and I was sitting at the kitchen table working on a last-minute homework assignment. I hadn't seen Benita since the night of the party on East Cordova. Whenever I tried to phone her, she wasn't home and did not return my calls, and, to my shame, what I felt about that was mostly relief mixed with some guilt.

"You know it's only God who can save her, Pet. And you're not God."

Poor Mom. She was only trying to make me feel better, but instead she made me mad.

"Mom, I'm sick and tired of hearing that God is always there when people are in need. Know what I think? I think praying for help is a waste of time and that religion is nothing more than a myth."

If she was shocked or hurt by my words, she did not show it.

"Now, Pet, you're upset I know, but it's no use getting mad at God. God isn't the cause of Benita's problems. Poor little girl. Life isn't going to be easy for her I'd say. Now how about a nice cup of tea before you finish that homework of yours?"

The basketball season came to a glorious end, with our team winning the provincial championship yet again and myself being voted Most Valuable Player. I was a star in the classroom again as well, which made my teachers and parents happy. I didn't have a lot of free time, but what there was I spent with Renzo, Molly, and the rest of the gang. In our last few months at St. Mike's, we clung together and there was a kind of wistfulness about us because we knew that, come September, our little group would disband and scatter.

Benita was not part of that group, and as time passed she became a stranger to me. When I thought about her at all it was the hostile, withdrawn girl who drank too much that came to mind rather than the Benita who read poetry and argued about movies and cared about ideas and smiled a lot and, although I missed *that* Benita, I sometimes wondered if she had really existed, or if I had invented her to match my own requirements. I found myself envying Renzo who had never had to re-think his Molly.

I still phoned Benita from time to time—more out of politeness than ardour—and asked her how she was doing. She always answered that she was fine, studying hard for final exams, staying home most of the time.

Then she would ask me how I was doing, how were my parents, polite questions like that. Once she told me that she had given up drinking for Lent. Once she told me she missed me. But when I asked her over to the house for a meal, she said she had too much homework that weekend, and when I invited her to a basketball match, she said she couldn't make it, and when I asked her to a movie she said she was busy that night, so after a while I quit worrying about her. Then one evening in April, she phoned me out of the blue, and on Easter Monday we went for a walk around Lost Lagoon and suddenly it was like old times again.

CHAPTER THIRTEEN

Senior prom at the St. Rita's Academy For Girls would turn out to be quite different from what was planned for St Michael's. Their prom was a sedate and sober affair. When Benita chose to invite me to accompany her to the dance, Dr. O'Carroll himself had to assure the principal that I could be relied upon to behave as befitting the occasion. And there were no after-Prom parties for the St. Rita's girls. Instead, after the last dance in the school hall, parents drove their daughters home, and shortly afterwards everyone went to bed. It wasn't dull exactly, but it was far from being a riotous evening.

Benita looked spectacular that night, by far the most striking girl in the room. She wore a wine-red dress which in itself made her stand out in a field of convent girls wearing white or pale pink or baby blue, innocent colours, bridesmaid-bland. It wasn't just the dress, though, that set her apart. Benita moved through the room as if she owned it. I noticed that while all the brothers and cousins who had been imported as escorts for the evening were ogling their partners, many of the older men, the fathers of the girls, could not keep their eyes off Benita and that made me mad. They were married men for God's sake! They were here with their daughters! Benita seemed not to notice, and if she did, she did not comment on those furtive looks and neither did I, because what I felt most of all that night was pride.

I knew that John O'Carroll, the tall, good-looking hockey-playing university student, the pride and joy of his family, had been expected to accompany Benita to the dance, but she had chosen me instead. I didn't want anything to spoil the evening for her, especially not lecherous old men. They were a pathetic bunch anyway, and I felt sorry for their wives.

While we were consuming our baron of beef served with fresh asparagus and duchesse potatoes, Benita leaned toward me and whispered in my ear.

"This is kind of boring for you, huh, Larry?"

"No! I'm enjoying myself."

And I was, because I was there with her and she was back to being the Benita I knew and understood. We were easy together, and I could see from the laughter in her eyes that she was amused by the whole scene. I was finally learning to read her, but I understood why some of her classmates, those tightly curled, lightly scented, discreetly lipsticked, chattering, giggling, pastel-gowned princesses of Shaughnessy, might have felt uneasy in her presence.

"What's so funny?" I asked her while we were waiting to be served our strawberry shortcake. I expected her to answer, "Oh, nothing" as she so often did, but that night she did not shut me out.

"This whole thing is funny. Just sitting here eating fancy food and being with all these rich people seems funny to me. I think about my other life, I mean my life on the Dena'dzlie Reserve, and I just have to laugh at all of this. Know what I mean?"

I looked around and saw a room full of wealthy parents, fathers in tailored double-breasted suits, mothers in floral silks and pearl earrings, their daughters with their expensive convent school brand of good manners and eager, open faces. I saw white linen tablecloths, formal place settings, bowls of white roses and camellias, and up at the head table a formidable line-up of priests, nuns, and school counsellors.

It was certainly far more elegant and sophisticated a gathering than any prom at St. Michael's would ever be, and these people—the *Shaughnessy Set*—were far more affluent than their counterparts on the east side of town, yet I did not feel out of place if only because I was in my home city. Like most Canadians, I had never so much as set foot on an Indian reserve, and all I knew about Blanchette at that time was what Benita had told me. I tried to imagine myself in that remote village on the shore of a vast, unknown northern lake and failed. That would be the place where I would feel like a stranger.

After the speeches, the girls danced with their fathers and then with their escorts, while their mothers nervously attempted to capture the moment on film, and when the evening came to its official end, the O'Carrolls drove the two of us back to their place. Despite the late hour their house was far from quiet. Not that this was unusual. Their home always seemed to be full of people and talk and laughter and music.

When Benita had fallen apart after the death of her father, the entire family had rallied round and supported her in a way that I had failed to do myself. When she decided to give up alcohol for Lent, they did the same, at least the ones who were old enough to drink, and even on the night of her prom all the O'Carrolls, parents as well as children and family friends, sat around drinking tea or Pepsi or Orange Fanta, and I stayed there enjoying their company until well after midnight. When I got home I found my parents waiting up for me just as they always did, and as soon as I walked in I read the question that was hovering over the kitchen table as if it were printed in bold type on a poster.

"The whole evening was perfect. I had a great time."

But they needed further reassurance. "No problems then, son?" Dad asked.

"None at all."

My mother smiled, clearly relieved. "Go on then," she said. "Tell us all about it."

And I did.

CHAPTER FOURTEEN

When it came time for my own prom, instead of pairing up with one of my classmates I caused a bit of a stir by inviting an *outsider* to be my guest. A few of my friends had already met Benita of course, but among the rest of the grads there was a great deal of speculation about the mysterious stranger who would be coming to the dance with me. This might have intimidated some girls, or at least made them feel self-conscious, but I knew it wouldn't worry Benita. She wore the dark red dress she had worn to her own prom, but this time with her hair unpinned and falling straight and darkly shining to her shoulders. In a room full of careful curls, her hair was remarkable. My mother, one of the battalion of parents in charge of flowers and decorations for the evening, saw us enter the room together and said what I had neglected to say.

"Benita, you look lovely!"

Why hadn't those words come from me instead of my mother? I don't know. Not original enough perhaps, not smart enough for a wit like me? I stood there feeling gauche and was grateful when my tactful mother threw me a lifeline. "Isn't she beautiful in her red dress, Larry?"

"Yes," I said, looking at Benita. "Yes, truly beautiful." And she heard in my tone that I meant it and gave me a smile.

As members of the grad council, Molly and I, together with our dates for the evening, Renzo and Benita, had to sit at the head table during dinner and make small talk with the guests of honour. This was no problem at all for the outgoing and self-assured Molly, but I wondered how Benita would handle being seated next to Father Martindale. I wasn't in a position to help her out because I had to devote myself, entirely and at high volume, to old Father Fitzwilliam while Renzo did his best with the Chairman of the Board. But when I was finally able to turn toward her, I saw that she looked poised and relaxed and that Father Martindale appeared to be unusually animated.

There were other after-prom parties that night, but the one at my house was the main event. My parents did not get back from cleaning up the hall until almost midnight, but even at that hour people were still arriving, and the entire basement was jammed solid. My mother brought down a tray of sandwiches: roast beef, egg salad, cheese and tomato, and a platter of sausage rolls and fancy little vol-au-vents filled with something savoury. There was a huge chocolate cake too, but she was afraid that in the crush someone might sit on it, so she left it in the kitchen and told Benita to bring it downstairs whenever it was needed. Renzo brought four bottles of his father's wine for the girls because most girls did not like beer, and somebody else had brought along a stack of 45s to add to my own collection of Theresa Brewer, Perry Como, Tony Bennett, and Frankie Laine. I turned up the volume as high as it would go, and Eartha Kitt rasped her way through "C'est si Bon" followed by Joni James complaining about "Your Cheating Heart." There was no room to dance, but people danced anyway, some with a lit cigarette in one hand and the other draped around the neck of their partner. The room grew noisy and hot and smoky, and Renzo went around topping up wine glasses and handing out cold bottles of Kokanee that had been standing in a bucket of ice.

Benita was drinking Orange Crush, and when Renzo noticed her empty glass, he went and fetched another bottle of wine.

"You'll end up with an orange tongue if you drink any more of that stuff, Benita. Try some of this instead."

"No thanks. I know your dad's wine is great, but I better stick to soda tonight."

She wasn't the only one. When I noticed Annabelle Russo drinking Pepsi, I asked her if it was because her parents had made her promise to stay away from alcohol. She rolled her eyes at me.

"Hey, aren't we supposed to be adults now? No, I'm just one of those strange people who doesn't like the taste of alcohol. Probably the same with you, hey Benita?"

"Uh-uh. I like the taste alright, but it's not a great idea for me to drink, right, Larry?"

She laughed as she spoke, and I answered with the first thing that came into my head.

"Lent's over now, Benita. One glass of wine won't do you any harm."

She stared at me. Then she leaned closer and said so that only I could hear.

"You sure about that, Larry? You sure you're not afraid I might start acting like a drunken Indian again, huh?"

She raised her empty glass and I had a brief moment of doubt, a moment when I wished it was Lent again, but then the voice of Little Richard and the insistent beat of very early rock 'n roll took over and the talking stopped and everybody danced. Was there a point at which the orange in Benita's glass turned red? The lights were dim, and I'd already downed a few beers myself, so I didn't notice. By that time there wasn't much wine left anyway, at least not enough for her to get drunk on.

Things began to quieten down. Little Richard gave way to Nat King Cole and Perry Como, and when somebody switched off the overhead light, there was only the glow from a couple of lamps in the corner. Couples drew closer, and when I held Benita I could feel the heat of her body and the curve of her breast as she pressed herself against me. Renzo had long since tired of dancing and would have happily stretched out in a corner and fallen asleep if Molly had let him. Instead she prodded him awake and came bustling over to tell Benita it was time to serve the coffee and cake. Bossy Molly.

Everyone groaned when she switched on the lights and pranced upstairs to organize things in the kitchen, followed reluctantly by Benita, Renzo, and myself, but when we served up the rich chocolate cake it was well received and the coffee that followed it revived us all, even Renzo. Soon the music was back at high volume and the party was back in full swing, and that's how it stayed until four in the morning when I took Benita to my bedroom and we lay down together on a jumble of coats and jackets and I undressed her and touched her body, every part of her, and made love to her for the first time.

"Are you sure, Benita, are you sure?"

I asked her, but I didn't wait for an answer. Later she told me that she wished I had at least spoken her name as I entered her, but my need for release made me heedless of everything but the rhythmic drive and surge of my own body inside the velvety warmth of hers. Afterwards, she slept in my arms for a while and then I gently woke her. We gathered up our clothes and were still pulling them on when Renzo came barging in to look for his and Molly's coats.

He made a good show of not seeming to notice that Benita was half naked and that I had no shirt on, but I could tell he was shocked and deeply embarrassed. He resolutely kept his gaze on the wall above the bed and muttered something about coming back later in the day to help clean up. Benita had wrapped herself in somebody's coat and she stood at the foot of the bed with one hand holding it closed, the other covering her mouth. I thought at first that she might be shedding tears of humiliation but when I moved towards her I saw that she was trying to hold back the laughter that shook her whole body.

Renzo had fled with only Molly's coat over his arm and then I saw that it was his jacket that was covering Benita's nakedness. I found her dress on the floor and she stepped into it and turned her back to me so that I could draw up the zipper.

"Are you okay?" I asked her when she had stopped laughing.

"I'm fine. Just can't believe I grabbed poor old Renzo's jacket is all."

"I'm really sorry, Benita."

"About Renzo? Ah, he'll get over it. Too bad your bedroom doesn't have a lock on the door, though"

"No, I mean I'm sorry about what just happened, what we just did. I guess I lost control. I swear I didn't mean it to happen like that."

She turned to face me and her expression was inscrutable.

"Are you telling me you regret it?"

"I'm just saying what we did was wrong, Benita."

"What was so wrong about it?"

"Why would you even ask me that? We're eighteen years old and we're not married. That means we've committed a sin."

When she opened the door, her profile was illuminated by the light from the hallway. For a moment she stood there motionless, and when she turned to look at me I saw something in her eyes that I didn't like. *Scorn*; I thought it might be scorn. I waited for her to say something but she remained silent.

"What are you thinking, Benita?" I asked her.

"What am I thinking? I guess I'm thinking that you'd better get yourself to confession, Larry."

And she was gone, leaving me to straighten out the bed and wonder if Renzo would tell Molly what he had seen. Then I wondered whether my parents would notice anything different about us. Would they guess when they saw us that we had left innocence behind and acquired what the priests liked to call carnal knowledge?

I needn't have worried. When I went downstairs my parents were hard at work in the kitchen serving up pancakes and bacon, and there were eight people already crowded around the chrome table eating in bleary-eyed silence. Benita was nowhere to be seen.

"She went home, Larry," my dad told me. "Said she was too tired to stay and go to Mass with us and phoned home for a ride. John O'Carroll picked her up and they left just a few minutes ago. Now how many pancakes can you handle?"

I ate without appetite, drank three cups of strong coffee and waited for the caffeine to jolt me back to normality. That was what I wanted more than anything, a normal day, the familiar routine of going to Mass with my parents, seeing my friends, even catching up on homework.

In truth I was relieved that Benita was gone. I did not want to deal with the aftermath of the night before. I did not want life to get complicated. At the same time I felt elated, proud that I was no longer a sexual innocent, but it didn't take long before I began to think ahead to the confession I knew I'd have to make before the following Sunday, and that was not a happy prospect. I wasn't worried about Mass later that morning. Every one of us Grads had already broken the fast and nobody expected to see us up at the altar rail after partying all night. It would be a different matter the following week though, and there would be all kinds of speculation if I were to miss Holy Communion two weeks in a row.

CHAPTER FIFTEEN

The week following the prom passed uneventfully. With only a month left before final exams, the mood at school was serious and focused, and I stayed up late each night studying. Benita had little to say when I phoned her. Dr. O'Carroll had engaged a tutor for her, a university student who came to the house three times a week and coached her in math and science, her two weakest subjects. Her marks had improved steadily throughout the spring term, and she was back on course to start at UBC in September.

On Saturday afternoon, I headed for the church and was glad to see the light on above Father Cooper's confessional. He was old, getting a bit doddery, but could be relied on for speed and efficiency. And of course this time I had rehearsed my lines.

"Bless me, Father, for I have sinned. It has been six weeks since my last confession. Since then I have often been selfish and impatient. I have had occasional impure thoughts. I have been inattentive during Mass a couple of times. I have sinned against chastity, and I have used bad language on at least five occasions."

Father Cooper pounced like a terrier on a rat.

"This sin against chastity. Was it alone or with others my son?"

And there it was! The question we all dreaded. For the first time in my life I told the confessor that my sin against chastity had been committed 'with others', which meant that I had not masturbated.

"I see. Tell me about these *others*, my boy."

"Uh, there was only *one* other, Father."

"One time, or one person?"

"Both, Father"

"Male or female?"

"Huh? I mean, I beg your pardon, Father?"

"This *other* you sinned with? Male or female?"

"Oh, female, Father, definitely female. A girl."

"Okay, we've got that much established. And this girl, is she all right?"

"Um, how do you mean, Father?"

"I mean there's no chance you could have got her pregnant, is there?"

That caught me off guard. Father cooper didn't wait long.

"Ah, I can tell from your silence that you didn't think about that. Well, you should. You know, Larry, there's a good reason why sex before marriage is forbidden by the Church. The sacrament of holy matrimony confers God's blessing on the sexual union of two people who love each other and who commit their whole lives to each other and who are ready to welcome children into their relationship. Do you and this girl want to get married?"

Wait a minute! Did he just call me by name? Can the old guy see through that grille? So much for the anonymity of the confessional, I thought bitterly. *And what did marriage have to do with this anyway?*

"No, Father. She's only seventeen and I'm eighteen."

"Then to have a sexual relationship with her is not only sinful, it is very unfair to her. Can't you see that, son?"

"Yes, Father." And I could. What he said made sense. At least it did right at that moment.

"So are you able to make a firm purpose of amendment and resolve to commit that sin no more?"

"Yes, Father."

"Then say the Act of contrition now while I give you absolution from all your sins. For your penance say three Our Fathers, three Hail Marys and three Glory Be's." God forgives you, my son."

"Ego te absolvo..."

The thing about the sacrament of Penance which will never be understood by those who are not of the Catholic faith is that it really does confer a sense of forgiveness and lightness of being that makes the penitent feel unburdened. When I made that particular confession all those years ago I knelt in what was essentially a wooden cupboard divided into two compartments by a wire grille. On the other side of the grille sat the priest almost hidden from view, wearing the sacerdotal stole around his shoulders. In the great cathedrals of the world those traditional confessionals are still in use, but ever since the reforms of Vatican Two most churches have done away with them and the sacrament of reconciliation, which for the majority of Catholics now occurs only at Christmas and Easter, takes place in a well-lit room, usually face to face with the priest.

When I was growing up, we went to confession at least once a month, and those who were especially devout went every week. At some point in the sixties the notion of sin fell out of favour and the word itself out of popular usage. Psychiatrists, psychologists, and a host of psychotherapists took over where priests left off, and a whole new industry was born. People stopped taking responsibility for their transgressions once they learned they were not wrong at all, merely *human,* and that the blame might well be placed on others, such as their parents. Catholics who abandoned the Church often went into counselling, no longer to confess their sins but to rid themselves of emotional baggage or to work through problems, or to deal with issues of co-dependency, difficulties with relationships, alienation, low self-esteem, anxiety, loneliness, and depression. And when the Talking Cure did not work they turned to drugs, alcohol, plastic surgery, botox, de-tox, herbal supplements, breast implants, and Viagra.

I would like to be able to say that people are happier now, but I know they are not. They are spiritually empty. Some of them, after years of wandering in the wilderness, return to the Church. Often they are parched and broken people, lost sheep with nowhere else to go for healing and redemption. And it is the true gift of priesthood, an incomparable gift, to be able to absolve them in the name of God, to tell them: "Your sins are forgiven. Go and sin no more."

Of course all of us, being human, do sin again. Despite my truthful and sincere confession, despite my firm purpose of amendment, and, alas, despite the sanctifying grace of absolution, I myself most certainly sinned again at every available opportunity, which was usually whenever Dr. and Mrs. O'Carroll went out to dinner with friends.

I wish I could say that on those occasions Benita and I made love, but although there was plenty of passion, it did not feel like love. The whole thing was too rushed, too furtive, too desperate to have been love, although it is also true that I did not know much about love then, about how to love another person. And I had no idea how Benita felt because I never thought to ask her.

Then I stopped thinking about Benita altogether and turned my mind to preparing for my final exams. When they were over, there was a trip to the Calgary Stampede with my parents, and not too long after that the exam results arrived in the mail, and I had the thrill of tearing open the envelope and finding that I had achieved distinction in almost every subject.

"Well, we won't have to worry now, Larry. It'll be scholarships all the way for you! McGill University will be begging for your presence." That was Dad of course.

It was my mother who reminded me to phone Benita.

"Please God, she'll have done as well as you, Pet. I've been praying for her too, you know."

It seemed as if Mum's prayers had been answered because Benita's marks were outstanding, although there was no trace of excitement in her voice as she read them out to me over the phone, only a tentative question when she got to the end.

"When will I be able to see you, Larry?"

"As soon as I get home for the Christmas break. But I'll write to you often, and I'll try to phone as often as I can too. It's going to be great, Benita. Aren't you over the moon about it? I know I am!"

Silence. I waited.

"I meant, can I see you *before* you go away?"

"Sure. How about tonight? Let's go somewhere to celebrate."

We met at the little park near the O'Carrolls' house. The evening sun shimmered softly above the stand of leafy maples where Benita stood waiting. The branches were shot through with apricot light, and the leaves rustled and glimmered and held tight to the dying day, and I saw that her hair was tied back in a single braid and that her eyes were dark and watchful like those of a stranger. I wanted to bring a sparkle to those eyes, to share my elation with her, to make her smile.

"Well, we got the marks we wanted, both of us. Let's go and celebrate at the White Spot, shall we? I've got fifty bucks on me, a gift from my parents, so you can go ahead and order anything you want."

She stepped out from the shadow of the trees and stood before me, solemn and immobile.

"Why so serious, Benita? Don't tell me you're not happy with your marks? They were outstanding. So why the glum face?"

"I'm pregnant."

The two words fell on my ears like a foreign language. What was she saying?

"Larry, did you hear me? I'm pregnant."

"But you can't be! That's impossible."

My voice sounded thick and muffled and seemed to come from far away. I felt as if I were caught up in a terrible dream. I turned away from her and stared up into the branches above us as if they offered an escape. They did not.

"I've seen a doctor and had the test. There's no doubt about it, Larry."

I was well aware that language can be distorted by the perception of the person who hears it. Until that moment, though, I had not understood that the spoken word, once uttered, cannot be unsaid and that words used as weapons almost always find their target.

"But how can you be pregnant, Benita? We only did it a few times, for God's sake and I was always careful. How could you have let it happen?"

When she replied I heard only anger in her voice. Not until much later did I allow myself to consider the hurt that must have been there too.

"You're blaming *me*? I always thought it took two people to make a baby, and I've never been with anyone but you."

"Uh-huh. If you say so. Okay, so what happens now?"

"I don't know."

"Well you need to figure out something fast. We're all set to go to university, not to be parents! I guess you could get the baby adopted, but then you'd have to turn down your place at UBC. And my parents..."

I felt sick when I thought what this would do to them, their disappointment in me, their shame, my father's anger. A thought came to me then and I felt a flicker of hope.

"Listen, Benita. Maybe there's a way we can fix things. I have some money saved up from my job at Woodwards. It's yours if you want it."

She looked confused for a moment, then shocked.

"What for? You don't mean to pay for an abortion, do you?"

I must have winced at the word, and she lashed out at me.

"What's wrong, Larry? Did I just say a bad word? Let me try to think up a nicer one for you. No, sorry, nothing comes to mind right now. Wait a minute, though. Isn't abortion illegal? And isn't it supposed to be what you call a mortal sin? Of course I would be the one going to hell, right? Not you. All *you* need to do is go to confession, say a couple Our Fathers, and show up for Mass on Sunday with a clear conscience. Not me, though, Larry. I'd be at the mercy of some backstreet hack who could kill me along with the baby—and send me to hell at the same time. But you know something? You're right. For sure it would solve the problem."

I tried to collect my jumbled, panicky thoughts and say something rational, but Benita gave me no chance to speak.

"Okay, give me the money, Larry. I'll take it. Sounds like a deal. Oh, by the way, congratulations on your exams." And she walked away.

I thought about going after her, but my body refused to obey what my mind told it to do, and by the time I was able to force myself out from the shelter of the trees and start moving, Benita had disappeared.

CHAPTER SIXTEEN

Margaret O'Carroll took the envelope upstairs and handed it to Benita who was awake but still in bed.

"Larry came by to drop this off, Dear. He said to tell you that even if you change your mind you're still to keep the money. What money is he talking about, Benita? I think you'd better explain."

Benita opened the envelope and shook out ten fifty-dollar bills.

"Blood money," she said. "He's talking about blood money." Then she closed her eyes and would say no more.

Later that day, she told the O'Carrolls that she wanted to visit her mother and grandmother. They did not attempt to dissuade her, and in the evening, the oldest of the O'Carroll boys, John, drove her downtown to the bus station. She took the overnight Greyhound to Prince George, and from there she hitched a ride in a logging truck headed for Blanchette. When she climbed down from the truck, she breathed in the familiar smells of fresh-cut timber and burning sawdust and then walked the short distance down to the lakeshore.

The sun blazed down from a clear blue sky, and the air was still in a way that it never was in Vancouver. When she had first moved to the coast, she was struck by the constant motion and clamour of everything, Always the wind in your face, the sea sighing and surging, waves pounding the shore, battering the sea wall, hurling huge trees and logs up onto the sand. She had never seen those tall coastal trees at rest. They were always bending, swaying, tossing their branches around, sometimes crashing and falling to the ground in the wake of a storm, but never still. Even the sky was full of movement; all those clouds scudding to and fro on their endless journeys to nowhere.

Here, all was motionless; water, trees, air, sky. Benita stood in the stillness of a northern summer and was glad to be back. She looked at Sturgeon Lake, now serene, its calm blue surface a mirror for the trees along its shoreline, and thought how deceptive it was, how unpredictable and how dangerous. A wind could come out of nowhere, whipping the water into a frenzy, creating a savage maelstrom that could capsize the sturdiest of boats, swallow up the most seasoned of fishermen. Her father had known the lake better than almost anyone, and yet he had perished, or maybe had *wanted* to perish. Had he chosen to give himself to the lake? Could death by drowning have seemed like a better deal to him than life? She would never know now. Nor did she much care. Either way, the Lake had taken him.

She turned away from the water and looked back at the town of Blanchette where the little white church of St. Gabriel stood out in the afternoon sun. She heard the clatter of the two saw mills and the occasional roar from the fire in the belly of the beehive burner. Pretty soon, she figured, the day shift would be ending, although the burner would remain active all night. To the east of the lake, the Dena'dzlie Reserve straggled up one side of the hill and down the other all the way over to the bridge. From where she stood, she could not see the house she had grown up in, but her Grandmother Pigeon's house was unmistakable, and so was the house where her father's sister lived, her Aunt Emma.

She had seen enough. She walked along Sturgeon Road toward the hotel and spotted Jericho George's beat-up old pickup truck parked outside the grocery store. The doors were unlocked as always, and on this hot day he had left the windows wide open. Benita climbed in and waited, knowing that sooner or later he would come and take her to LaPierre where her mother lived now, and her grandmother, Hepzibah.

When Jericho found her, she was fast asleep, her head against the door-frame. He put the two bags of groceries he was carrying in the back of the truck, rolled up the window on the passenger side, made a pillow from the old plaid jacket that always travelled with him, and placed it beneath her head. She barely stirred, slept all the way up to LaPierre despite the constant bumps and jolts from potholes in the rough, deeply rutted road.

At the sound of the truck, Hepzibah came to the door and took the bags from Jericho.

"Wait up, Hepzibah," he said. "I got something else to deliver to you today."

He opened the door of the truck and helped Benita out, handling her carefully, as if she were fragile, as if she were something precious.

Her grandmother smiled when she saw her.

"How were the exams?" she said.

"Good," said Benita. "Real good." And then she began to cry.

Clara came out and put her arms around her daughter.

"It's okay, Benny. You're home now," she said, and led her into the house. There was no further talk until Benita had cried herself out. Then Clara and Hepzibah fixed a meal, and the three of them sat down to eat. Benita found that she was hungry, and as she ate, she felt all the tension and strain of the past days dissipate, and she was suddenly overcome with lassitude. She saw the question in her mother's eyes but felt too weary to embark on explanations. She was exhausted.

Hepzibah stood up and began to stack the dishes.

"You need to sleep now, Child," she said. "Plenty time for talking in the morning."

But it was almost noon the next day when Benita woke up, and the little house was empty. She filled the bath, washed her hair, and lay in the tub until her skin shrivelled and the water grew cool. When she was dressed, she made tea and drank it outdoors while her hair dried in the sun. She was still sitting on the doorstep when Hepzibah and Clara came back from the forest laden with the wicker baskets she recognized from long ago. She saw that her grandmother had been gathering bulbs, leaves, and shoots, while her mother carried only berries. A hot summer like this one always produced a bumper crop, and it looked as if they would be well supplied for the winter.

When Clara saw her daughter sitting on the step, she set her basket down and sat beside her.

"Pregnant, huh?"

"Yeah, but I won't be needing those sumac berries, Ma."

"You gonna keep it?"

"I guess so."

"What about school? You gonna give up on all of that?"

"Don't really know what I'm gonna do, Ma. I'm eighteen. Wasn't planning on getting pregnant."

"Who's the father?"

"Just some white guy. Doesn't matter. He doesn't wanna know."

Benita's voice grew tight, and she took perverse pleasure in breaking Larry's rules of proper speech. She wasn't going to talk like a white person any more. She thought about the money he had given her to get rid of the child he had made with her, and felt only hatred for him.

"So what are you gonna do?"

It was Clara who asked the question, but Benita looked over at Hepzibah, still standing impassive and watchful, asking nothing, saying nothing.

"Granny, you still think you're young enough to raise another child?"

Before Hepzibah could answer Clara said, "Between the two of us, we're plenty young enough to take care of our own grandchild. You quit your worrying now. Everything's gonna be okay."

CHAPTER SEVENTEEN

The long, hot days of summer passed slowly and languorously. Benita made a few trips to the lending library in Blanchette and read her way through dozens of books. At home she helped her mother and grandmother with the mundane tasks of cooking and cleaning as well as drying, sorting, classifying and storing the berries and bulbs that had been taken from the forest. She felt strong and healthy and, under the care of Hepzibah, had no need to see a doctor.

September arrived, bringing with it cooler mornings and shorter days. Shadows grew longer, and the light took on a golden lustre as summer surrendered to fall. The birch trees that lined the edge of the lake and grew in scattered stands at the foot of Mount Cardinal proclaimed their presence with a showy display of vibrant gold, standing like lit candles among the sombre evergreens. When the yellow leaves began to fall, the men left to set up camp at the keyoh, just as the women and children had done earlier in the summer.

Isaac King, Clara's older brother, was the first to return to the village with a moose, a large bull in its prime. He brought it to his mother's house and hung it for her on a scaffold made of birch branches so that the blood could drain before the hide was stripped from the flesh. When she was growing up, Benita had always been away at school when the moose hides were stripped and tanned, but now she watched Clara and Hepzibah so that in the future she would be able to take her place with them and help them with their task.

It was not easy work, requiring time and endless patience as well as skill.

Once the meat had been removed, Isaac distributed it among the relatives while his mother and sister prepared their portion for the roast. Then they removed the hide from the birch frame and put it in a wooden barrel to soak for three days so that the hair and remaining flesh could be scraped off more easily.

In the afternoon, Isaac's wife Cecile came over with baskets of fresh corn and potatoes, and the aroma of roasting meat and vegetables drifted into the air and brought people out of their homes long before it was time to eat. One of the men brought a case of beer and a few bottles were passed around together with jugs of Kool-Aid for the kids and hot tea for the women.

Benita recognized most of them from childhood berry-picking expeditions. Many of them now had children of their own and already looked middle-aged, although she knew that the oldest among them could not be more than twenty-five. She saw that they were at ease with each other but not with her, despite her efforts to engage them in conversation. At first they seemed curious about her life in the city, but she found that she could not hold their interest for long; Vancouver held no reality for them. A couple of them were pregnant, and that gave her hope that she might find companionship in the coming months. One of them, Violet Thomas, only a year older than Benita, was expecting her second child. As a little girl she had been lithe and mischievous, full of animation and quick to laugh. Now she was heavy and inert and her voice was flat and lifeless.

"So who's the father of your kid, huh?" she asked.

"Just some guy down in the city."

"White guy?"

"Yup."

And that was the end of the conversation. What did these young women do all day? Benita wondered. Did they read books? Sew? Acquire knowledge of healing like her grandmother? What did they talk about when they got together? How would she establish her position among them if she were to spend the rest of her life here? Her years of education were of little use in a place where the only knowledge that was respected was that of healing or tanning or beadwork. Pretty soon they all drifted away, leaving her alone by the fire until her grandmother came and stood beside her.

"Right now you are like a stranger to them, Benny." Hepzibah spoke quietly. "They are thinking you've maybe spent too much time with white folk. It'll be easier when the baby comes, you'll see."

"I'm not too sure about that, Granny. Don't forget my baby will be half-white. Could be they'll never accept my child, or me either. I feel like I have nothing in common with them any more. Maybe I don't belong here any more."

"You must be patient, Benita. Everything changes if you wait long enough," said Hepzibah. "You need to give them time."

A couple of days after the moose roast, Cecile King arrived with her sister Francesca Jack to help Clara and Hepzibah work on the hide. They took it from the barrel, two of them twisting it around a stick to squeeze the water from it. Then they stretched it by hand to remove the wrinkles and speed up the drying process. Clara made a series of small holes along the outer edge so that they could string up the hide in the birch frame and leave it there to dry. They were lucky with the weather, which continued warm, so that by the next day they were able to start on the laborious task of scraping the rest of the flesh and hair from the skin. It was messy work and could not be rushed since it was all too easy to pierce the hide with the tip of the knife. When her mother showed signs of fatigue, Benita took her place and eventually found a rhythm that allowed the knife to scrape away the tough hair that clung stubbornly to the thick hide. She was glad it was a bull moose. Had it been a cow, the skin would have been considerably thinner and all the more fragile. When they had finished scraping the hide, they soaked it once more to remove any traces of blood, and then it was squeezed dry and re-hung to dry out thoroughly before it was smoked.

Work stopped late in the afternoon and by then Benita was tired. She was thankful that neither her mother nor her grandmother were big talkers. They were restful to be with. After the evening meal they sat for a while on the porch thinking their own thoughts as daylight faded and stars appeared and later they slept a deep and dreamless sleep.

On the following day, while Hepzibah sewed canvas to the bottom of the hide and stitched the sides together to make a skirt, Clara made a smudge fire from the embers of rotten spruce wood. Then Hepzibah threaded heavy twine through the holes in the hide and hung it so that it surrounded the coals. It took four hours for the cool smoke to permeate the hide, slowly turning it to honey gold. Clara said that when they got the next hide they would make the smudge from dry cones instead of spruce wood so that it would take on a more reddish tone.

It was Benita's task to keep the fire going all day while Hepzibah and Clara cooked the brain of the animal and mashed it with water. In the afternoon the three of them turned the hide to smoke the other side, and then Benita was left by herself to keep the embers aglow and to make sure they did not produce a flame that would brown and ruin the hide. It was peaceful work, and her thoughts drifted like the smoke rising from the embers. Larry came often to her mind, but as an intruder, an unwanted alien in this peaceful place. Each time he appeared, she fought with herself to banish his image, fearing that her dark thoughts might somehow reach the child growing within her. She looked up through the smoky haze, and when she saw the slender trees reaching toward the sky, she felt her spirit rise up like a branch seeking light. Larry vanished from her thoughts and she grew calm again, her baby at peace in the safety of her womb.

When the smoke had fully permeated both sides, the hide was soaked again, then wrung out and left to dry throughout the still and starry night. Early the next day, as she massaged it with the mashed brain, Hepzibah told Benita that some of the women now used a solution of soap and fat for the process. She herself, though, still preferred to use cooked brain because it contained just the right amount of fat needed to soften the hide and combine with the protein in the skin so that it could not return to its raw state again. Benita tried not to think too much about mashed brains as she worked the mixture into the smoked hide, but the pungent smell made her queasy. Clara laughed when she noticed her holding her breath and turning her face away.

"It's 'cause you're pregnant," she said. "You'll get used to it."

Benita was glad to hear her mother's laughter. Clara's scars had healed, and she had had new teeth fitted by the dentist in Blanchette, although she rarely used them. She remained withdrawn though, preferring to stay in the background, always in the shadow of her mother, Hepzibah.

The three of them stretched the treated hide and scraped both sides before massaging it once more. Then it was given a final soak before it was stretched and hung on its frame to dry thoroughly. When they took it down, Hepzibah told Benita to stroke it and feel how supple it was so that next time she would be able to judge for herself when a hide was ready. It was felt-like and slightly fuzzy to her touch, and a creamy-gold in colour. At this stage, Hepzibah told her it could be used for ceremonial cloaks, but to make it waterproof they would need to smoke it thoroughly again.

They laid the finished hide over the carved cedar chest that Saul King had made for Hepzibah when he married her, and the little house took on its smoky, acrid smell. To Benita this would always be the smell of the north and of the tribes who followed the ancient trails in search of game. When she smelled the hide she had helped tan, she felt connected with the past, and perhaps for the first time in her life, she thought of herself as a Carrier woman, like her mother and her grandmother.

October brought crisp mornings and shorter days. Isaac King and Jericho George came home with two more moose and three White-Tail deer, and Benita's days were busy helping Clara and Hepzibah with the tanning of them. When they were finished and piled up on the cedar chest, Benita felt no less pride than when she had passed her final exams. It seemed to her that this might even be a greater accomplishment because, through her own skill and knowledge, she had produced something lasting and beautiful. Her grandmother had always been slow with her praise, but now when she inspected the hides one last time, she was pleased.

"This is good work. You helped a lot, Benny. Now you will be one of those with the skill, like me and your mother. Not so many of us left, you know."

"That's because you're a good teacher, Granny," Benita said. "I learn everything from you."

Over the next few days they were visited by other women, some of them masters of the tanning process but now too old for the strenuous work involved in soaking, scraping, and smoking. They fingered the hides laid out for inspection and murmured their approval. The younger women came too, but Benita thought they were there more to inspect her than the hides. Her mother pushed her forward.

"She sure is a fast learner," she said to the little group surrounding the cedar chest. "Benita did a lotta the work and finished this one all by herself."

Clara pointed to a red-gold deer hide, soft and supple as a blanket, and Benita saw that she was proud of her daughter's work and more animated than she had been for a long time. For a moment, the women stayed silent, their faces expressionless. Then Violet Charlie smiled.

"You did real good, Benita. Better'n me."

Clara made tea, and they sat around for a while and talked about the good hunting season, the dry weather, the prospect of early snow, the fish that Isaac King had caught with his son the other day. And for the first time since she had come home again, Benita felt herself to be a part of things.

CHAPTER EIGHTEEN

I am embarrassed to confess that at the age of eighteen I still kept my money in a sock in my bedroom drawer. Several socks, in fact, because I had managed to accumulate over nine hundred dollars from my job at Woodwards, and socks seemed as good a place as any to stash it. Those were the days when nobody bothered to lock up when they left the house for a short time. Had a stranger approached when the occupants were away, the neighbours would have been over like a shot to ask him his business. In the late fifties, homes were considered sacrosanct, even by thieves, and anyway there was nothing much worth stealing in Mount Pleasant. Shaughnessy was the place for that.

Still, I had once overheard my mother comment to my father that with the house wide open all the time, anyone who so desired could stroll in off the street and rob them blind. For some reason her casual remark had alarmed me, and I began to stash my weekly allowance in a sock for safekeeping. When my mother complained that I was going through socks at a preposterous rate I told her to think of them as my safety deposit box, and she said she was glad to hear that I was saving my money at last and not "splashing it around like a movie star."

The night Benita told me she was pregnant I did not sleep at all, and it was still dark when I jumped out of bed the next morning. In a frenzy, I pulled out the money socks and emptied them all over the bed. I counted out ten fifty-dollar bills, stuffed them into an envelope and scrawled her name on the front.

Dad was still snoring, but I could hear my mother stirring about so I crept downstairs like a thief. Rice, curled up in his basket in the alcove and looking like a misplaced marshmallow, opened one eye hopefully and closed it again when I did not reach for his leash. Instead, I took the car keys from the hook and left by the back door.

When I arrived at the house, it was Mrs O'Carroll who came to the door and took the envelope. She promised to give it to Benita as soon as she woke up, politely wished me a pleasant day, and closed the door. I was dismissed.

When I got back to the car, I sat for a while filled with shame and self-disgust because, in truth, I did not want to talk to Benita, did not want her to call me, did not care if I ever saw her again. I wanted this calamity never to have happened, but now that it had, I desperately wanted to make it disappear again so that I could get on with the rest of my life.

When I got home, my mother was frying bacon, and Dad was still in bed. I had forgotten that it was Saturday, the one morning in the week when she cooked what she called "a proper fry-up" with eggs, bacon, mushrooms, sausages, tomatoes, and potatoes. It was my father's favourite meal and usually mine too. Today though, the smell made me nauseous, and I knew I wouldn't be able to eat a bite. I tried to hang the keys back on the hook without Mum noticing, but of course it didn't work.

"Well and good morning to you, Larry! And where were you off to at the crack of dawn might I ask?"

"Benita left her jacket in the car last night," I said. "I thought I'd better drop it off early in case she needs it today."

"You're a true gentleman is what you are, Son. I hope she appreciates your chivalry."

I felt my face turn red. *If you only knew what a gentleman I really am, Ma.* I trudged up the stairs to seek refuge in my bedroom.

I stood by the window and watched a lone robin fly from branch to branch in the cedar tree that had shot up in recent years and now screened us from our neighbours' house. The roses were in full bloom, lush and vibrant, and the dahlias were a riot of colour. Other than tulips and daffodils in the spring, and pansies in the winter, those were the only flowers my mother grew, but they gave her pleasure, and she took pride in them. I felt numb as I watched the bird fly back and forth, and I envied it because it was free from all anxiety and responsibility; it didn't have to do anything at all except simply be a bird.

I heard the creak of my parents' bed as Dad heaved himself out and made his laborious way to the bathroom. He always whistled while he shaved, had a whole repertoire of traditional favourites that saw him through the morning ritual and let my mother and I know the kind of mood he was in. He was usually pretty cheerful first thing in the morning, but if he started his day with "If I Were a Blackbird" we'd know we were in for a gloomy breakfast, and God help us if his choice for the day was "The Auld Triangle." We were on happier ground with "Phil The Fluters' Ball" and, today's selection, "The Garden Where the Praties Grow."

The whistling came to an end, and I listened to his heavy tread as he clomped his way down the stairs to the kitchen. His entrance was followed immediately by the Saturday morning mess call:

"Breakfast, Larry! Come and get it while it's good and hot!"

Down I went, and a huge plate of greasy food was placed in front of me. My mother rattled off a quick "Grace Before Meals" as she did each weekend, and my father tucked in with his usual hearty appetite. My mother was a dainty eater of small portions, but she liked to see my father and me clean our plates. Normally I had no trouble complying, but today I could manage no more than a couple of mouthfuls. After that I toyed with my food like a sulky seven-year-old. My dad stopped eating, his laden fork poised en route to his mouth.

"What's this then, Larry? Are you on a diet now or what?"

"No, I'm just not hungry this morning."

He looked scandalized.

"What do you mean, *not hungry*? A growing boy like you? When I was your age, I was hungry all the time, never got enough to eat. Were you out drinking last night, son? Maybe it's a bit hungover you are this morning? That'll take away the old appetite every time."

"It's not that at all, Dad. I just don't feel like eating right now. Sorry, Ma."

"Give me over your plate then. It's a sin to let good food go to waste, sure it is. And after your mother getting up early to cook it and all."

He reached for my plate and slid the whole mess onto his. I watched three slimy mushrooms swim in a pool of black juice and slither from my plate to join the mound of coagulated yolk on his. The sight made me gag, and as I turned my head away from the sight my mother caught my eye.

"What's wrong, Pet? If there's a problem, you'd better tell us about it. You know what they say, don't you? A problem shared is a problem halved."

Not this problem, I thought. But they were going to find out sooner or later, and far better they hear it from me than from someone else. I waited until they had finished eating and Mum had refilled the teapot. Then I told them the whole story, leaving out nothing except my offer to pay for an abortion.

When I stopped speaking, my mother sat in shocked silence. My father did not.

"Didn't I tell you right from the start that girl was no good, Larry? You damn well should have listened to me, you nincompoop you. Now you've got yourself into a right old mess and a half."

He pounded the table with his fist, making the plates jump and tea slosh over the side of his half-filled cup.

"For Christ's sake, boy, did you never hear tell of Durex? If you had to screw her, couldn't you at least have used a bloody safe?"

My mother, who had been examining the contents of her cup as if it might contain some noxious substance rather than Irish breakfast tea, finally looked up.

"This has come as a terrible shock, Larry. I'll not deny it. How is poor Benita dealing with it?"

But before I could answer, Dad jumped in again.

"For God's sake, Kathleen, let's not get side tracked here. Larry screwed an Indian who likes to drink. No surprise there—don't they all? Now she's going to have a kid at the ripe old age of what, seventeen? Well, nothing new there either. Unless of course she's smarter than the rest of them, and I'm sure as hell hoping she is."

"What do you mean?" I asked. My voice sounded weak and shaky even to my own ears.

"What do I *mean*? I mean let's hope she uses that money you gave her to do the right thing and get rid of it."

My mother's expression slowly changed from hopeful to horrified.

"Oh, God, Charlie, please don't tell me you're talking about abortion."

"At a time like this, why the hell *wouldn't* I talk about it?"

My mother stood up and crossed her arms. She rarely showed anger, but whenever she did, Dad would run for cover. He'd escape to the racetrack or the beer parlour, and when he felt brave enough to show his face again, he'd be bearing flowers or chocolates or some other kind of peace offering. Now though, there was no avoiding her wrath.

"Well, Charlie, I'll give you three good reasons, and I'm sure Larry can probably give you three more. Number one, abortion is still a crime in this country. Number two, it is and always will be against the teaching of the Church. And number three, you are talking about destroying a child, your son's child. I'm absolutely certain that Larry doesn't want that to happen, right, Pet?"

I didn't need to answer because by that time Dad was on his feet too.

"Is this what you want, Larry? You really want the girl to have this kid? Let me ask you, then, how you see things working out? Do you see the two of you getting married, living here with the two of us, say, perhaps with the young one running round the yard in a feather headdress? I hope not, son, because I promise you, you'll regret that decision for the rest of your life."

He ran out of steam, and my mother jumped in again.

"Larry, would Benita consider putting the baby up for adoption? I'm sure there's a lovely couple out there somewhere who can't have a child of their own and would give anything to take this baby.

I remembered how much she had longed for a second child, how she had prayed to become pregnant again, how she had *begged* my father to consider adoption, and how he had adamantly refused.

"To hell with adoption!" was what he said now. "It would mean that Larry would have to hang around till after the kid was born. He'd lose his place at university for sure, and the opportunity might never come again. I don't give a tinker's curse if Holy Mother Church puts us all on a guilt trip, and as for it being a crime, well there are ways around that. It's not as if she'd be the first girl in Vancouver to have an abortion, you can be sure of that."

"But what about the child itself, Charlie? Would you have it destroyed for the sake of convenience?"

"Right now it's just a foetus in a womb, Kathleen, not a child at all, and that foetus is not wanted." Dad thumped the table again for emphasis.

"Not *wanted*?" my mother said fiercely. "Of course, it's wanted!"

My father rolled his eyes. "Wanted by whom? By the Catholic Church?"

"No, you stupid man. Wanted by *me*, this baby's grandmother. Larry, you can tell Benita that I would be honoured and happy to help raise my own grandchild."

Suddenly all the fight went out of her, and she rushed from the room in tears. We heard her footsteps on the stairs and then the click of the bathroom door as she locked it behind her.

Dad sighed heavily. He looked at me, and I saw a flicker of contempt in his eyes before he pushed past me and slammed out of the house.

I wish I could say that the remorse I felt then was because of Benita or because of the unwanted child, but it was the sight and sound of my mother in tears that filled me with shame. *What have I done?* I thought. *What have I done?*

I collected the dishes and was stacking them in the sink when I heard her come downstairs. Through the open door, I saw her pick up the phone and dial a number. When she spoke, she kept her voice low, but I knew she was talking to the O'Carrolls, maybe even to Benita herself. She caught sight of me standing in the doorway and turned away, dropping her voice still further and then growing silent as she listened to the voice at the other end of the line. Then there was a click as the call came to an end, and when I heard the receiver being replaced on its perch, I understood my father's need to escape. Rice trotted over and looked up at me imploringly, and I was reaching for his leash as my mother came into the kitchen.

"Not so fast, Larry. The dog can wait. We've some talking to do, you and me. Benita left last night. John O'Carroll dropped her off at the Greyhound station, but he didn't wait to see her get on the bus. They've just found the letter she left for them, and now they're not sure what to think.

"Do they know?" I blurted out, feeling as sick as if I had just consumed two fried breakfasts while suffering from a hangover.

"Know *what*?" my mother snapped, no longer weepy now but impatient and anxious.

"That Benita is pregnant".

"Of course, they do! The man's a doctor for God's sake, and he's also the poor girl's guardian."

"What did she say in the letter?"

"She said she had a decision to make and a problem to solve. She thanked them for all they had done, told them not to worry about her, that she'd be in touch as soon as she could. Now Larry, in light of our conversation this morning—what your father was talking about—I'm feeling very uneasy about this whole situation. You know Benita better than any of us. Is it possible that she might be thinking of ending the pregnancy? Could that be the decision she's talking about?"

My mother's hands were clenched, her posture rigid.

"Why would you ask me that, Ma?"

"I'll tell you why, Larry. And I'm guessing that Peggy O'Carroll is asking the same question herself. She said that when Benita opened your envelope yesterday and found the five hundred dollars, she called it blood money. What did she mean by that, Larry? That's what I want to know."

There was an African violet in a glazed pot at the end of the kitchen counter where it caught the light from the window but was protected from direct sunlight. It was in deep purple bloom. I focused on it for a moment, noticing for the first time the tiny golden stamens at the centre of each flower, the dark velvety green of each heart-shaped leaf. It was a peaceful thing to be looking at, and I wished that I could gaze at it a while longer, but there was to be no reprieve.

"Larry, snap out of it! This is no time to be drifting off into one of your daydreams. Hard enough as this might be for you, it's *much* harder for Benita. If she didn't get on that bus last night, she could be out there alone somewhere in this big city with nobody to turn to for support. Tell me something now, Larry, and I want to hear the truth from you. Did you talk to Benita about having an abortion?"

For a moment I knew how a rabbit must feel when it is caught in the headlights of a speeding car.

"Answer me. Did the two of you discuss abortion?"

I nodded. Here came the car bearing down on me. I could almost smell the heated metal, hear the screech of tires.

"Did *you* suggest it, Larry? Or did she?"

"I did. It was my suggestion. I'm sorry, Ma."

"Save your sorrow for God, Larry. May He forgive you for what you might have led that poor girl to do."

And for the first time in my life, my mother turned away from me in disgust and reached for the phone again.

CHAPTER NINETEEN

Had I been eight years old instead of eighteen, I might have put my head down on the kitchen table and bawled. Instead, I took Rice for a walk. It was fortunate that he was on his leash because for all the attention I paid him that morning he could have gone chasing after a squirrel or a cat and met his end under the wheels of a car. As it was, he trotted gamely along at my heels, his stump of a tail bobbing jauntily, pointy ears pricked, little currant eyes darting a glance upward every once in a while to check on me. He knew something was wrong. He always knew. He knew too that there was nothing he could do about it but stick around and wait it out.

I set out in the direction of Fairfield Park where I used to play soccer as a kid, but when I got to the intersection of Renfrew and Oxford, I turned left instead of right and a few minutes later found myself in front of Renzo's house. Then I stopped. What if somebody else was visiting, even at this early hour? While I stood there debating with myself, the question was answered by the appearance of Molly at the front door. I tugged sharply at the leash and turned on my heel. Too late.

"Yoo-hoo! Larry!" she bellowed, as if I was two blocks away rather than mere steps. "Aren't you going to come in? I was on my way out, but now that you're here maybe I'll stay a bit longer."

She bounded down the path and bent to ruffle Rice's curly head which he hated and tried his best to back away from. Molly had always been hopeless with dignified, soldierly dogs like Rice.

"Who's a good little doggy then?" she cooed. Then Renzo appeared at the front door.

"What's up, buddy?" he said. "You're looking a little green around the gills. Were you into your dad's whiskey last night or what?"

When I didn't answer, Molly shifted her attention from Rice to me.

"Are you okay, Larry?"

She shot a warning glance at Renzo, a clear signal for him to stop joking around.

"Do you guys want to talk by yourselves for a bit? I should really get going anyway. I promised to help Mom with the grocery shopping for the weekend."

I don't know why I should have been surprised by her tact and sensitivity. Despite her ebullience Molly had always been astute and intuitive. Of course she was well aware that whatever I told Renzo that morning "in confidence" would, with a bit of prompting, get passed along to her later in the day. There were no secrets between those two. Renzo gave her a chaste peck on the cheek and she took off down the street at a purposeful clip.

"Want to come in for a while, Larry?" Renzo held open the gate for me.

"No," I said. "Rice didn't get his walk yesterday, so it's better if I keep him moving. I wouldn't mind some company for a while though."

We must have walked a good six blocks before I reached the end of my story, and when I did Renzo spent no time at all on what has come to be called *emotional support*.

"Larry, this is unacceptable. You can't just leave Benita to deal with the situation on her own. If you do, you'll have it on your conscience for the rest of your life. Even if you feel nothing at all for her, you have to accept responsibility for what has happened. You're just going to have to face up to it, buddy."

Renzo sounded far older than his age, and for a moment I felt like a kid being chastised by an adult. He might be only eighteen years old, but he was already thinking about marriage, the very thought of which horrified me. I did not like what he was telling me but, still, I knew that he was right

When I got home, the house was empty. I filled Rice's bowl with water and gave him a biscuit to crunch in the comfort of his basket. It was past lunchtime, but I still couldn't eat. I noticed the car keys dangling from their hook and thought briefly about throwing a few clothes in a suitcase, driving to California, and spending the rest of my life on some out-of-the-way beach. Instead, I left a note for my mother telling her that I was on my way to talk to the O'Carrolls and would be back in a couple of hours.

It was not a happy visit. John O'Carroll opened the door and gave me a long look.

"Come in," he said, as though there was a lot he wanted to say but wouldn't. "Dad's out at the moment, but I'll tell Mom you're here."

Left to wait by myself in the formal living-room, I listened to the relentless ticking of the clock on the wall and stared at a crystal bowl of white flowers I could not name. Their heavy, cloying scent filled the space and heightened my queasiness. I wondered if Benita was suffering from morning sickness. The clock ticked on, and the minutes passed slowly in a house that for once felt devoid of life

When she finally appeared, Peggy O'Carroll seemed tense and flustered, although she greeted me with her customary courtesy. We spent a couple of minutes in meaningless chit-chat and then she took a breath and got down to the matter at hand.

"I'm afraid none of us saw this coming, Larry. I'm sure I don't need to tell you how anxious we are about Benita. We haven't been able to reach anyone up in Blanchette yet, so we still don't know if she even got there. Cormac is out looking for her now, and Kevin and the girls are spending the day with our neighbours. I've been calling Benita's friends, but maybe you can tell me if I've overlooked anyone."

She rattled off a list of names, but I wasn't able to add to it, and we sat there in awkward silence until I finally found some words.

"I'm to blame for all of this, Mrs. O'Carroll, but I don't really know what I should do right now."

She stood up and came over to where I sat. Her expression was kind, and when she put her hand on my shoulder, I felt as if I might cry.

"No, of course you don't. How could you? Don't be too hard on yourself, Larry. You're young yourself, and this is a very adult predicament to find yourself in. Go home now and try to relax. I've promised your mother I'll phone her as soon as there's any news."

She saw me to the door. When I was partway down the drive she called my name and I turned back hopefully.

"You know, there *is* something that you could that might help, Larry."

"Anything," I said. "I'll do anything."

"You can pray. That's the best thing you can do for now."

It was the kind of thing my own mother might have advised me to do. To her, prayer was the antidote to all of life's problems, every tricky situation that might crop up along the highway to heaven. My own view was that prayer, even prayer to St. Anthony the patron saint of lost things, would not help to find Benita, nor would it solve the problem of an unwanted pregnancy. In the past year I had come round more to my father's way of thinking.

His view was that the Catholic Church was moribund and that all its sacred rituals were nothing more than what he called mumbo-jumbo, only a step away from jungle hocus-pocus orchestrated by witch doctors. This was not a view he ever expressed in the presence of my mother, of course, so it never reached the point of discussion, but somehow I had begun to absorb it to the point that I now looked upon my faith with a fair degree of cynicism.

I did not want to go home to a house filled with blame and tension and disappointment, so for a while I drove around aimlessly until I noticed that the gas was running low. I had no money for a fill-up, so

I headed to South Granville, followed it to Broadway and ended up back on Main Street where I discovered that old habits really do die hard, especially those we are trying to kick. I say this because when I reached St. Anthony's Church, I parked the car and went inside.

The church was dimly lit, and I crept into a pew near the back, sinking into the silence and stillness of the place with an audible sigh of relief. I knelt and gazed at the red glow of the sanctuary lamp, wondering not for the first time whether it really did signify the living presence of Christ here in this old brick building in the heart of Mount Pleasant. If it were true, then surely all those who came close to that presence would be leading extraordinary lives, lives that were inspired and holy. If I myself, say, had been in the presence of Christ at least once a week since I was born, if I had consumed His sacred Body in holy communion since the age of seven, would I not have been able to resist sexual temptation? Would I not have wanted to protect Benita instead of making her pregnant? And would I have paid for her to have an abortion?

Then I stopped struggling with the unfathomable and just sat there, believing nothing at all except that this battered old building on the east side of the city, this plain-Jane church with no steeple or bell tower or rose window to boast of, was, at that precise moment in my life, what I needed most, a refuge and a safe haven from a world I could not cope with. To anyone watching, I would have appeared to be deep in prayer, but my thoughts were not centred on God at all, they were just the wanderings and driftings of a troubled mind.

After a while, I became aware of the presence of others in the church. There were a couple of old Italian ladies dressed in widow's black, clacking away at their beads as they prayed the rosary, and a woman standing at one of the side altars where rows of candles flickered before a life-sized statue of Our Lady of Lourdes. I watched her light three new candles and bow her head in prayer, and when she turned to genuflect before the main altar, I saw that it was my mother. I bowed my head in the hope that she would not notice me on her way out of the church, and when I looked up again she was gone.

My mother possessed what non-believers refer to as blind faith. If the Holy Father were to ask Catholic women to erect a shrine to the Blessed Virgin Mary in their front yards, she would happily have gone in search of the largest statue she could find and planted it in the middle of the lawn. Usually I was embarrassed by that kind of faith and thought of it as simplistic and superstitious, but at this point in my life, I saw it as something to be envied, something you could rely on to get you through the tough stuff.

The red light was on above two of the confessionals, and I saw that both Father Vanelli and Father Cooper were at the service of the steady line-up of penitents near the back of the church. I felt weary, tired from all of the thinking and talking that had gone on in the past twenty-four hours. What I was looking for was not absolution, but a solution to a very real problem, and there was only one person I could think of who might be able to offer some practical advice.

I left the church and headed straight for the rectory where I found Father McGowan finishing a late lunch. He had just come from a visit to St. Paul's Hospital he told me, where he had been called to administer the last rites to an elderly parishioner.

I did not want to eat, wanted only to unload my tale of woe, but when he insisted on making me a ham and cheese sandwich, I found that I was ravenously hungry. Father McGowan handed me a glass of Coke and made me finish eating before he allowed me to tell my story. I found it easy to talk to someone who was removed from the situation, and therefore impartial and objective in a way that my parents could not be. Father McGowan asked no questions until I came to the end of my account, and when he spoke, I heard nothing judgmental in his tone; certainly nothing condemnatory.

"So a bit of a mess all round then, huh, Larry?"

"Yes, Father."

"It's a difficult situation to be in at your age. Hard for your parents too, of course. But the person I am *most* concerned about is the girl. Do you care for her at all?"

"Of course I do, Father."

"I have to ask that because it seems to me that you have put your own feelings first in this matter with not too much regard for Benita at all. That's normal and natural at your age, and it's the reason why most young people choose to wait before they embark on a serious relationship. They need to grow up a bit before they are ready to make a commitment that is based on love and not just sexual attraction. When it comes right down to it, love is everything, Larry. That's what Christ tried to teach us. Would you say that you love Benita?"

Did he think me incapable of love because I was eighteen and not twenty-eight, or thirty-eight? His question offended me, and I did not reply.

When Father McGowan spoke again, his tone was measured and reasonable.

"If I were hearing your confession, you'd be waiting now for me to absolve you from your sins and send you on your way with a clear conscience, right, Larry? But then you'd be missing the whole point of the sacrament. Confession is only one part. There's also what we call the firm purpose of amendment, and I don't need to tell you about that. But sometimes it's easy for us to forget the final component, which is doing penance. It's unfortunate that people have come to think of it as simply rattling off a few Hail Marys or Our Fathers before they leave the church. There was once a time when penance had to be performed and witnessed by the rest of the community, not that I'm advocating that of course!"

I felt my mind drifting and stifled a yawn, which didn't escape his notice.

"Tedious as it might be, this is no small thing, Larry. And I won't trivialize it by sending you on your way with a pat on the shoulder and my good wishes. You're going to have to deal with this wisely. Otherwise I'm afraid that guilt will come to roost within you and lay an egg as cold and heavy as a stone, and you will carry it with you for the rest of your life. Are you with me, Larry?"

"Yes, Father."

"Just suppose you'd gone to confession this afternoon and confessed to shoplifting. What would the priest have told you to do, do you think?"

"He'd have told me to return the stuff I took."

"How about if you'd confessed to stealing money from someone?"

"The same. I'd have to return it."

"That's right. And if that wasn't possible, say you had taken the money years ago and the person had since died or moved away, then you would have to donate the equivalent amount to some charity. Do you see where I'm going with this, Larry?"

"Are you talking about making restitution?"

Father McGowan pushed his empty plate to one side and leaned forward, elbows on the table.

"I'm talking about *atonement*. Restitution is something you will need to figure out for yourself. You don't need me to tell you that you have taken something from Benita that you had no right to take. Harsh as this might sound, I think you'll agree that you have robbed Benita of her honour, her dignity, maybe her self-respect, and almost certainly her trust in you. And tell me if I'm wrong here, but it seems to me that so far you haven't given much thought to Benita, nor her foster guardians, and you have pretty much overlooked both your own parents and the parents of the girl. Neither have you considered the unborn child, *your* child, Larry, that Benita is carrying. That's just how *I* see things here, but that's of no importance at all. What matters in the end is the way *you* see things."

I sat at the table and was overcome by shame for my self-indulgence and selfishness. Everything Father McGowan said was true. I looked up at him.

"What should I do, Father? What can I do to make restitution?"

"Start by asking Benita to forgive you, but be prepared to accept that she may not be able to do so. Spend some time in prayer, and ask God to show you the way to atone for your failure to love. Because that's what this is about, Larry. And always remember this. You are not a bad person because of this mistake you made. Every single one of us does things that are wrong, but here's the great thing, God forgives and loves us all. Accept that and be grateful for it. Then, Larry, and this is important, you need to forgive yourself."

I thought about what Father McGowan had said and the advice he had given me, but I knew I would not be able to forgive myself until I had made amends, until I had made restitution. I thought about Benita, still adrift and out of touch. How could I give back to her the honour and dignity and self-respect I had taken from her? How could I win back her trust? I could not. Then I thought about the child I had been so willing to dispose of. How does one make restitution for a life destroyed?

Each day for a week, I took Rice for a marathon walk as I struggled with questions and prayed for answers. By Saturday, he was exhausted and made his views known by scurrying to his basket and glaring at me when I showed him his leash. That morning, I walked by myself and by the time I got back to the house I had come up with, if not an answer, then at least a decision and a plan for the future.

CHAPTER TWENTY

Cold, grey November crept in, bringing with it short days and long, dark nights. Benita spent her time keeping the wood stove burning, preparing simple meals, and watching her mother and grandmother cut out patterns for moccasins, mukluks, and two ceremonial jackets from the hides they had tanned in the early fall. Hepzibah used thick waxed thread to sew the parts together, and then Clara brought out tins of coloured glass beads which she double-sewed to create intricate spirals and lavish flower designs. She gave Benita her scraps and remnants on which to practice, and it helped to pass the hours although it did not take long to establish that she would never join the ranks of tribal elders famed for their artistry. Her attempts at traditional beadwork revealed that she lacked the patience, skill, and talent to ever be able to produce saleable items, and she marvelled at the meticulous work done by her mother and grandmother.

While the lake was still free of ice, they went across in Isaac King's big sturdy boat and delivered the jackets and moccasins and mukluks to the Hudson Bay Company's outpost in Blanchette. Most of what they had produced would be sent by truck to Prince George to be sold in the big department store downtown, but some items would remain for the few tourists who might find their way to Blanchette the following spring and summer. Any work done by Clara and Hepzibah was highly valued and in constant demand, but they set a strict limit on what they produced each year.

"We're not a factory," Hepzibah said when Benita asked why they did not increase their output. "Each piece is unique and entirely made by hand. If we try to meet the demand, the quality will suffer and our hearts won't be in what we do no more. That's what happened to Amelia Prince and Celina Jack. They got greedy. Now the moccasins they make all have the same two patterns and get sold for next to nothing to tourists who just want something cheap and Indian to take back to the city with them. Those two women, they are like machines. There's no more joy in their work. Big mistake."

They spent a full week in Blanchette, and on the last day the weather changed suddenly. A vicious wind came out of nowhere and whipped the lake into a frenzy of heaving water and wild waves that lashed the shore and surged across the sandy beach. In the forest that surrounded the town on three sides, trees bowed their heads and moaned and surrendered their branches with a fearsome crack and snap. It was the kind of storm that caught people unaware, powerful enough to capsize boats and toss the occupants overboard plunging them into the dark swell of the surging water, the kind of storm that had made Sturgeon Lake notorious for its many drownings.

At the height of the storm, late in the afternoon, Benita left her mother's house and walked down to the lakeshore. Already encumbered by her swelling breasts and belly, she stood heavy and squat, rooted in place by her own weight. She watched the lake writhe and roil like a living thing, grey, amorphous, and threatening, and she thought about her father whose body it had tossed about and swallowed up and spat out again, and about those countless others who had lost their lives fishing these waters. And then into her mind, unbidden, unwanted, floated the image of another body, this one hard, and lean, and sinewy, a body that had once shaped itself to hers and penetrated her inmost sanctuary. Now she thought of it as an invasion because he had abandoned her, leaving her cold and empty and desolate. What a fool she had been to trust a white guy! Bitterness welled up within her and submerged Larry's image until it grew blurred and distorted and was swept away so that it was as if he too had drowned. She would not speak his name again. She would not allow herself to mourn him.

By Christmas the lake had frozen solid and snow frosted the trees and carpeted the forest floor. Father Hines slipped and fell on an icy patch outside the rectory and had to go to Vancouver for surgery on his badly broken arm. His replacement, a young Oblate missionary from Ottawa, drove up to Blanchette and crossed the iced-up lake by sled and snowshoes to say Mass in LaPierre on Christmas morning.

He was young and enthusiastic with all the fervour of the newly ordained, and his sermon had been well prepared. It was also lengthy and delivered entirely in English. The little chapel was tightly packed, and Benita, sitting with Hepzibah, Clara and Jericho George, was moved to see the congregation listening stoically and respectfully while understanding very little of what the visiting priest said.

Many of the older people spoke no English at all, and Benita wondered if young Father Butler was aware of that. Did he not realize that people living along this remote chain of lakes might speak only the Carrier language? He stood at the simple wooden lectern and she watched him struggle to make a connection with those who had walked from their homes on this bitterly cold morning to attend Christmas Mass.

She was close enough to see beads of sweat appear on his brow even though the chapel still felt frigid to her, and she felt sorry for him, a stranger in their midst. She was startled when he suddenly stopped speaking mid-way through another long, convoluted sentence. Nobody moved, just watched impassively as the young priest picked up the typed pages of his sermon, ripped the bundle in two, and scrunched it up into a tight wad in his fist. He looked down at his little congregation .

"I am so sorry, people. Can you put it down to my lack of experience and forgive me? I promise I'll do better if you let me come here again." Then he smiled. "God's blessing be upon us all and may He make our Christmas holy."

A faint murmur went through the chapel and Benita, turning in her seat, saw that everyone was smiling and that this raw young priest from far away had been made welcome and was a stranger no more.

At the end of Mass, Benita went and knelt before the créche. She gazed at the baby lying in the straw-filled manger and wondered about the actual birth of Jesus Christ. Had his cradle really been a manger? Had friendly animals—sheep, cows, a donkey—actually come in from the fields to pay their respects to the baby? Had angels circled overhead? Had three kings followed a star that stopped right above the place of birth?

Not very likely, she concluded.

She looked at the statue of Mary. Well, that part at least was real, she thought. Jesus definitely had a mother, and by all accounts she had given birth when she was even younger than Benita was now. She wondered if Mary, too, had been scared. Had she worried because she knew nothing about motherhood, nothing at all about raising a child? Had she ever felt like a failure? Surely not the Mother of God. Mary would have had no reason to pity the child growing inside her. Mary's child had two parents on earth and God his father in heaven. Her own child would be born on a reserve to the unmarried seventeen year-old daughter of a drunken Indian. What kind of life would it have, already cursed and not yet even born?

Still on her knees she prayed for her unborn child, asked Mary to spare it from a life of misery, and prayed that she would be a good mother when the time came.

For their Christmas dinner, they ate roast venison. The little house was crowded, and people sat all over the place with plates balanced on their knees. After the meal, Hepzibah gave her brother Isaac King one of the ceremonial jackets they had made, and Clara gave the other one to Jericho George. He accepted it gravely and wore it for the rest of the day despite the heat from the stove which eventually caused one of the cousins to open the door and let the winter air drift inside to cool things down.

Benita had noticed that Jericho's visits to the house were becoming more frequent. Whenever he dropped off groceries, her mother would make tea and sit with him while he drank it. There was never much talk between the two of them but she saw that they were easy with each other and seemed to have no need of words. It was restful to see them together. Jericho George had always been a patient man, and her mother was still not fully healed.

The baby was born on March 19th, delivered at home by Hepzibah and weighing a healthy eight pounds. When Father Hines, broken arm now fully healed, came to say Mass in the village a couple of weeks after the birth, they took the child to the chapel to be baptized. The name they gave her was Miriam Josephine. Miriam, because that had been the name of the sister of Moses and Aaron, and Benita thought that was a pretty impressive family to belong to; Josephine, because she had been born on the feast of St. Joseph. Miriam Josephine Pigeon sounded like a good name to all of them.

She was a placid, contented baby who rarely cried and smiled a great deal. For a while she had three mothers attending to her every need, with Benita to nurse her when she needed to be fed and Hepzibah and Clara to bathe her and change her and rock her to sleep in their arms. For the first few weeks of her life, she was passed around and examined like a precious little parcel and spent almost no time in the rocking cradle that Jericho George had carved for her out of fragrant cedar.

Without a child of his own, he was in awe of the baby. He refused to pick her up, said he was afraid he might drop her, or crush her with his big, clumsy hands. Not until she was two weeks old did he allow himself to stroke with a thumb her silky black hair, and after a month she seemed to know his touch and the sound of his voice. He arrived one afternoon and found her whimpering in her cradle and when he lifted her out and held her up she smiled at him. After that he came every day, and when she was weaned from the breast he would sit and hold her and give her the bottle. Clara laughed at him, said he should have been born a woman, but she said it kindly and anyway he did not care. So for a time, Miriam was loved by three mothers and one adoring substitute grandfather.

Shortly after Easter, a package arrived at the post office in Blanchette and sat there unclaimed until May when the lake was finally free of ice and Isaac King was able to run his boat again. It was Clara who brought it back from town and laid it on the kitchen table, and when Hepzibah and Benita saw it they both laughed. It was addressed to BABY PIGEON, c/o MISS BENITA PIGEON, BLANCHETTE B.C. But when Benita saw the sender's name she stopped laughing, went and fetched a pen from the drawer and scrawled across the label, RETURN TO SENDER.

Her grandmother looked over at her.

"You are behaving now like a child instead of a mother. This gift is for my great-granddaughter, and I am going to open the box if you will not."

She used the kitchen scissors to cut the string and then she carefully removed the brown paper wrapping from the package. She opened the box, took out a bundle wrapped in many layers of tissue paper and handed it to Benita.

"Open it," she said.

It was a shawl, soft and white and knitted by hand. Clara exclaimed at the intricacy of the pattern, the delicacy of the stitching, the hours that must have gone into the making of it.

"It's real beautiful," she said. "Was it her other grandmother that made it for her?"

Benita said nothing, but Hepzibah lifted Miriam from her cradle and wrapped her in the shawl and held her up to be admired, and when Jericho George arrived later in the afternoon he said she looked like a royal baby, a little princess.

Hepzibah did not make the trip across the lake until mid-June, but the first thing she did when she got into town was to buy a card. It had a white rose on the front and was blank inside. She took it across to the post office and borrowed a pen from the counter. She opened the card and painstakingly printed her message.

    THANK YOU FOR THE NICE GIFT.
    HER NAME IS MIRIAM JOSEPHINE.

She did not sign her name, just closed and sealed the envelope, addressed it to Mrs Kathleen Kinsella, 56 Winchester Avenue, Vancouver B.C., and dropped it in the post box. Then she walked over to the Hudson Bay Store and picked up her moccasin money.

PART TWO

CHAPTER TWENTY-ONE

The card with the white rose was kept in a shoebox on the shelf above the radio. My mother showed it to me the day after Dad's funeral, when the two of us were sitting in the front-room, she, exhausted by grief, and I still in shock over the suddenness of my father's death from a massive stroke.

Even though my mother called me less than an hour after it had happened, by the time I had booked myself onto the first available flight from Rome and endured a five-hour stopover in Toronto, my father was dead and I had been lucky to get home in time for his funeral. When I saw the flower-covered casket before the altar, it was not grief I felt at first but outrage that he had not waited to say goodbye to me, that he had not been able to delay his passing from this world until I reached his bedside at St. Paul's. Any nurse will tell you that the dying, by dint of sheer willpower, are often able to hold onto life until their loved ones are assembled around them. I wondered if Dad, in the end, had just given up on me.

But of course he hadn't waited till the moment of death to do that. He had given up on me eight years earlier when he learned of my decision to enter the seminary and become a priest.

I had approached my mother first, and her reaction had been predictable: she had wept tears of joy that God had chosen her only son for the priesthood, and she did not doubt for a moment that my vocation was a true one. By that time we knew that Benita had gone back up north, and I assumed had had an abortion. I had decided that the blame was wholly mine, and that the only way to atone for the destruction of another life was to offer my own life to God and to spend it in the service of my fellow human beings. I had given the matter much thought and the decision, once made, filled me with a sense of relief and certainty, which made Father McGowan's reaction all the more perplexing. He didn't actually laugh out loud, but I could almost hear the smile in his voice when he spoke.

"Larry, Larry, that's a pretty drastic course of action to be choosing. Tell me now, did you ever entertain the notion, even fleetingly, of becoming a priest before all this happened?"

My silence was sufficient answer.

"I thought not. You know, when I told you to look for a way to atone, I was thinking in practical terms, hoping that you would find a way to heal the rift you created between yourself and the girl. I certainly wasn't suggesting that you run off to the seminary."

"You make it sound like I'm running away, Father." I spoke defensively, but I was confused rather than angry.

"I know that's not your intention, Larry. But I still want you to question your motives before you make a final decision. You need to be absolutely certain that you don't end up using the priesthood to escape from life's complexities and hurdles. It's far from an easy road to travel, you know, and no life is ever free of problems."

But my mind was made up, and the questions Father McGowan had raised only served to strengthen my conviction. My father, though, when I broke the news to him and my mother the following day, raised more than questions: he raised hell.

"Jesus, Mary and Joseph, don't be telling me you're serious!" he roared when I broke the news to him. "Sure, life on a reservation would be a better choice than that. You've your whole life ahead of you, son. Why would you want to spend it singing hymns and wearing a frock, listening to old ladies confessing that they said yes to a second glass of wine or that they kicked the cat when it pissed in the house?"

Dad was staunchly anti-clerical in the way of many of his generation of the Irish poor. A frequent victim of savage beatings by the Irish Christian Brothers who had taught him in Ireland, he harboured a deep-seated mistrust of any man in clerical garb.

"Why in God's name would you want to throw your life away like that? Your mother and I didn't scrimp and save for your education so that the Church could snap you up and put you to work for them."

"You make it sound as if the Church is some gang in Rome, Dad, but the Church is people like you and me and Mum too, ordinary people, not just priests and nuns."

"Don't be telling me about priests! A bunch of queers who never did an honest day's work in their lives, the whole sorry lot of them."

"We should be proud to have a son who is willing to give his life to God, Charlie", my mother said, attempting to intercede on my behalf. "It's not every—"

"*Proud?*" he bellowed. "Proud, did you say? Cathleen, I could give you a list a mile long of things that would make me proud, and my only son going off to join the Roman Queer Brigade isn't one of them."

My poor mother stood up, her hands over her ears. "For God's sake stop, Charlie! God forgive you for your blasphemy. How can you go to Mass with me every Sunday and yet talk like this?"

"I've been going to Mass my whole life, Kathleen. And I'll continue to go till the day I die. But I don't want any son of mine joining those fags in frocks!"

There was nothing left to say. I walked out of the room and, a week later, left home to enter the seminary and begin studies at St Michael's College at the University of Toronto. When I was ordained four years later, my parents made the trip back east for the ceremony at the Cathedral, and at the reception that followed, my father was at his genial best, charming the cardinal and other dignitaries with stories about me as a kid and making them laugh at a mildly outrageous story about an Irish priest he had known who had bet the entire Sunday collection on a horse at the Leopardstown races.

Since then I'd been home only twice, first for Renzo and Molly's wedding in 1955, and a second time in the summer of 1960 after I had completed my Master's degree in scripture at Notre Dame University. Both times Dad had been welcoming and affectionate, but I suspected he was under strict orders not to say anything that might ruin the visit. There were even times when I found myself wishing he would let fly with some vitriolic remark that would put me in touch with my "real" father again, because the man I found when I went back to 56 Winchester Avenue was not the man I had grown up with—this was not the man I had once respected and later spurned. This man was almost a stranger to me.

Of course, at the time, I had no way of knowing that both he and my mother were deceiving me, that they had conspired to keep me in ignorance of the fact that I had a child. I still couldn't believe it. I stared at the card while my mother tried to explain.

"You were almost at the end of your first year in the seminary when the O'Carroll's phoned us with the news. Your dad and I thought it best not to tell you. What good would it have done anyway?"

What good indeed? That was the question that was tearing me apart. I stayed silent while my mother struggled to continue.

"You'd already made the decision to give your life to God. It would have been a dreadful thing to take it back again."

I was no longer the impulsive, hot-headed teenager I once had been. I kept my voice calm, my tone measured.

"But Ma," I said, "it was *my* life to give or to take back. It should have been my decision, not yours."

My mother didn't see it like that.

"But our lives are *not* our own, Larry. We all belong to God. Besides, your father insisted that we didn't tell you."

At last I was hearing something that made sense to me.

"Too worried about the teepee on the front lawn, was he?" I asked her.

It was unkind of me and I knew it. We had only just laid the man to rest, yet I had let anger get the better of me.

"No," said my loyal mother. "He just thought it would have destroyed your life. You were only eighteen, love. You had no education, no job. What could you have done at that time?"

I wondered if she had been trying to convince herself of that for the past seven years. Listening to her now, I wasn't sure she had succeeded. But then, maybe for the first time, it struck me that in escaping from the turmoil I had created, first by leaving Vancouver, and later, Canada, I had abandoned my parents. I looked at my mother and saw that in my absence she had begun to grow old.

"Did we do the wrong thing then, Larry?"

She was sitting in her favourite armchair by the window, the tea she had insisted on making growing cool on the table beside her. She had developed a mild tremor in her hand, and her teacup shook when she picked it up, rattled when she placed it back on the saucer. It was the sight of her hands and the rattle of the cup that made me let go of the anger that had been building up inside me. I sat down again, drank my tea, and waited until I was fully calm before I spoke. When I did, it was not to answer her question. Instead, I asked one of my own.

"So how is Benita doing?"

My mother stood up slowly, stiff from sitting so long. She bent to pick up the tea things, hers and mine, so that I could not see her face when she answered.

"I couldn't tell you, Larry. We've had no further contact with her. She left LaPierre a couple of years ago and I don't know if she's still in touch with her people. I don't hear from the old lady any more anyway."

"Which old lady?" I asked.

"Benita's grandmother up in Blanchette, the one I figured sent me the card. She stopped writing to me a long time ago."

"And the child?" I said, unwilling to speak her name. Saying her name would make her real, bring the reality of her existence crashing into my life to tear it apart, and I couldn't let that happen.

My mother handed me the tea things and I followed her into the kitchen and put them into a sink full of dirty dishes. I had never before seen the kitchen less than sparkling clean, and I was dismayed by the mess around me. She noticed my glance.

"Ah, now, don't be worrying about the disorder, Larry. What does it matter anyway? I've all the time in the world ahead of me now."

But of course both of us knew—I perhaps for the first time—that wasn't true. At some point my mother would follow my father into the next life, maybe not for years yet, but one day it would happen. You would think with all my training in philosophy and theology that I would have already come to terms with the inevitability of death, but it remained an intellectual concept and had never, until now, touched me personally.

Rice's blue leash was still hanging on the hook next to the car keys, although he had died in his sleep years before. Even the death of my little dog seemed unreal. I think I had been expecting him to live forever, always to be waiting at the kitchen door, white tail wagging, ready for his walk.

My mother saw me looking at the empty place where his basket had been.

"Ah, I still miss the little fellow. He was always cheerful, and he had a way of getting me on my feet and out the door that I could never resist."

She was standing in front of the fridge as she spoke. She seemed jittery, and I thought that I should not have allowed the memory of Rice to intrude on her mourning for my father. But it wasn't the dog that was the cause of her agitation.

"Larry, I told you, didn't I, that the old woman had stopped writing?"

"Yes." I was confused by the sudden change of subject. "You told me."

"But I didn't tell you that I still get news from LaPierre. Take a look."

She stepped aside and I saw then that the fridge was covered from top to bottom with brightly coloured art work, printed cards and illustrated letters. I was looking at a mini-art gallery.

My mother smiled. "Start here," she said proudly. "I have them all in order for you."

The first few pictures were of shaky stick figures, box-like houses, dwarf trees and giant animals. Then came a large portrait of a scarecrow figure with stringy black hair, eyes like two coals, a button nose and a violent red slash of a mouth. This one had been signed by the artist:

M I R I A M.

I turned to my mother but there was no need to voice the question. "Yes," she said. "Yes."

I felt dizzy, from jet lag maybe, but also from shock. I tried to focus on the pictorial display before my eyes and little by little, picture by picture, letter by letter, it drew me into her life, Miriam's life.

> *I am in grade one.*
> *My teacher says I print real good*
> *I picked lots of berries with Clara and Jericho.*
> *Thank you for the nice clothes. I am*
> *saving them for school.*

As the rows descended, the display gradually became more sophisticated. I had to bend down to see what must have been the most recent additions.

> *On my birthday it snowed all day. Jericho made me some snowshoes and they fit me just fine. Me and Jericho went on a walk in our snowshoes. We had fun.*

"Who's Jericho?" I asked my mother.

"I'm not sure. An uncle, perhaps. A friend of the family?"

"Do you have photographs?"

She shook her head. "No. I don't expect they have a camera up there."

The last entry was at floor level and I read it in disbelief.

> *Dear Grampa Charlie,*
> *Thank you for the doll. She is sure pretty. More prettier then me. She sleeps on my bed.*
> *With love from Miriam.*

"That's the last letter she wrote to your dad."

"Dad sent her a doll?"

"Indeed he did. He was thrilled when he finally found it in Eaton's toy department. Hiawatha, he called her."

"Hiawatha? Don't tell me he actually sent her an Indian doll! A racist to the end of his life. How could he do that to a little girl?"

My mother's proud smile faded. She stepped back and folded her arms in front of her.

"Well for all you're a priest, Larry, I'd say you haven't lost any of your arrogance. Don't you *dare* accuse your father of hurting that child. He did nothing but dote on her from the moment we got news of her birth. He wrote to her, sent her little surprises, told her jokes. He kept every one of her notes in the drawer by his bed, said he was going to put them all in an album and give it to her on her wedding day. When he had the first stroke, I took the whole lot of them to the hospital, read them aloud to him when there was still a chance he might recover. I'd say he died a better man than you are right now, and may God forgive me for saying that."

She turned her back on me, marched out the door and up the stairs, and I was reminded of that other time years ago when she had left the room in high dudgeon.

I washed and dried the dishes mechanically. I cleaned the kitchen until it was restored to the immaculate condition I remembered. I emptied the trash can into a bin bag, carried the bag out to the garden shed and deposited it in the bin, came back to the kitchen and put the dish towels to soak in bleach. I rinsed out the teapot and filled the kettle and couldn't think of anything else to do. Only then did I allow myself to stand before the fridge and contemplate my daughter's life.

My daughter, Miriam.

When my mother came downstairs and stood silently beside me, I turned and put my arms around her.

"I'm sorry, Ma," I said. "I spoke in ignorance and, okay, maybe with a bit of arrogance."

"How about ignorance and a *lot* of arrogance? No, I'm just teasing you now. What I was thinking up in my room there was that you've had a real shock today, Larry. And on top of that you're still jet-lagged from that long flight from Rome. No wonder you're a bit snappy."

In the evening, I took Mum to the White Spot over on West Georgia. We had burgers and fries with a small green salad on the side purely for show. Then we drove over the Lion's Gate Bridge to North Van for ice cream at Peter's. We talked about my life in Rome and the friends I had made there. We talked about the magnificence of Italian churches. We talked about Italian cuisine, Italian wine, Italian opera. We talked about everything except the existence of Miss Miriam Pigeon, daughter of Benita Pigeon and Larry Kinsella, granddaughter of Kathleen Kinsella and the late Charlie Kinsella.

By the time we got home again, jet-lag was starting to set in. I made a quick call to Renzo and Molly, but the moment I sat down with my mother to watch the late news on TV, my eyes closed and I was out like a light. I wearily dragged myself up the stairs to bed but then tossed and turned for the rest of the night, and it was not until dawn that I was able to sleep at last.

It was mid-morning when I woke up, and while I was saying my prayers the aroma of percolating coffee came drifting up from downstairs, a sure sign that my mother was up and about and no doubt waiting for me to put in an appearance below. I found her in the kitchen and was relieved to see that she looked well rested and less frail than she had seemed yesterday. When she saw me, she bustled over to the stove and took out a stack of warm pancakes.

"Sit yourself down now, son, and get these into you while they're still good and hot. You must be starved altogether."

She brought the coffee pot over to the table and while we were eating I broached the subject of a lightning trip up to Kamloops to see Molly and Renzo's new baby girl. Mum had every right to protest at my leaving her again so soon after the funeral, but unselfish as always, she asked no questions, just told me to drive safely and to give her love to Renzo and Molly and the baby.

"Take Dad's camera with you, Larry. I'd love a picture of them, the new little one especially, I haven't seen her yet. We'll get a copy made at the drugstore and I'll give it to Renzo's parents."

When I got back three days later I brought with me an eight-week old West Highland White puppy who made himself at home immediately. My mother named him Trice, which stood for Rice Two, but also because whenever he caught a whiff of food he was there in a trice.

On the morning I left to return to Rome, I handed her the snapshots I had taken with Dad's camera: one of me and Renzo sitting on his porch, another one of me holding baby Mirella, one of Molly and Renzo and the children, and finally a photo of a solemn little dark-haired girl in a white beaded dress.

"Here, Ma," I said. "Here's your granddaughter."

CHAPTER TWENTY-TWO

Ever since the birth of the grandchild they had never seen, Charlie and Kathleen Kinsella had sent her gifts. When she was a baby, Miriam had been indifferent to the clothes and toys that arrived for her in the mail, and even as a toddler she preferred to play with an old plaything of her mother's. Had it been up to Benita, every package would have been returned unopened, but her grandmother would not hear of it. Hepzibah said that whatever had been sent with love, should be received with grace, that even if Miriam grew up without ever meeting her grandparents in Vancouver, she had the right to know they existed, and that they cared for her.

"So how come her father, their own son, has never acknowledged her!" Benita asked. "And what use are grandparents who would put up with that?"

Clara was removing the final layer of tissue paper from the porcelain Beatrix Potter bowl and cup which had arrived just in time for Miriam's first birthday. Hepzibah took the bowl, felt the weight of it, examined the hand painted rabbits that encircled it, turned it over and read aloud from the bottom of the dish.

"Made in England," she said. "Some long trip for this one dish and cup, huh? You know, Benny, some kids, their fathers die when they are small, like Peter Cardinal. Remember him, Clara? Went out to hunt moose with old Henry Matthias?"

"Yup," said Clara. "Old Henry, he was half blind but he never wanted to stay home. That one time he thought it was a moose coming out of the bush but it was Peter Cardinal, and Henry Matthias shot him dead. That little Pauline Cardinal, she was just a tiny baby when he died, and she never knew her dad. She lived with her mom and her grandparents right up to the day she married Charlie Baptiste."

"No," said Benita. "That's different. Pauline Cardinal grew up knowing who she was and she got to hear lots about her father."

But Hepzibah, as usual, had the last word.

"Every life is its own, Benny. Miriam will grow up knowing she is loved by a whole bunch of people, and that's what counts the most."

So of all the gifts that were sent to Miriam, only one had ever been refused. When she was three years old, a birthday card arrived in the mail. It had a baby elephant on the front holding three pink balloons in its trunk. Inside the card there were two fifty-dollar bills and a message: "With love and best wishes from Grandfather Charlie and Grandmother Kathleen."

Jericho George whistled through his teeth when he saw the money.

"Holy Cow! One hundred bucks! Thassa lot of money!"

Benita ran and got a pen from the kitchen drawer, took the card and scrawled on the blank page next to the message: "We do not need your money." While she was searching for an envelope Hepzibah reached over and added the words, "You are very kind. Thank you but...."in front of Benita's angry message. The card and money were returned in the next post, and since then Miriam had received toys, games, blocks, clothes, and many books, but never again money.

The books were especially welcome. By the time she was three, Miriam was accustomed to spending time by herself with her picture books. In the early days, Benita had turned the pages for her and together they looked at elephants, tigers, palm trees, sailing ships, castles, and dragons. Then Miriam began to point to things she recognized.

"Truck," she would say. "Jericho truck."

Her first storybook arrived just before she turned four, and Benita sat her on her lap and read it to her. When she reached the end, Miriam said, "again!" The second time, Benita read more slowly, pointing to each word as she spoke it. The third time, she held Miriam's finger and moved it across the line as she pronounced the words. By the fourth reading Benita was sick and tired of hearing about the little red hen, but Miriam had memorized the story and spoke the words along with her. Clara came to watch and listen. She laughed and clapped her hands when Benita finally closed the book.

"Hah! That one's gonna be a reader for sure, just like her ma."

And Jericho George patted Miriam on the head.

"Yup, she's one smart little girl," he said.

The next time he went to town, he came back with two more books for Miriam. Benita put *Heidi* aside.

"This one's for when she's bigger," she said. "It's too hard for her right now, but this other one's perfect."

So *Little Red Riding Hood* was the first book Miriam read by herself, and for weeks she read the story aloud to anyone who would listen.

"Just you watch out for that Big Bad Wolf, huh, Mirri? He's pretty tricky." Benita said one day.

Miriam laughed. "Hah. He could never fool me, that wolf. I'm way too smart."

"Maybe. I used to think I was smart, too, but I got fooled all the same."

Miriam stopped laughing and looked alarmed.

"You got fooled by the Big Bad Wolf? What did he do to you, Ma?"

Hepzibah frowned at Benita.

"Your mother is teasing you, Miriam. It's a story is all. Wolves are animals and they got fur to cover them and keep them warm. That's how come they don't need clothes like us folk. Besides, that Little Red Riding Hood was kinda dumb anyways. You're way smarter than her."

While Miriam was learning to read, Hepzibah, ever a watcher of people, noticed signs of restlessness in Benita. She said nothing, just went on watching. She saw that Benita was a loving mother to Miriam, that she did her best to take her place with the younger women of the community, and that she had become accomplished at tanning hides and even working with the beads she claimed to despise. But her heart simply was not in it. Nor, thought Hepzibah, would it ever be. She was far more interested in learning about plants and had grown skilled at collecting, sorting, and classifying those that could be used to heal. Often, she took Miriam with her and had already begun to teach her about the *good plants* that could be used to treat people when they were ill. Hepzibah watched them as they learned together and thought that one day both of them might be healers.

In late summer, while Isaac King and Jericho George and some of the other men fished further down the lake, the women gathered to pick berries at the keyoh which had been used by the King family for many years. Miriam, tall for her age and agile, had lots of kids to play with, but the one she chose to be her best friend was Cecile Baptiste, granddaughter of Pauline Cardinal.

The days were getting shorter, but the sky stayed blue, the sun was still hot, and the smell of ripe berries and cedar bark hung in the still air. The kids ran wild while the women roamed the keyoh in search of salal bushes ripe for picking, and at night it was warm enough to sleep out in the open with just a light blanket as covering.

On the night of Cecile Baptiste's fifth birthday, Miriam was wakeful and restless, and Benita waited for her to settle.

"Stop your tossing and turning now," she said at last. "You're keeping me awake."

"I'm just not sleepy, Ma. My eyes, they won't stay closed. See? They keep on popping open every time."

"Okay, keep them open then. Look up at the sky and try to count all the stars you see."

"Is that what you used to do when you were a little girl?"

"Uh-huh. Sshh. Start counting."

Miriam counted aloud, lost count, started again, reached fifty-nine.

"That's as high as I go, Ma," she said.

Benita turned on her side and peered at her daughter.

"What are you talking about? I bet you there's a thousand stars up there, Miriam. Just keep counting."

"No, I mean I don't know what comes after fifty-nine." Miriam said.

"Sixty," said Benita. "Then seventy, then eighty, then ninety, then a hundred. After that you start all over again."

But Miriam didn't want to start over.

"I'm sick of counting stars," she said. "Who cares how many are up there anyway? Know what I really want to know?"

"What do you really want to know?" Benita asked sleepily.

"How come I don't got no dad?"

Benita was jolted awake by the question she had been expecting for a long time, but now found herself unprepared for.

"Hey, you've got me, you've got Hepzibah, you've got Clara, and you've got Jericho. That's plenty people to raise one kid. You don't need a dad."

"All kids got to have a dad. That's what Samuel said, Cecile's big brother."

"Well, Samuel's wrong. Lots of kids have no dad."

"Did I used to have a dad when I was just a baby?"

"No, you never had a dad."

"Never?"

"Never."

"How did I get made then?" Miriam asked triumphantly. "You told me babies get made by a mother and a father, remember? Like a hen and a rooster make a chick, a buck and a doe make a fawn. Same thing with people, you said."

Benita lay on her back and looked at the stars while, beside her, Miriam waited, wide awake and watching her.

"Well," said Benita after a while. "You got made that way too, but then he had to go away."

"Who?"

Miriam was waiting for the word her mother did not want to say. "Your father."

"Why did he go away? Didn't he want me?"

"He never knew about you."

"But he knows now, right?"

"I'm pretty sure he knows by now." But even as she answered her persistent daughter, Benita realized that she wasn't sure at all. "Yeah, I'd say he knows about you."

"So why doesn't he come and see us?"

"I don't know," Benita said. "Okay, enough questions now, little girl. We gotta sleep now. How about we both count the stars? You and me together. You start…"

CHAPTER TWENTY-THREE

When all the berries had been picked and dried and stored for the winter, the weather grew colder. Miriam began to spend more time indoors, sometimes at Cecile's house, sometimes at home with Benita and Hepzibah and Clara, although Clara had begun to accompany Jericho George on his trips to Blanchette where she stayed at what she referred to as "The Pigeon House." It was Clara who suggested one day that Miriam make a picture for her "other grandparents," and it was Clara who, when the picture was done, carefully folded it, put it in an envelope, addressed it, and took it with her when she crossed the lake in Jericho George's boat.

A few weeks later there was a letter in the post addressed to Miss Miriam Pigeon, LaPierre, B.C.

> *Dear Miriam,*
> *We like the picture of your house very much and we will keep it always. We have put it on the door of the fridge so that we can look at it all the time and think of you.*
> *Can you send us another picture some time?*
> *With love from Grandfather Charlie*
> *and Grandmother Kathleen.*

Hepzibah read the note to Miriam, showed her her own name and the names of her Vancouver grandparents. Benita put a pile of scrap paper on the kitchen table alongside a plastic tub of pencil crayons, and Miriam sat at the table to draw a stick-like figure with blackcurrant eyes, button nose, long black hair, and a mouth like a red slash. She handed the finished portrait to her mother.

"Send them this," she said.

"Who is it?"

"Me!" Miriam was shocked that her mother did not recognize her instantly.

"Can't you see it's me? Here's my smile. And my hair. See me *now*?"

"Oh, yeah, now I see you," Benita said apologetically. "Okay, how about we print your name underneath your picture? We can do it like this."

She put a pencil in Miriam's hand, wrapped her own hand around it and printed 'MIRIAM' on a blank sheet of paper.

"No. I want to do it by myself," said Miriam.

The pile of scrap paper diminished as the number of failed attempts to reproduce the six letters of her name grew. Miriam got mad because, she said, she had to make the hardest letter of all of them, the 'M', twice. She complained bitterly that the top half of the 'R' was "too round." She said that she wished her whole name was made up of 'I's because 'I' was her favourite letter. She asked them why they had chosen such a hard name for her in the first place, and added that it was a stupid name and she hated it. When Clara told her it was perfect, that she could read it just fine, Miriam glared at her balefully.

"It's not perfect! Can't you see it's all wobbly? Go away!"

In the end it was Benita who put an end to things. "Okay," she said decisively. "It's good enough. Now copy it in the space under your picture and we'll send it to Vancouver."

Not long after that, Jericho took Miriam into town with him, and Clara and let her choose three storybooks from the children's section of the lending library, and by Christmas she was reading aloud to anyone who would listen to her.

"Told you she was smart," Jericho said with pride, and Hepzibah smiled.

"She's like her mother," she said. "But could be she's like her father too."

Then, in March, one week after her fifth birthday, Benita told Miriam that she was going to Vancouver.

"Why?" her daughter asked her.

"Because," said Benita.

"When will you come back?"

"Soon."

"Will I be a big girl when you come back?"

"No. You'll still be a little girl."

The next morning she was gone, taking with her almost nothing, and leaving a lonely space in Miriam's life. She filled it with books and pictures and daydreams, rarely played with Cecile, often spent her time curled up in a chair doing nothing at all. Clara started to fuss.

"She's way too quiet," she told Hepzibah. "And she's lost her appetite."

"She'll be okay," Hepzibah said. "She's just gotta get used to things being different."

Jericho George arrived one morning to pick up Clara for the trip into town and found Miriam sucking her thumb.

"Hey!" he said. "Take that thing out of your mouth. Big girls don't suck their thumbs."

"I'm not a big girl," said Miriam. "I'm still a little girl."

Jericho stroked her hair. "Well, I guess it's okay then." But when he and Clara were on their way across the lake he said, "That Miriam, she's one sad little girl now."

"Uh-Huh, that's what I'm thinking too," said Clara. "You got any ideas what to do about it, Jericho?"

When Clara returned to LaPierre, she came with Isaac King's son, Solomon.

"Where's Jericho?" was the first thing Miriam said.

"Hey, don't I even get a hello from my own granddaughter?" Clara said.

"Hello, Grandma. So where's Jericho?"

Clara laughed. "He had to take care of something in town,"

"When's he coming back?"

"Soon as he can, Miriam. I can't tell you more than that. Now go and read a book or something. I've got stuff to do."

Over the next few days, Miriam trailed around after Clara, demanding to know exactly when Jericho would get back to LaPierre until Clara, exasperated, snapped at her.

"God damn it, Miriam, just stop your pestering! He'll come back when he's good and ready."

Miriam burst into tears.

"Everybody keeps on leaving," she sobbed inconsolably. "I just don't want people to be going away all the time."

But Jericho George showed up the next day. Miriam heard him talking to Clara outside the house and rushed to greet him.

"Hey, little girl," he said, smiling his big smile. "I got something for you".

There was a cardboard box on the ground by his feet and he stooped to flip it open. "Come and see," he said.

Miriam looked inside, took a step backwards, looked up at Jericho, knelt down on the ground and bent over the box again.

"Oh!" she said, and expelled the breath she had been holding since her first glimpse of something wonderful. "Oh…"

Jericho George scooped up two puppies and placed them on the ground in front of Miriam, two fat furry balls that tumbled around on the patchy grass, whimpering and bumping into each other.

"Me and Clara found them in town," Jericho told Miriam. "They were real little, and almost starving. I had to stay in town and feed them with a bottle. Clara, she didn't want to say nothing to you because she thought they might not make it. It was touch and go there for a while."

"Why didn't their mother feed them?" Miriam asked.

Jericho George did not want to tell her that they had discovered the bitch with her litter of five underneath an abandoned truck on the reserve in Blanchette. Three of the pups were already dead, and the mother was covered with mange and close to lifeless. He had shot her with his hunting rifle and removed the two remaining pups.

"She was too sick," he said.

"What about their dad?"

"They don't got no dad," Jericho said.

"Huh," said Miriam. "Kinda like me then."

Then Jericho told her to pick the puppy that she liked the best while he and Clara went indoors to fix them something to eat.

Miriam sat down on the dusty ground and the puppies crawled over her legs. Hepzibah came out from the shack and watched as she lifted them up one at a time and examined them closely. She looked into their eyes, spoke to them softly, stroked them gently. Then she stood up, moved to a different spot, sat down again, watched the two puppies, and waited. One of the pups tottered off to explore the long grass by Hepzibah's plant shack, but the other one made its way over to her, clambered onto her lap, and went to sleep curled up in a ball.

Hepzibah smiled. "Guess you found your pup then."

"No," said Miriam, "He found me."

"How do you know it's a he?" Hepzibah asked her.

"I checked," Miriam said matter-of-factly. "Both of them are boys. Boy dogs have a thing sticking out underneath and girl dogs don't. Clara showed me on Isaac King's dogs."

"Okay," said Hepzibah. "You thought of a name for him yet?"

"Nope," said Miriam. "I'm busy thinking."

She sat in silence with the sleeping puppy and pondered. Then she said, "I got an idea. He kind of looks like a furry berry. My idea is to call him Berry. Would that be an okay name for a dog?"

Hepzibah looked at the red-gold puppy and thought for a moment before replying.

"Berry? Yup, sounds like a pretty fine name to me. He does have the look of a nice plump berry. Might turn into a real big one when he's full-grown though, I'm thinking."

Miriam laughed. "Then I'll call him Big Berry!"

"Well," said Hepzibah, "looks like little Berry's waking up. You take him inside now, Miriam, and feed him while I go get the other one. Tomorrow we have to find a home for that one. How about we give him to your friend Cecile, okay?"

"Okay," said Miriam.

CHAPTER TWENTY-FOUR

On the day Benita left LaPierre, Jericho George had driven her all the way to Prince George, with Clara sitting alongside him and Benita next to her mother, duffel bag at her feet. She was planning to take the overnight Greyhound, and it was almost dark by the time they found a place to park the truck a couple of blocks away from the bus station.

The acrid smell of wood pulp hung in the chill air, and apart from the constant comings and goings at the beer parlour on the corner, the streets were deserted. Jericho lifted out Benita's bag and slammed the door shut. He did not lock it. Anyone looking at Jericho's beat-up old truck would know there was nothing in it worth stealing.

Outside the beer parlour, there was an Indian passed out cold on the sidewalk and Benita could smell the reek of booze even before they reached him. His buddy leaned against the wall, barely able to stay upright. As they approached, he muttered something to himself, his gaze bleary-eyed and unfocused.

Jericho George stopped, bent over the guy on the sidewalk, lifted his head off the ground and tried to wake him. The other drunk staggered over.

"Hey, tha's my buddy," he said. "You leave him be, he just gotta sleep awhile, okay?"

"Best leave him be, Jericho," Clara said. "He'll be okay. He's real drunk is all."

But Jericho stayed put. "You and Benita wait up for me at the Greyhound station, Clara. Get the bus ticket, okay? I'll be right there."

He reached into his pocket, took out some money, and handed it to Benita. She looked at it for a moment, hesitated, then put it in her own pocket.

"Thanks, Jericho, but I'm in no big rush. I'm staying right here with you."

"No, you and Clara better get going," he said firmly. "I gotta find out where these two guys come from, get them home safe."

Clara said, "Let's just move this one guy over to the wall. More safe that way and he can sleep it off." She bent down and took hold of an arm. "Benita, grab his other arm, okay? Jericho, you grab his legs."

Between them they managed to shift the drunk from the centre of the sidewalk. As they were turning him onto his side, the saloon door swung open and three white guys spilled out onto the street.

Trouble, thought Benita, noting the lurch and swagger of them. They were big, bulky guys in their late twenties, loggers by the look of them and strong as bull moose, not pie-eyed yet but well on the way and spoiling for a Saturday night fight. One of them caught sight of Benita.

"Hey, lookie, lookie! What have we here?"

His drinking buddy took in the rest of the group on the sidewalk.

"Looks like another bunch of injuns wandered off the reserve. You're in *our* territory now, Big Chief, and you're in the way. Move your ass, you drunken bum!"

He lifted his steel-toed work boot and aimed a vicious kick at the prone figure lying by the wall, the blow landing full-force in his belly.

"Jesus Christ!" Jericho yelled. "Why'd you have to go and do that? He can't even stand up! You hurt him bad, most likely."

"Is that right? You wanna do something about it, Big Man?" The third guy stepped forward, fists raised, dancing on the balls of his feet, fuelled by booze and adrenaline.

"Come on, Red Man, let's go!"

When Jericho did not respond, he turned his attention to Clara and Benita.

"These your women? Looks like one ugly squaw and her juicy daughter. How many beers you want for the loan of the young one, huh? You can have her back in an hour."

Jericho and Clara ignored the taunts and tried to raise the injured man to a sitting position.

"Now ain't that a pretty picture? One big happy Indian family."

Suddenly the tone changed from a sneer to something more threatening. A mean drunk, wanting to liven up a dull Saturday night in town.

"Hey, Indian, you deaf or something? I asked you a question, and I'm waiting for an answer."

Jericho spoke quietly to Clara. "Time for you to get out of here now. You and Benita get going to the bus station. These guys are just a bunch of drunks. I can handle them."

Clara stood up and turned to Benita. "You go," she said. "I'm not leaving Jericho. We'll catch up with you when we get rid of these clowns."

Benita thought that maybe her mother had intended to be overheard, but maybe not. Too late to wonder about it, anyway.

"Did I just hear you call me a clown, you dirty squaw?" The mouthy one grabbed Clara by the shoulder, yanked her head towards him and spat the contents of his mouth into her face. Clara gasped and pulled herself free. She wiped her mouth with her sleeve and got shoved to the ground while the other guy smashed his fist into the side of Jericho George's head.

Benita wondered briefly why anger was associated with heat. The fury that overtook her when she witnessed her mother's degradation felt like ice, freezing her in place. Then it seemed to her that she was moving through thick, heavy mud and getting nowhere, but the truck was close by and she had barely any distance to cover. No thought was involved, no actual decision made. She opened the door, reached into the cab, and slid out Jericho's hunting knife from the leather sheath that was strapped to the base of the driver's seat.

The guy who had sent Clara flying was standing over her, one booted foot on her chest, posing for his snickering buddies.

"Me Big White Hunter," he said, and then caught sight of Benita, knife raised in her hand.

"See this, you fat, ugly pig?" she said. "You better take off real fast or I'm gonna cut off your balls, if you have any, and you can bet I'm really gonna enjoy doing it"

One of the white men started to snigger, but was silenced by the stillness of Benita, the coiled and deadly tension in her body, the rage and hatred that radiated from her.

Later, when she thought back to the event, Benita never doubted that she would have carried out her threat. She had been ready to attack. She only wondered what would have happened if she had used the knife, if she had inflicted a serious injury on the white guy—if she had killed him.

The one thing she was certain of was the intensity of her desire to hurt the men who had spat on her mother and pushed her to the ground, punched Jericho George, and kicked the helpless drunk. She would never remember their faces, but she would hate the memory of them forever. What scared her was not the hatred she had felt, but the sure knowledge that she was capable of violence.

A police car rolled up in response to a call from the beer parlour, a call the barman was used to making on a Friday or Saturday night when the loggers came into town. Within minutes, the three white guys, fun over for the night, had been sent on their way, leaving Benita to explain the incident.

"Want to come along to the police station and lodge a formal complaint, Miss?" the older of the two officers asked, a half smile on his face.

"No," said Benita. "I have to catch the bus to Vancouver."

"Uh-huh," he said. "How about the rest of you guys? Like to make a formal complaint about what just happened?"

Jericho George and Clara looked at him wordlessly. The guy on the ground lay groaning in a pool of his own vomit. His drinking buddy lurched forward, leaned heavily against Jericho and leered at the cop.

"Hey, pal, wanna come for a beer?"

Benita said, "I don't think anyone here is going to be filing a complaint, Officer, Thanks for your concern though."

He looked at her sharply, not sure if he detected sarcasm in her tone.

"Okay, you all get yourselves back to the Reserve then," he said, nodding in the direction of the guy on the sidewalk. "And don't let me come back later and find you guys still here, or you'll be spending the night in jail."

In the end Benita walked by herself to the Greyhound Station. By the time she had boarded the overnight bus to Vancouver, Jericho George and Clara were on the road again, the two drunks sleeping it off in the back of the truck, already half way back to their Reserve near Lejac.

When she stepped off the bus the next morning, Benita felt as if she were trapped in a dream. She had not slept all night. The noise of the constant shifts in speed played beneath the sporadic conversation and occasional bursts of laughter from her fellow travellers. Gusts of cold air blew in through the open door whenever the bus stopped to disgorge a passenger or admit a new one. All this, together with an hour-long stopover at the Husky Roadside cafe in Hope, had conspired to keep her wide awake for the entire thirteen-hour journey.

In Vancouver she was met by rain and wind. The city was shrouded in grey mist, and there was no sign of the majestic snow-capped Coast Mountains over on the North Shore. Gulls wheeled overhead screaming, a sound she had not heard in years. There were no trees in the vicinity of the dingy bus station, and without even a glimpse of their budding and greening and blossoming, it was hard to believe it was already springtime here on the West Coast. Benita pulled up the hood of her quilted jacket and started out on the long walk down Dunsmuir Street to Hastings, and then along Main until she reached Mount Pleasant.

There were more cars on the roads now than when she had last been here, but Winchester Avenue was just as she remembered it, a quiet, sedate side street of neatly kept houses and trim gardens where, today, armies of daffodils battled the wind and bowed before it.

The outside of Number 56 looked as if it had recently received a fresh coat of paint, but indoors all was the same. She was greeted rapturously by Kathleen, and almost as warmly by Charlie who had gained weight since she had last seen him. He took her coat and Kathleen sat her down in the front room, and after a few minutes of small talk, an uneasy silence fell upon the three of them. Benita broke it.

"Why I'm here is because Miriam has started to ask me about her father; who he is, where he is, why he has never come to see her. I want to go back with something to tell her so that she doesn't have to spend her whole life wondering."

Kathleen was visibly nervous.

"He's not here any more, Pet. He lives abroad now, you see."

Abroad. The word was strange to her ears. She let it slide around in her mind for a few moments

"Where, abroad?"

"Italy."

"Italy? What's he doing there? He's not Italian."

Charlie Kinsella laughed mirthlessly. "You got that right, Benita! Larry's as Irish as any Canadian can be."

Kathleen warned him with her eyes.

"Don't be starting now, Charlie," she said. And then, "Let me just go and make a pot of tea for you, Pet. And how about a nice sandwich? You must be starved altogether after that long old bus trip."

She bustled out to the kitchen, leaving Charlie and Benita marooned on their chintz-covered armchairs, adrift on the brightly coloured Axminster rug. Benita struck out for shore.

"Does he know?"

Her words sank into the silence, and Charlie gazed at the door, willing it to open on his wife bearing a plate of ham and cheese sandwiches. It remained firmly closed.

"Does Larry know about Miriam?" she asked again.

He looked down at the carpet and stared at the pattern.

"No," he said finally. "We never told him. Now why don't I go and check on those damn sandwiches for you? They're a hell of a long time coming."

He heaved himself out of his chair and launched himself across the room like a drowning man reaching for a lifeboat. Benita heard him say something to his wife in the kitchen but couldn't make out the words, nor could she hear Kathleen's reply.

It struck her that the two of them were hiding out like a couple of guilty kids. Well, if they had kept the news of his own daughter's birth from Larry then they deserved to feel as guilty as sin, she thought. How could they live with themselves and the choice they had made? How could they be sending gifts and letters to Miriam as if they genuinely cared about her? They had never wanted her to be born, and they did not want her now. They were ashamed of her.

There was no sound from the kitchen. Benita stood up, crossed the room, and opened the door. In the tiny hallway she took her coat from the tallboy at the foot of the stairs, shrugged it on, opened the front door, and started up the path. She was already through the garden gate when Charlie came lumbering after her, followed closely by Kathleen.

"Benita, wait," he said, red in the face from exertion. "Don't go rushing off now. We need to explain something to you."

As far as Benita was concerned, there was nothing to explain. She understood the situation perfectly. They had not told their son about his daughter because they did not want his life to be messed up by a youthful error which had resulted in a half-breed child born on a reserve. They were willing to acknowledge Miriam as their grandchild, but only at a distance so that they need never be confronted by her native and illegitimate heritage. She and her daughter would never be seen as anything but the flotsam of a downtrodden, inferior race. She trudged through the rain and silently cursed the whole lot of them, even people like the O'Carrolls who had undoubtedly been motivated by pity, and maybe by the desire to win a place in Heaven. Well, to hell with them all!

She arrived at the bus stop, reached into her pocket for change, and pulled out a folded envelope with the Kinsella's phone number scrawled on the front, along with a single sentence.

We are here any time you need us.

One of them had slipped it into her pocket. When she opened it she found two fifty-dollar bills. She screwed the envelope into a tight ball, hurled it into the gutter, and tossed the money after it. A moment later she heard the voice of her grandmother chiding her for such foolish behaviour, and when a gust of wind sent the notes flying into an overflowing gutter, she was forced to chase them down. She scooped up the sodden bills and dried them on the inside flap of her jacket. Then she took her place in the queue for the bus to downtown.

CHAPTER TWENTY-FIVE

The day Miriam started school she was accompanied by Jericho George and Berry, with a rope tied around his neck because he had no collar. The puppy fought the rope every step of the way, and Miriam begged Jericho to take it off.

"He's not used to it," she moaned. "Can't you see it's hurting him?"

"It's to stop him from running away," Jericho said calmly, reeling the pup in again.

"But he won't run away, Jericho. He'll just stay with me."

"Maybe," said Jericho. "But what'll happen when you get to school and he can't go in with you and I gotta get him home again? Think he'll follow me?"

Miriam laughed. "Never! He's smart. He already knows he's my dog."

"That's why we gotta use the rope to train him. After that he can take you to school whenever I'm not here to bring you."

By the end of September, the puppy was trotting to school each morning at Miriam's heel and following Jericho back home, the rope no longer needed. By Hallowe'en, he could be trusted to return by himself, and after that there was no real need for Jericho to walk the short distance with Miriam or to meet her again at noon, although he was always happy enough to do it.

Miriam loved kindergarten and wished it lasted the whole day instead of just the morning. There were only the four of them in her year, Zachary Joseph's twin boys, Teddy and Tommy, her friend Cecile Jerome, and herself. Mostly they kept themselves busy with toys and games while the teacher worked with the bigger kids, and at first Miriam was happy to draw pictures or play with the sand and playdough. Her favourite part of the day, though, was story time when all fifteen students in the primary division would sit in a circle on the floor and listen while their teacher, Kristin, read aloud to them and showed them pictures. Next door, in the second of the school's two rooms, Kristin's husband Max did his best to keep the older children occupied and quiet until the story finished and the little ones were dismissed for the day.

Recent immigrants from Germany, Max and Kristin Hoffmann were young, adventurous, and idealistic. They saw themselves as progressive educators and were opposed to all forms of discipline, routine, and structure. As a result, their happy band of students did pretty much whatever they felt like doing, and the loosely designed curriculum largely favoured arts, crafts, and outdoor sports interspersed with extended periods of recreation.

The young teachers were deeply respectful of the native people they had come to live among, especially the elders who still followed the traditional way of life and seemed fully at home in the land they had occupied for more than a thousand years. Before signing up to teach at the school in LaPierre, they had spent a summer driving through the central region of the province, going as far south as Williams Lake and Merritt, and northwest all the way up to Prince Rupert. Their journey allowed them glimpses of a forgotten people who lived in sometimes squalid conditions on barren reserves on the outskirts of towns. Many of the men, and even some of the women who found their way into town, seemed to be in thrall to alcohol, and Max had been shocked to see people sprawled out drunk in front of beer parlours. Nothing like it existed in their homeland, and they were appalled by the wide gulf that apparently existed between White Canadians and the Native community. Only in some of the remoter communities did they encounter people who appeared to be happy and were clearly leading a healthy and productive life in harmony with nature, which was exactly the kind of life that Max deeply desired for himself and his young wife.

As soon as they arrived in LaPierre, they set out to embrace the native lifestyle, and even though the local people saw that the Hoffmanns were well-meaning and sincere, their efforts to live off the land and lead a traditional way of life became a source of great amusement to them, especially whene they encountered Max in the forest, hunting with his bow and arrow. His wife Kristin, a striking blue-eyed blonde, was regarded by the women with a mixture of envy and admiration, and despite her efforts to befriend them, she was seen as a member of an alien tribe, which, indeed, she was.

When Max and Kristin Hoffmann first encountered Miriam Pigeon, they did not know quite what to do with her. From the start, it was clear that she was different. When Kristin arrived late for class one day she had been amazed to discover Miriam sitting crossed-legged in the kindergarten corner, reading aloud to the twins and Cecile. She read clearly and confidently, holding up the book before turning the page so that her listeners could see the pictures of Jack and his adventures with the Beanstalk.

"Miriam, you are reading already!" she said in her formal, slightly stilted English. "Who taught you to read?"

"My mother," said Miriam. "She learned me when I was real little."

Kristin and Max discussed their new student at some length and with a genuine desire to do what was right for her. In the end, the decision was taken out of their hands because Miriam began to direct her own learning, wandering freely between the primary and intermediate divisions, which is to say between the two rooms of the school. With the younger students she often acted more as a tutor than peer, reading aloud to them or helping them with their phonics and vocabulary. In Max's class she was tolerated by the older children who were of the opinion that Miriam was "too smart for kiddiegarden." It helped that she was tall for her age, articulate, opinionated, and somewhat bossy. And if there were times when a few of the older girls might have wished to put Miriam in her proper place in the rankings, she had serious back-up in the form of Berry. A puppy no longer, he had grown into a very large, very protective guardian whose demeanour signalled to the world around him, "Don't mess with me or my girl."

First Holy Communion did not take place in LaPierre until mid-July when the lake was free of ice and the mud had dried up and the little girls could wear their white dresses without a winter coat, and without mukluks or rubber boots on their feet. Miriam did not especially care about wearing a white dress, even though hers, stitched and elaborately beaded by Clara, was lovely. She looked forward to the event only because Benita had promised to be there, had told her in a letter that she would make up for her absence at Christmas by making a special trip to see Miriam make her First Communion, but as the days passed, hope began to fade until, in the end, there was no hope left, just bitter disappointment that came to rest within her like a cold, heavy stone.

Clara was angry with her daughter, but Hepzibah stopped the flow of harsh words.

"This is not the time for anger, Clara," she said.

"We have to do our best to make it a happy day for Miriam so that she will have a good memory of it. If her mother is not here with her, it's because she couldn't make it, not because she didn't want to. We don't know the reason, but Benita surely has one. That's good enough for right now, okay?"

On the eve of Miriam's communion day, a grey pall drifted across the summer sky and there was an acrid tang in the air. Clara said it was smoke from one of the big fires that were burning up the forest around Prince George and creeping northward to Blanchette. Everyone was saying it was a bad year for bush fires.

"Could it reach here?" Miriam asked, looking at the tall trees that surrounded the house and stretched back into the forest as far as she could see like battalions of soldiers standing at attention. She had thought of them as guardians of the village. Now she wondered if they were putting them all in the path of danger.

"No," said Clara. "We have the lake between us and the fire."

But that night, the night before her first communion, Miriam dreamt of a giant tongue of fire stretching across the lake and lapping up the water, blazing a path of flames that reached all the way to the village, burning and destroying the homes and the people of LaPierre. She woke at dawn, screaming in terror, and found Hepzibah standing beside her bed.

"A terrible fire was coming for us," she sobbed in her great-grandmother's arms.

"There's no fire, Miriam. Everything is alright. Shhh. Do you hear Berry barking?"

"No."

"If there was a fire, he'd be barking his head off to warn us, and we'd have plenty of time to get to the lake. There's nothing to worry about, I promise you. We're safe in the hands of God. He's watching out for us."

"How do you know that?"

Hepzibah lay down beside her on the bed.

"Because He's the One who taught the stars to sing when they see the light of morning and know their watch is done."

"The stars sing?" Miriam laughed at the thought.

"Softly they sing at the coming of the day. Listen now and be still. In a little while you will hear their song."

When Miriam woke up again, she had forgotten the fire dream, but she remembered that her mother still had not come. Jericho George arrived early with Berry at his heels, wearing a large white bow tied around his neck, but even that did not bring a smile to Miriam's face. When they entered the church she looked around hopefully, and then, finally accepting that her mother would not come, she took her place in the front pew with the other first communicants.

There were only the four of them that year, Teddy and Tommy Joseph, Cecile Jerome, and Miriam, but the altar was full of flowers, and John Prince was already in place at the organ. He never missed a First Communion and travelled to every settlement along Sturgeon Lake to lead the hymns and play the organ, if there was one. When John Prince was a boy in the Residential School at Lejac, one of the

Oblate Fathers had heard him sing and pronounced him musical. The priest had taught him to read music and persuaded him to join the boys' choir which had been established to promote the singing of hymns in the Carrier language. Most of the boys abandoned the choir as soon as their voices broke, but John Prince turned into a splendid bass-baritone and went right on singing. He was a natural musician and devout in his faith. Now a widower in his mid-fifties, he could be relied upon to show up for weddings, funerals, baptisms, and First Communions, except for those times when he was too hung over to get himself to the church at all.

It was the wakes that were his downfall. One of the mourners would offer him a drink, and then somebody else would pour him another. By nightfall John Prince could barely stand up, let alone play the organ the next day at the funeral. But for every problem there is a solution. One of the Sisters of St. Joseph took to showing up at his house well before the bell began to toll for the funeral Mass. Sister Imelda would rap briskly on the front door, and if there was no reply, she would stride into the house, rouse him from his stupor, heat the coffee while he was getting dressed, wait for him to gulp it down, and then strong-arm him over to the church to take his place at the organ. Even when hung-over and bleary-eyed, John Prince was amiable and good-natured and never failed to thank the nun for getting him to the church on time.

Miriam knew she was supposed to feel joy when she received the Lord for the first time, but she felt nothing but sadness, and the flicker of a small spark of resentment. Maybe Benita had plain forgotten all about Miriam's special day. Maybe she was having such a good time in the big city that she couldn't be bothered to get on the bus and get herself home for her own daughter's First Holy Communion. Whatever the reason, she could have come. Should have come, thought Miriam as she swallowed the host.

John Prince cranked up the organ, and the congregation rose in song as the four young communicants followed the priest up the aisle and out the door, their families trailing behind them. When they emerged from the church, Father Hines was standing at the foot of the wooden steps beside a tall, dark-haired man with a camera.

"Boys and girls," he said. "This gentleman has come all the way from Vancouver, and he has very kindly offered to take a photograph of each of you. When he goes back to the city he'll get the pictures developed and send them to you. Would you guys like that?"

Teddy and Tommy Joseph were camera shy and hung their heads until they received a sharp reprimand from their father, Zachary, at which point they managed to produce a toothy grimace that passed for a smile. Cecile Jerome posed willingly, smiling enthusiastically and displaying her frilly white dress. When it was Miriam's turn, she came forward reluctantly and stood stiffly on the bottom step of the little white church, refusing to smile even when Jericho George made faces at her and got Berry, still decked out in his white bow, to stand up on his hind legs and wave his paws in the air. Everyone urged her to smile on the day of her First Holy Communion, but the man with the camera said nothing, just waited patiently, and in the end settled for a picture of Miriam looking solemn and a little bit sad.

CHAPTER TWENTY-SIX

The black and white snapshots that I left with my mother were from the roll of film I had had developed in Vancouver before my return to Italy. Four others were mailed to Father Hines in Blanchette, along with a note asking him to distribute them to the First Communicants in LaPierre, and there was one more that I kept for myself.

When I got back to Rome, I put the photo of Miriam in a frame and stood it on the bedside table next to the picture of my parents on their silver wedding anniversary, the last time they had posed for a photo together. Each morning when I woke up, I saw the faces of my parents and my daughter, and each night before I slept, I prayed for them, for the soul of my father, for the continued good health of my mother, and for Miriam—that the sadness be lifted from her face and from her life, and that her future be blessed with happiness. And always I prayed for the one who was missing, the one I could not see. Always, I prayed for Benita.

Shortly after my ordination, I had begun my studies in theology and cannon law at the Pontifical Gregorian University in Rome and was now well on my way to obtaining my PhD. I loved everything about the Holy City and felt thoroughly at home in it. In those days, priests in continental Europe, in particular in Italy, could be identified by their soutanes, the long-skirted, many-buttoned black robes they wore when out in public. In Rome I was one of a thousand whom my father would have called "fags in frocks," and the thought made me smile. I suppose that amongst us there must have been some who were homosexual, although I had not met any, at least not to my knowledge, and I had never had the slightest doubt about my own sexual orientation. In fact, I was strongly attracted by the beautiful women who surrounded me and had had to learn how to switch off desire. What worked best for me was to look at them as though they were my sisters rather than as objects of sexual desire. It was a matter of will power and self-control, and if those sometimes failed me, then all I had to do was recall that it was surrender to sexual desire that had created havoc in several lives, and had almost led to the destruction of a life in the making.

Now though, for the first time since my ordination, I found myself unsettled and distracted, my thoughts frequently turning back to Canada and to the frenzied dash to LaPierre that had resulted in my first sight of Miriam. Perhaps I had not quite believed the evidence on display in my mother's kitchen. Maybe she had fallen for a kind of fairy-tale grandchild and established a wishful relationship with a little native girl who had no real link to me or to our family. I had needed to know the truth, to find out for myself if the child I had helped to create had survived in spite of me.

I had left Vancouver wearing a clerical suit and white collar and was still wearing it when I arrived at the rectory in Blanchette and introduced myself as Father Larry Kinsella, on leave from Rome. I asked Father Hines if he knew of anyone who could take me across the Lake to LaPierre, and he said he did, and that person was himself, that he'd be going across the next morning to say a special Mass there for the four children who were to make their First Holy Communion. When I asked for their names he gave them willingly enough, though he was clearly puzzled by my interest. I spent that night at the rectory, and when I appeared for breakfast the next morning I was wearing civilian clothing. While we were eating, I explained to Father Hines that for personal reasons I wished to remain incognito. He looked at me quizzically but asked no questions, and for that I admired him.

The lake was choppy when we set out and the wind was brisk. The light sparkled off the water as we bounced and rocked our way to the other side, with myself in awe of the beauty of the day and the elderly priest keeping a wary eye on the waves.

"A dangerous body of water, this" he told me, "deceptive and unpredictable. The wind can come from nowhere and flip a fishing boat as if it were a child's toy. A lot of lives have been lost in these waters."

I was tempted to ask him how well he had known Johnny Pigeon, but he was a shrewd old bird and might have started asking some questions of his own. I guessed that his loyalties lay entirely with the Carrier people he served, and there was a chance that, had I told him my story, he would have turned the boat around and dumped me back in Blanchette. So I said nothing but my morning prayers, and those too were silent.

When we reached LaPierre, we crossed the rocky beach and followed the trail through the woods to the little white chapel on the hill. It was a simple structure, but it served as the heart of the community, bringing people together to mark the joyous heights and the solemn depths of life on this earth. I handed Father Hines the black leather bag containing the sacramentals, and went to kneel at the back of the church while he put on his vestments. I asked God to bless my presence here among His people and to make of it something good and holy. I asked Him to show me a way to atone for the sins of my past and to grant me His forgiveness, but what I had really come for, I knew, was the forgiveness of Benita and for a glimpse of my daughter, if she really existed.

I was alone in the church for some time and was beginning to wonder if Father Hines might have got the date wrong when he appeared before me fully robed and smiling.

"Don't worry, Larry. The people will come when they're good and ready. They don't have too much use for clocks up here."

He began setting up the altar by himself but was interrupted by the clatter and scurry of two little boys on their way to the sacristy. Moments later, they appeared on the altar wearing white surplices, and Father Hines himself tied their corded cinctures before they took up their duties as servers for the Mass.

When the people started to arrive, I fully expected Benita to be among them. Surely she would be here for her own daughter's First Communion. When I did not see her, I began to wonder if her appearance could have changed to such a degree that I no longer recognized her. Was it possible that she had cut her hair short perhaps, or maybe gained a great deal of weight after her pregnancy? I scrutinized every woman in the church until I was certain that none of them was Benita, and by that time Mass had begun.

I did not spot Miriam until after she had received the host and was on her way back to her place in the front pew, but as soon as I saw her I knew that she could only be my daughter. It was not so much that she resembled me, but that in her I recognized something of myself, and when she looked around expectantly I knew that she was searching for her mother. Then she sat down with the other kids, and I did not see her face again until she was standing in front of me refusing to smile for the camera. I took her picture and watched her walk away with a tall old lady whom I took to be her great-grandmother, Hepzibah, and a younger woman who might have been Benita's mother. A man was with them too, and a big ferocious looking red dog with a white ribbon tied around his neck. The man took Miriam's hand and the little group set off toward the cluster of houses at the foot of the hill. I stood watching them until they disappeared, and then went to help Father Hines strip the altar and re-pack his case for the trip back across Sturgeon Lake to Blanchette.

I woke before dawn the next morning and was soon on the lonely stretch of road back to Prince George. As I approached the city, smoke hung heavy in the air and drifted through the open windows of the car, and when the sun rose, it burned unseen, fierce and hot in a sky that was like a thick yellow-grey blanket. I pulled into the Husky station on the outskirts of town and got gas and coffee to go.

On my way out of the store I picked up the morning edition of the *Prince George Citizen* and read the front page while drinking the worst cup of coffee of my life. I would have dumped it after the first mouthful had I not needed an infusion of caffeine to keep me going for the long trip ahead. The news that morning was all about the forest fires, one thousand acres burning out of control to the east of the city. On the previous day, thirty-five unemployed men had been rushed to the Buckhorn Lake area to join the fifty-five man firefighting crew. The fire there had been caused by a spark from a power saw, and the blaze, fanned by the wind, had sent smoke billowing 10,000 feet into the air. I could see it from where I stood drinking my coffee.

I read that at Tabor Mountain the 190 men fighting the blaze were being fed three times a day by women using a tiny wood-burning stove, doing the best they could with facilities designed for only twelve men. The Forestry Service lookout at the top of the mountain reported that the woods were like gunpowder, and a firefighter was quoted as saying "the wind holds the key to the fire. It has us all at its mercy. We don't know which way it's going to blow."

With the heat, the wind, and the tinder-dry condition of vast stretches of forest, fires had broken out all over the region. Some, like the one at Frost Lake, had been caused by "devil winds" created by the fire itself, and the Grove fire had flared up on two fronts, jumping guards and forcing the crew to flee to safety. The report stated that during a single month well over a thousand men from the Prince George Forest District had been employed as fire fighters, most of them untrained. The good news was that unemployment in Prince George was at an all-time low. The bad news was that experts were predicting that the worst of the fires would continue to smoulder until the first snowfall at the earliest.

I tossed the gritty dregs of my coffee into the trash, and the guy parked next to me leaned out of his truck and asked which way I was headed. When I told him, he whistled through his teeth.

"You might want to take a different route, buddy. I hear they're pulling drivers off the road to join the fire-fighting crews. Kind of like conscription." Then he caught sight of my black suit and clerical collar.

"Although in your case, Father, I kind of doubt that'll happen."

He tooted his horn and pulled out, and I followed him onto the Cariboo Highway, heading south to Quesnel. The smoke grew denser, and I drove through a stretch of road where flames were visible on either side. It was an alarming sight, especially as there was no evidence of fire-fighting crews in the vicinity, and no sign of anyone stationed at the side of the road conscripting drivers to fight the blaze. For a moment I was tempted to stop in town and offer my services, but then I recognized the notion for what it was, nothing more than a vain and childish desire to play the hero. By the time I reached Hope, the sky was a clear blue again and the fires well behind me.

Two days later I returned to Rome, and once back in that crowded, clamorous city, the memory of the forest ablaze near a distant lake slowly began to drift away like smoke from the fire.

But I was restless and unsettled. I didn't know how to get myself back onto the path that I believed would lead me to God, the path I had thus far stuck to by staying focused on my studies. I had encountered no obstacles until now, but suddenly the road before me seemed impassable. I was a Roman Catholic priest with a seven-year old daughter. It is true that these days many Anglican pastors have converted to Roman Catholicism and have been ordained as priests, and it is no longer unknown for the pastor of a parish to be married with children. In my day, though, it was not only unacceptable for an ordained priest to have a child, it was unheard of.

In between classes and assignments, I spent hours walking the narrow, labyrinthine streets of Rome, driven by the need to be on the move.

I walked fast, head down, oblivious of the sights and sounds of the city, just pounding along, stopping every hour or so to down an espresso to keep the adrenalin surging and the energy level high. It seemed to me that whether I was attending a tutorial, socializing with my confrères, or even offering Mass, I was now set apart from other priests, a sheep that had not wanted to stray from the flock but had got lost all the same. Inevitably, I began to question my vocation, and since I found it impossible to pray, I took to the streets.

Walking in an ancient, overcrowded European capital is very different from walking in tranquil Vancouver, a city blessed with an abundance of lush green space and panoramic views of ocean and mountains. For those in need of solitude, there is Stanley Park where you can stride along the sea wall or amble through hidden forest trails, often without meeting another soul. Rome, though, is always rackety, and the Romans themselves, voluble, gregarious and garrulous, make it impossible to walk far without being jostled and distracted. If you leave the narrow, crowded side-streets in search of space and wider roads, you are engulfed by cars driven at a frenzied pace, horns blaring non-stop, and traffic police who contribute to the din with their piercing whistles. The Holy City was far from peaceful, but I had always thrived on its high spirits and vitality and its endless surge of cheerful humanity. Now it only made me feel jaded and claustrophobic, and I longed for the rainy streets and tall trees of home.

One day my wanderings led me south of the Vatican to the blue-collar district of Trastevere, once home to Rome's Jewish community and now a maze of narrow cobbled streets filled with bars, restaurants, and tenement buildings worn by time and neglect. Sergio Leone, the director of spaghetti westerns, grew up in this neighbourhood as did Ennio Morricone the composer, but tourists rarely crossed the Tiber to discover its charms, at least not back when I was a resident of Rome.

I walked till I grew tired and then I sought refuge from the clatter of the street in the ancient church of Santa Cecilia. It was dimly lit and mercifully quiet, apart from the clacking of an old woman's rosary beads and the mumbled drone of her Aves. I sat in silence for a long time and let my muddled thoughts come and go in the hope that God would help me unravel them—although truth to tell, I was no longer sure of God's presence in the world, either in this old church in Trastevere or anywhere else. Maybe the naysayers were right and God was nothing but a comforting myth dreamed up by those who feared death and the unknown. Doubt slithered and coiled its way into my mind, and I wrestled with it while the candles flickered in the gloom and the old woman rose from her knees and made her way to the lady altar to say more prayers.

I had already consulted my spiritual director, a lanky Bostonian in his late fifties. At the time I was convinced that my situation was extraordinary, but later it struck me that there was probably nothing he had not heard before, no sin, no crime even. He had established a rock-solid reputation for giving wise counsel, and I trusted him. So I stumbled through my story from start to finish, and when I reached the end, I sat back in relief and waited for his words of wisdom, certain that he would tell me what to do to put matters right. He did not. Instead he placed the ball firmly in my court.

"So what do you want to do now, Larry?"

"Well, I was rather hoping that you'd be able to advise me, Father."

"You want me to solve the problem for you, is that what you mean?"

He asked the question gently enough, and there was kindness in his eyes, but still I felt that I had been reproved.

"Well, no Father. I am simply asking for your advice."

"Are you perhaps questioning your vocation to the priesthood, Larry?"

"I'm afraid I am. Yes, Father."

"Why be afraid? Life is full of questions. If we never encounter rough patches on the road we're on, whatever our calling in life may be, we will never reach spiritual maturity. It was Socrates, remember, who told us that the unexamined life is not worth living, and

I'm in full agreement. So here's the only advice I have to offer you, Larry. Go directly to the source of all counsel and wisdom. Ask God for guidance. Put yourself humbly in His presence and the answer will come to you. That I can promise."

So there I was in that dark old church in Trastevere. I sat for a bit and doubted the existence of God. Then I got down on my knees and asked Him what I should do. I knelt, and after a while I thought of nothing at all, just put myself in the presence of the Holy One and waited.

When I emerged it was evening, and the harsh glare of the sun had softened to a gentle bronze that made the old buildings glow. I set out briskly on the long walk back across the city to my flat near the Piazza Navona, and when I got there I phoned my mother in and told her what I wanted to do.

CHAPTER TWENTY-SEVEN

When Benita got off the bus at the corner of Hastings and Main, she saw at once that there was no shortage of cheap rooming houses in the area, and after a bit of searching she found a vacancy in one of the old brick buildings on Carrall Street. She was given a room on the third floor, and when she saw the condition it had been left in, she went in search of bleach, soap, a scrubbing brush, and insecticide. At the St. Vincent de Paul thrift store, she used some of the money she had rescued from the gutter to buy herself a pillow, a set of sheets and a sleeping bag, two towels, and some basic cookware and utensils. She hauled everything back with her, scrubbed the room from top to bottom, and laid out her stuff. Then she opened the window and let the sounds of the street drift into the room, along with a cold sea breeze which she breathed in thankfully. Nothing else seemed clean here in the city, only the air and the snow on the distant mountains that were just visible above the rooftops. Benita did not care. She did not plan to stay for long.

For the next few days, she drifted around the streets without a sense of purpose, hoping to find one, but not sure how. She only knew that she could not go back to LaPierre with nothing to tell Miriam except that her father did not know she existed. She was no longer a high school student in a uniform that set her apart as privileged and privately educated. She was a Carrier Indian and she had come back to the city as a stranger. She would not be staying for long, but while she was here she would take note of things. She would keep a record of what she saw, and when she went home again she would have stories to tell her daughter.

She bought herself a Hilroy scribbler, and each time she returned to her room after an outing, she made a list of all the things she had seen or heard or sometimes even smelled. In her first letter to Miriam, she used short sentences and simple language to tell her about the long bus ride to Vancouver and about the streets and cars and traffic lights, and the two bridges that spanned the harbour. She tried to tell her about all the people in the big department stores and how much noise they made. She could not draw, but did little drawings anyway because she knew they would make her daughter laugh. When she was done, she mailed the letter and spent the rest of that day wandering the streets of her new neighbourhood: Hastings, Pender, Cordova, Powell, Dunleavy, Carrall, and Main, the whole of the Downtown Eastside, and it was here that she encountered her own people.

For the most part they were a sorry lot. Ravaged by alcohol and disease, they shuffled along Main Street, skinny and malnourished, or with bellies swollen by beer and cheap wine and poor food. Benita saw them sprawled on the sidewalk outside seedy beer parlours that reminded her of Prince George, or propped against a wall clutching bottles of Calona Red in a brown paper bags. She guessed that many of them survived on handouts provided by the Union Gospel Mission or the Franciscan Sisters of the Atonement who lived in an old house on Dunleavy Street and dispensed soup and sandwiches every day. When she walked by the food line, she saw her people among those waiting to be fed, some of them her own age or younger. She wondered what had made them leave their homes, why they had not stayed where they belonged. Then she thought about her father, Johnny Pigeon, and about herself, and understood how someone could easily end up here among the flotsam and jetsam of white society.

There were nights when a fight would break out on the street below her room, and the racket would wake her up. Almost always, there would be a couple of winos yelling and cursing and rolling around on the sidewalk. Sometimes the cops would come and haul one or both of them away in the paddy wagon, but on the whole the police turned a blind eye on the drunks. Most of them were harmless, too far gone in alcoholism to be a danger to anyone but themselves, although once she saw the glint of metal in the dark, and when she heard a scream of pain she ran down to the lobby to phone for an ambulance. She waited in the street until it arrived, but by the time the police got there, the guy with the knife had disappeared into the night.

When her money started to run out, Benita went to the library and scanned the situations vacant column in the Vancouver Sun. She eliminated anything that required a resumé or references, narrowed her search to jobs that were within walking distance, and eventually came up with three possibilities, the most hopeful of which was a posting for a receptionist to cover the night shift at a local hotel. She phoned the number listed and was told to come for an interview the following day.

Back in her room, she looked through the meagre contents of her wardrobe, decided that nothing would do, and took herself to the charity shop where she found a charcoal-grey fitted skirt for three dollars and a plum coloured vee-necked sweater for a dollar-fifty. Shoes were more of a problem, and in the end, she had to settle for a scuffed pair of navy pumps that were too narrow for her feet and pinched her toes.

The Kazbah Hotel on Kingsway was a long way from the rooming house, and by the time Benita arrived she had blisters on both heels and her toes were on fire. In daylight, without the rainbow glow from the neon palm trees that surrounded the entrance, the place looked run-down and seedy, and the lobby stank of stale beer and cigarette smoke. The man behind the reception desk was pasty-faced and flabby, with a greasy comb-over and a yellowish food stain on his tie. His lizard eyes raked her from head to toe.

"Help you?" he asked.

"I'm here to see the manager."

"What for?"

His breath stank of booze and raw onion, and Benita held her breath until the fumes drifted past her into the fog of the lobby behind her. She took a couple of steps back before she answered.

"About the job that was posted in the newspaper, the night reception job? I was told to come for an interview."

His eyes drifted away from her to the entrance although the street outside was clearly empty.

"Yeah, well, you came too late. That position's already been filled."

"But that's impossible. The ad was in yesterday's paper, and I spoke to the manager in the afternoon. He definitely said to come in this morning. Can I at least speak to him?"

Bad Breath grinned across the desk revealing small yellow teeth.

"You're already speaking to him," he said. "I'm the manager of this establishment, and I've hired someone else for the job. Too bad you had a wasted journey"

He walked around the desk and stood next to Benita, close enough for his breath to make her recoil and step back once more .

"But hey now, wait a minute. I got an idea. You look like you got a pretty good body under that outfit, and you need a job, right? How'd you like to work in the bar?"

"What? You mean pouring drinks?"

He smirked. "No, I got plenty staff to do that," he said. "I'm talking about a different kind of service. You know, stripping. Course I'd have to see you without your clothes on before I could go ahead and hire you. Y'know, to make sure you fit the bill okay. Know what I'm saying?"

Benita spent all of two seconds reflecting on the offer.

"Yeah, I know what you're saying, Scumbag, and here's what I'm saying to you. Why don't you go drink a bottle of mouthwash and keep your sleazy job?"

She turned for the entrance and heard him laugh.

"Okay, Running Deer, but you'll be back. I give you three months max."

She was halfway out the door when he added, "Unless you end up turning tricks on the street first. You people usually do."

Out on the street again, anger and adrenaline came in hot waves and she wanted to run, but her shoes would not let her. Instead, she hobbled as far as the nearest beer parlour, ordered a Kokanee, and took it to a table in the back. The place was empty apart from a couple of old guys sitting at the bar. One of them turned to look at her, slid off his stool and crossed the floor to where she was sitting with her shoes off, her throbbing feet stretched out in front of her.

"Buy you a drink, Miss?" he said, hopefully. "Pretty young lady like yourself shouldn't be drinking alone."

"No thanks," Benita said. "I'm fine." She waited for him to take the hint and leave her alone, saw that it wasn't going to happen, stuffed her feet back into her shoes, and got up leaving her beer untouched.

Her admirer followed her to the door.

"Hey, little lady. Don't go running away now. I got lots of money, see?" He pulled out a wad of twenties and waved it in her face. Stick around for a while, and I'll show you a good time."

Benita pushed past him into the street, took off her shoes and walked in her stockinged feet. She felt a sob well up inside her and make its way to her throat. She refused to let it escape, swallowed it back, and kept walking until she was back in her room where she threw herself on the bed and lay, fully clothed, reflecting on her options. The one that held the most appeal, of course, was to go straight home again, back to LaPierre, where she could be a mother to Miriam and a helper for Hepzibah. She could learn the art of healing from her grandmother, maybe even some day become a wise woman. But she knew that if she went now, she would not be returning by choice; she would be driven back by fear and humiliation. She did not want that. What she wanted was to create her own story so that she could feel like she was somebody, not a faceless, nameless reject, but a mother that Miriam could be proud of. The decision was made. She would stay.

The next morning she made a phone call to the Knight and Day restaurant and applied for a job as a waitress. She was asked to show up as soon as she could as they were desperately short-staffed and keen to hire. The manager's name was Elsie. She was in her forties, as lean and stringy as a boiler hen and as tough and worn as the naugahyde banquettes in the booths along the walls. The place was open twenty-four hours a day and breakfast was still being served, even though it was already lunchtime.

Elsie wasted no time on diplomacy.

"You're an Indian, right?"

Benita nodded.

"Yeah, well, I'm sure you're a real nice girl, but that's what I thought when I hired the last one, and the one before that. I'm sorry, hon, but I've been burned twice already, and I'm not going to take a chance again."

"Why? What happened with the last two?" Benita asked.

"Just plain unreliable right from the start. Showed up for work late, gave all kinds of lame excuses, or else went all silent and sullen. And sometimes they didn't show up at all, which made it real hard on the rest of us. As you can see, this is a busy place. The other thing about them was that they never smiled, never chatted to the customers, not even the regulars. We got some folk who come here for all their meals. Some of them are old. Some of them live by themselves and we're kind of like family to them. The waitress who serves them might be the only person they get to talk to all day. Anyways, the first gal lasted a month; the second one less than two weeks. Just didn't work out. Nothing personal, hon, but you people don't make good waitresses. You'll be happier in a job you're better suited to. Now I've got to run. Have a cup of coffee on the house before you leave and good luck with finding work."

Benita's next-door neighbour at the rooming house was Amelia Joe from St. Mary's Reserve in Cranbrook. She was moon-faced and short-sighted with heavy-breasts, skinny hips, and bow legs. On the day Benita moved in, Amelia knocked on her door and offered her a glass of wine. By the time the bottle was empty, there was very little Benita did not know about her neighbour's past. It was the present she was less clear about.

"So how did you end up here?"

They were in Amelia's room. Benita was sitting on the only chair, Amelia sprawled out on the bed. Apart from a rickety card table by the open window, there was no other furniture. Underwear was draped over the sill to dry. Clean dishes and mugs were stacked on the table and a collection of empty wine bottles stood by the door.

Amelia shrugged her thin shoulders. "I got a couple rides."

"But why come to Vancouver? It's a long way from Cranbrook."

Amelia giggled. "That's for sure. Guess I could'a gone to Calgary, but it's too damn cold there in the winter. Anyways, you can make a lot more money here. When I get rich I'm gonna drive back to Cranbrook in a big fancy car, wearing a real fur coat and flashy jewellery. I'm gonna buy drinks for the whole reserve, 'cept for the guys who were mean to me when I was a kid."

Benita stood up to leave.

"Uh-huh," she said. "Well, maybe that'll happen some day. You got a job here, eh?"

"Yuh. Sure do. Right now I'm working at a bar. I can get you free drinks any time you want. You just let me know when you plan on dropping in, okay?"

Since that initial meeting they chatted whenever they ran into each other on the stairs or in the hallway, but with Amelia being out every night and asleep all day, Benita rarely saw her.

When she got back from the Knight and Day restaurant, she stood outside her room, key in hand, reluctant to open the door to emptiness and the loss of hope. On impulse, she knocked at Amelia's door. She could hear Glen Campbell singing "Wichita Linesman." If the radio was playing, Amelia had to be awake. She knocked again, harder.

"Hey, it's Benita. Open up. I need some company"

Glen Campbell lowered his voice and Amelia opened the door. She was still in her robe. One of her eyes was half shut and surrounded by a deep purple bruise, her lower lip cracked and grotesquely swollen.

"C'mon in," she said, slurring the words, speaking painfully. "Hope you weren't standing outside too long. I can't hear a damn thing with the radio playing."

Benita sat by the window and watched Amelia climb back into bed.

"What happened?" Benita asked. "And don't give me any BS about walking into a door or something. I grew up looking at a face like yours, and it sure wasn't no door that did it."

"I look like shit, huh? How'm I supposed to go to work tonight like this?" Amelia started to cry.

Benita got up, filled the kettle from the plastic jug of water underneath the card table and plugged it into the outlet. She took two mugs from the window ledge, rinsed them out and looked around for tea or a jar of instant coffee.

"Wait right here," she said. "Don't go away, eh?"

Amelia stopped crying. "Hah, very funny." She smiled through swollen lips and revealed a badly broken front tooth. "Where you going anyways?"

"To get some tea bags. I'll be right back."

She fetched tea, sugar, a couple of cans of soup, and a bottle of aspirin from her own room. She made the tea, added sugar liberally and handed the cup to Amelia together with a couple of Aspirin. She had trouble getting her lips around the rim of the mug and the tea slopped out and dribbled down her chin. Benita handed her a clean tea towel.

"Okay," she said. "Who did it?"

"Just some drunk. Told me his name was Bob Williams, but I could tell he was just making that up."

"White guy?" Benita asked. Amelia nodded.

"Why'd he hit you?"

Amelia shrugged. "Drunks don't need no reason. Sometimes they just wanna slap someone around."

"Were you at work when it happened?"

Amelia looked up from her tea. "Work?" she said.

"I mean, did it happen at the bar where you work? What's the name of the place anyway?"

"S'called the Blue Flamingo. Here, I'm finished with this. Thanks." She handed her empty mug to Benita. "You know, I'm feeling kinda tired right now, Benny. I think I'm gonna sleep some more, okay?"

"In a minute. Finish telling me first. Were you in the bar when the guy beat you up? Did anyone see it happen? Why didn't anyone try to stop him?"

"Who cares?" Amelia said wearily. She closed her eyes, opened them again, then snapped. "Why all these questions, huh? You're not my mother!"

She sounded just like a petulant adolescent, and Benita wondered, not for the first time, how old she really was.

"Amelia, you need to tell me the truth. I'm not snooping. I'm just trying to find out if there were any witnesses, okay?"

Amelia closed her eyes again.

"Don't matter," she mumbled. "I got beat up, and that's all there is to it. It's no big deal. My dad used to beat me up all the time, my brother as well. I'm used to it."

Benita rinsed out the cups, wiped them dry, put them back on the window ledge.

"It's just that if there were any witnesses, we could report the guy to the police; let them go after him."

Amelia sat up in bed, threw off the covers, stood up groggily, then sat down again.

"Police? What's it got to do with them? Leave the cops out of it!" Her voice was strident, almost a shout.

"I don't wanna talk about it no more so just leave me alone and go away. I gotta sleep now. I'll be okay in the morning, honest. Thanks for the tea."

She turned her face to the wall and pulled the covers up around her ears, shutting out Benita and the rest of the world.

CHAPTER TWENTY-EIGHT

I won't say that I forgot about Miriam. How could I when I was paying thirty percent of my monthly salary into a trust fund for her? I had asked my mother to set up a family trust in her name, and at the beginning of each month, I sent her my contribution, and she took it to her local bank and deposited it. It was a tedious process, but in those days it was the easiest way things to get things done. At first she had been reluctant.

"It makes no sense, Larry," she said when I phoned to make my request. "Benita made it very clear that they don't want our money. They are proud people and this will only offend them."

"I know all that, Ma. And that's exactly why I want to set things up this way. What I'm proposing is to let the money accumulate for Miriam, either to pay for her education or to give her as a lump sum when she turns twenty-one. By that time she can decide for herself whether she wants to accept it or not, and nobody's ever going to know that the money came from me and not from you, her grandmother. We've got fourteen years to put together a nice little sum for her. I've given it a lot of thought, Ma. This is the best I can come up with."

Since then I had gone about stripping my life of any kind of luxury in order to make the monthly payments, and soon I was living frugally in a city devoted to pleasure. I found that I did not mind this at all. I was better able to focus on academics, and as a result I completed my PhD in theology earlier than expected. Then, to my great surprise, I was appointed Secretary of the Congregation for Catholic Education.

I wrote to Renzo and Molly to give them the news and received a congratulatory card to which Renzo had added a footnote:

Sounds like you've gone over to Rome completely, old friend! Will we ever see you back in Canada?

My mother was delighted. "You're on your way up the ladder for sure now, Pet, and well you deserve it. You'll have that red hat on your head before you know it. You'll make a great cardinal altogether."

I worked hard at my new job and soon acquired a reputation for being dedicated and serious. Those who worked with me probably saw me as a bit of a killjoy, but then nobody in Rome looked to Canadians for fun.

For the most part, we were viewed as earnest plodders rather than stars on the international stage, and that was just fine by me. I kept my head down, nose to the grindstone, and chose not to participate in the current wave of gossip and speculation that swirled around the Vatican and made it a hotbed of rumour. But it was impossible to avoid altogether.

It spread rapidly from the hierarchy of cardinals, bishops, and monsignori down through the clerical ranks and spilled over into the laity. In time the rumours proved to be well-founded because, in April 1962, Pope John XXIII declared the Second Vatican Council officially open, and I was one of the 25,000 priests who were present for the opening Mass. Those in attendance overflowed from St. Peter's Basilica out into Vatican Square, and all of us were swept up in a sense of awareness of history in the making. You would have to have been made of stone not to feel the energy that radiated from the Holy Father himself and almost bounced off the walls of the Basilica. I was thrilled to be there, to be part of a movement of change and growth in the Church after centuries of political intrigue, European dominance, and iron-clad protocol.

With all of the panoply and pageantry the Church of Rome was known for, the ranks of red-robed cardinals, princes of the Church, filed into the Basilica and took their places like the blue-blooded aristocrats that so many of them actually were. It was impossible to tell what was going through those noble old heads of theirs, but I'm sure I wasn't the only one who wondered what they thought of all this talk of change.

They had elected seventy-six year old Angelo Roncalli as a "caretaker-pope" whose papacy would be short and forgettable. But far from meekly taking his place as a benevolent figurehead, the Peasant Pope mounted the throne of St. Peter with an assurance built on a long and illustrious diplomatic career. He was fluent in no less than six languages and had acquired enviable skills as a negotiator. As Papal Nuncio to Istanbul, he had had the courage and temerity to funnel Nazi money directly to the aid of Jews fleeing Eastern Europe. Through his friendship with the German ambassador to Turkey, a Catholic strongly opposed to the Nazi regime, Cardinal Roncalli, as he was then, had been responsible for the safe passage of almost one thousand Jewish refugees on their way to Palestine. That alone should have alerted the electorate to the nature of the man, and perhaps it did. Perhaps he had indeed been chosen on the basis of his significant achievements. But nobody, not a single soul, could have predicted that this son of a tenant farmer from Bergamo, known more for his affability and concern for the poor than for his intellect, would have convened the only Council of the Church Universal to take place since the Council of Trent in 1545.

It was clear from his opening address that the Holy Father wanted this Council to bring about a renewal in the life of the Church, to adapt its organization and teaching to the needs of the modern world, and to have as its ultimate goal the eventual unity of all Christians. Huge goals. Brave goals. His large but humble presence and his hopeful words were inspirational to all but the most cynical of his vast audience. When the first session of the Council opened on October eleventh 1962, there were 2,860 bishops in attendance, and they came from all over the world. In addition to the active participants, there were observers from other faiths in attendance, as well as translators, advisors, and aides, bringing the total number of participants to three thousand.

It was my great good fortune to be asked to serve as an 'expert' in theology, a role, as it turned out, to which I was well suited. Most of the time I was simply an observer at each of the four sessions of the Council, but there were occasions when I was called upon to explain or clarify one of the more arcane points of theology. I found myself in exalted company. One of my fellow experts was the celebrated German academic, Josef Ratzinger. His was always the voice of authority, and I was happy to defer to his knowledge and scholarship, although it was evident, right from day one of that first session, that the Holy Father was set on maintaining an atmosphere of freedom and openness for all participants for the entire duration of the Council.

The Church, however, for all its emphasis on things heavenly, is very much of this world, and its members, clerical as well as lay, are just as likely to be driven by ambition, pride, and vanity as those of any large, powerful corporation. It did not take long for two extremist groups to emerge, the "Progressives" and the "Reactionaries," and they were bitterly opposed to each other. There was a shameful incident in which one of the elderly conservatives, Cardinal Ottaviani, was silenced and humiliated during his lengthy address calling for restraint. For the most part, though, participants did their best to put aside personal differences and let them selves be guided by their conscience and their sincere love for the Church. And as Pope John continually reminded them, whereas the Church in the past had felt it necessary to use severity and condemnation, what was required now was mercy and understanding. Their task, he told them, was to find the means by which the Church could present itself to the world in a way that was relevant and constructive.

The first session ended on a positive note, and Christmas seemed especially joyful that year. Early in 1963, however, it became apparent that the Holy Father was in poor health, and it turned out that he was suffering from an aggressive form of stomach cancer to which he succumbed at the beginning of June. He was deeply and, I think, genuinely, mourned throughout the world, and without his kindly presence the Church was at a loss, cast adrift without a leader at the helm.

At the time, everybody thought that the Council would come to a premature end, but after a lengthy break to allow for the funeral of Pope John XXIII and the election of Pope Paul VI, the second session opened on September 29th, 1963, and the work of renewal moved ahead. When the Council finally came to an end, there were some who claimed that John XXIII may have got all the glory, but that the actual spadework of Vatican II was done by the ascetic and aristocratic Paul VI. As far as most of us were concerned, though, none of that mattered as long as the work got done.

As the next three sessions were played out, there were heated debates and some bitter struggles. The more extreme of the liberal faction held the view that the changes were not radical enough, while the hardcore reactionary division reeled in horror and fear that the traditional Church, the Church Apostolic, had been virtually destroyed.

In the end, though, most people agreed that the council had accomplished a great deal, not least of which was that Bishops of every colour and nationality, speaking in many different languages, had participated as equals. No longer was the Church dominated by Europe, and no longer was Latin the language of communication among the hierarchy. The laity found themselves attending Mass where the sacred rite, for the first time in more than a thousand years, was celebrated in their own language, and this alone sent shock waves around the world.

A second major achievement was support for the ecumenical movement. It was Pope John himself who decided that non-Catholic observers should be invited to the Council, and at the final session there were almost one hundred non-Catholic and non-Christian delegates in attendance.

Vatican II also served to elevate the role of the laity. Up until 1962, the Church had operated on a two-tier system with the clergy on one side and the laity on the other. The Council re-established the Church as a single communion, with the clergy and the lay apostolate assuming roles of equal importance. In addition, the Church's relationship with Judaism, Islam, and other world religions became far more important, resulting in a significant increase in interfaith dialogue.

But the drastic changes to the liturgy of the Mass were upsetting to many, and critics were of the view that the faithful had not been sufficiently prepared. Many Catholics, including my mother, Renzo and Molly, and the O'Carroll clan of Vancouver were deeply attached to the liturgical forms they had known all their lives and were distressed to see them vanish virtually overnight. It was much the same for elderly priests who secretly felt that to replace the High Altar with a plain table and to say Mass facing the congregation was a desecration of all that was sacred.

In time, most people came to accept the changes, or at least tolerate them, although in recent years there has been a movement towards a return to the traditional Latin Rite. And there are still those, myself among them, who lament the demise of our great musical heritage, the exquisite and uplifting Masses of Bach, Haydn, Mozart, Beethoven, Schubert, Liszt, Gounod, Puccini, Rossini, and Bruckner, the requiems of Fauré, Mozart, and Verdi, all of them replaced by what I refer to as 'happy crappy' hymns accompanied by a couple of thumping chords on some maltreated guitar. Of course I only mutter these things to myself or to close friends; publicly, I grin and bear it and sing along with those appalling Carey Landry ditties we got stuck with. Does that make me a musical snob? Probably. Do I care? Not in the slightest. Bad music is bad music, whether it is performed onstage or in a church.

Music aside though, there is no doubt that Vatican Two succeeded in bringing a much-needed breath of fresh air to a church that had grown stale and calcified by outdated protocol. My zest and enthusiasm, together with the thrill of being an active participant in a historical event, never flagged in the three years of its duration, although I confess that I was shaken and thrown off course by the turn of events at home late in the summer of 1963.

CHAPTER TWENTY-NINE

Amelia had made it clear that she did not want anyone interfering in her life. Still, when Benita woke up the next morning, she found herself thinking about her battered face, and after she had washed and dressed, she went next door and knocked. There was no sound from inside, and the radio was silent, which meant that Amelia must still be asleep. Benita went back to her room, made tea, and drank it by the window overlooking the street below. At this early hour it was all but deserted.

There was a bum sprawled out in the doorway of a pawnshop surrounded by litter that had been tossed on the sidewalk the night before. He lay on bare concrete without even a layer of newspaper between himself and the ground. *Lucky for him the winter's over,* Benita thought. *At least he won't freeze.* She turned away from the window and removed two letters from between the pages of her note pad. One was from her sister. Martina had written to say that she had quit school and moved to Vanderhoof where she was spending a lot of time with a trapper from Fraser Lake.

> *...He's kind of wild, and sometimes he drinks too much. I don't think he's ever going to settle down enough to marry me but he sure is good-looking. I guess I wouldn't mind getting a bit of advice from my big sister. You're real lucky living in a big city like Vancouver. They say it never snows there. Is that true? It must be pretty*

nice down there with all of those fancy stores they got. Sometimes I feel jealous of you. But me, I'd most likely get lonesome so far away from home...

At the end of the page, almost as an afterthought:

> Benita, Mom told me that Miriam is missing you real bad. Sometimes she gets sad. They are pretty worried about her. I'm thinking that maybe you should come up and see her some time...

The second letter had arrived months ago and had been read so many times that the folds in the paper had worn thin. She took it now and carefully spread it open, examining the picture of the chapel in LaPierre as if for the first time. Miriam had drawn herself standing outside the door, a small figure in a long white dress with the dog, Berry, beside her. Her mouth was turned down at the corners and dark blue tears fell from her eyes. And printed in the space below the drawing:

> You said you were gonna come for my First Communion but you never showed up. That made me real sad. With love from Miriam.

Benita traced her daughter's face with one finger, gently, so as not to smudge the waxy blue tears. She gazed out the window and watched the drunk in the doorway beginning to stir. When he finally sat up, she saw that he was a Native, about the same age as Jericho George, she guessed, and scarecrow-thin.

She had not known how to answer her daughter's letter, and in the end she had sent her a post card with a picture of English Bay.

> Dear Miriam,
> I am very sorry I missed your First Communion. Don't worry. I'm working on a plan for us.
> With love from your mother, Benita.

The single tree she could see from her window must have been planted to bring some life and beauty to a derelict neighbourhood, but at some point all of its lower limbs had been hacked off and its trunk gouged and carved up. Somehow it had managed to stay alive, and now it lifted resilient branches high above the street displaying its bounty of tender green leaves.

She spent the rest of the day chasing down three more job possibilities, all of which proved to be dead ends. When she got back to the rooming house, she went straight to Amelia's room and rapped on the door.

"She ain't gonna answer because she's not there no more."

The old guy across the way was shuffling along to the shared bathroom at the end of the hallway. When Benita turned to look at him, he stopped, glad of any excuse to talk. His eyes were red-rimmed and watery, and he wiped them incessantly on a grubby handkerchief. His dentures had been badly fitted and when he spoke the words sloshed around in his mouth before finally sliding out.

"I seen her haul her stuff out late last night. She was looking pretty beat up. I figure she must've been moving on to some other place. She a friend or something?"

Benita thought about Amelia, her raucous laugh and skinny little legs, her broken tooth and swollen eye.

"Yeah," she said. "I guess you could say she's a friend."

Later that evening, when she walked through the door of the Blue Flamingo Bar and Grill she was enveloped in a thick haze of cigarette smoke and stale beer combined with the whiff of old sweat and unwashed bodies. It was still early, and the place was empty apart from a guy behind the bar.

He leant against the counter in a proprietorial way, not even pretending to look busy, and Benita took note of the heavy gold chain he wore around his thick neck and the thinning black hair slicked down with some kind of strong-smelling grease. *Manager*, she thought, *or maybe even owner*.

"I need to talk to Amelia," she said. "Is she here yet?"

He gestured at the empty space that surrounded them.

"Nobody here but you and me," he said. "Can I get you a drink?"

Benita hesitated, not sure if he was offering to buy or to sell her a drink. Either way her answer was the same. "Nothing right now, thanks." she said. Then, "Maybe I got here too early. What time should I come back?"

"What do you want her for?"

"Just to talk to her for a minute, make sure she's okay. I'm kind of worried about her, that's all."

"Why's that?" He took his weight off his elbows and raised himself to his full height. He was in his mid-thirties Benita thought, stocky rather than tall, already starting to go to seed but still with the look of a brawler.

"She got beat up pretty bad a couple of nights ago."

"That right, eh? Gee, that's too bad. Guess that explains why she hasn't been showing up for work." His eyes were small and black and shifted constantly like a couple of battery-driven raisins. Benita felt her mind drifting and snapped back to attention suddenly. Too suddenly. She should have taken more time with her next question.

"Did it happen here?"

"Here? No way! I take care of my girls, you ask anyone. No. If something bad happened to your friend you might want to consider her *other* place of work, know what I mean?"

Benita shook her head. "I don't think she has another job."

The raisin eyes shifted back and forth, back and forth, and he stretched his fleshy lips in a smile.

"Yeah? Well, let me tell you about it, honey. After she leaves here, she starts her night-shift. Corner of Kingsway and Main, that's where I usually see her on my way home, although sometimes she cruises the back alleys too. Guess she never told you about that, huh?"

He laughed, revealing unexpectedly white teeth. *False for sure*, Benita thought distractedly.

"If you wanna find her, I'd say check out the street later on tonight."

Benita turned to leave.

"Hey, lady, I'm just trying to help you out "

He laughed again and came out from behind the bar.

"But listen. Now that Amelia's moved on to outside work, I need a girl to replace her in here. You interested? It's easy money and you look like you've got the body for it. Pretty face, too, not like your young friend."

Benita reached the door, pushed it open and took a deep breath of fresh air.

He raised his voice.

"Think about it, eh? All you gotta do is take off a few clothes—not everything, mind you; I'm not running a nudie joint here—and move around a bit to the music. You could do that, couldn't you?"

Benita could feel his hard little eyes on her back as she passed through the door. Even as it swung shut behind her she could hear him:

"A hundred bucks the first week, more after that if you're any good…"

Out on the street, there was no sign of Amelia but it was still early, barely dark yet. In the fading light of an April evening, the squalor of the neighbourhood was less noticeable and even this wasteland of tawdry strip bars and dingy beer parlours, pool halls, pawn shops, and derelict rooming houses was somehow redeemed and transformed. But springtime breezes and drifting blossoms could not diffuse the stench of piss and decay that lay over the back alleys like a miasma. Benita moved past them quickly, barely glancing at the bums hunched over garbage bins, ransacking them as if they were treasure chests containing gold. Then she slowed her pace and began to search for Amelia. She did not find her.

Back in her room, she paced restlessly and once more considered her options. She had felt so hopeful at first; now she understood that she had only been naive. Her money was all but gone. What was left of it would cover either another week's rent or a bus ticket home. Buying the ticket would take her back to Miriam, which was where she belonged. But who would she be when she got to La Pierre? Just another reject chewed up and spat out by white people.

Benita had never before felt inferior. Now she did. Her recent experience in the city had shown her the 'Us' and 'Them' of Canada, and she had discovered which side she belonged to. She thought about Amelia and the goal she had set for herself, her determination to make a pile of money so that she could go back to the Reserve wearing fancy clothes and driving a big car. The clothes would be out of style within a year, the car would end up a rusted hulk in somebody's yard. Amelia's goals were not her goals.

She had no desire for stylish clothes or a big car. Couldn't drive one anyway, although maybe Jericho George could teach her. For a moment she imagined herself driving a shiny blue Cadillac across the iced-up lake in winter, getting stuck in a snow-drift and having to be towed to the other side; maybe having to abandon the car until Spring. And then would come the mud. The car would be no good to her for nine months of the year. She'd be able to drive it around the town's four paved streets only until the first snow arrived. A good-for-nothing Cadillac in Blanchette; the thought made her smile a bit.

Benita snapped back to attention, annoyed with herself for wasting time on a frivolous daydream and what she suspected was a severe dose of self-pity. She might not be the best mother in the world, but she was the only one that Miriam would ever have and her daughter needed to be with her. She sat by the widow and thought about things until she had come to a decision. Miriam was a bright kid and she made new friends easily. She would bring her to Vancouver and send her to school here in the city so that she could get a good education. Maybe she could even go back to school herself one day. Would they still give her a place at the University, or was she too old now? She'd have to look into that. First, though, she had to make some money.

CHAPTER THIRTY

The stage was small. When the three of them were up there, it felt like a cage without bars, which made her think of what Amelia had told her about a club in San Francisco where dancers called go-go girls performed in a real cage suspended from the ceiling. The first time Benita had put on the tight red bodice with its matching micro-skirt and pulled on the thigh-high black boots she stood before the mirror and wondered who she was looking at. The thought made her shiver suddenly. The manager, watching her, smiled.

"First night nerves, eh?" He handed her a shot glass. "Here, get this down you. It'll take the chill off."

Benita tossed back the rye whiskey. She had not eaten a proper meal all day, and the booze kicked in immediately, warming and numbing her until she felt like a different person, a tough girl who was able to climb up onto the circular stage and gyrate to the music as if she had been doing it all her life. The club was packed and noisy, and except for the stage lighting, the room was dim. Benita could see nothing beyond the floor she stood on, was only half aware of her two fellow dancers whose faces were without expression. In the harsh glare of the spotlight, she obeyed the beat of the music, one of three wind-up dolls rotating and swaying in front of strange men until she felt herself slip away to another place leaving just a body, nothing else. After that it was fine. She could do this. She had a job at last, and she was making money.

"You're good," Clive told her at the end of her first week. "But you gotta smile more. Loosen up a bit. Relate to the audience, know what I mean?"

"Sure," said the dancing doll who was not Benita Pigeon.

Each night Clive introduced the three of them as Miss Belle, Miss Miranda and Miss Rosita. Belle was the one who could switch on a smile that reached the dimmest corner of the room and could often elicit a roar of appreciation and applause.

"Whenever you turn sideways, bend right over," he told her half way through the second week.

"Why?"

"To give them a good view of your tits and ass."

"Okay," said Belle.

Men began to thrust dollar bills at her, sometimes even the odd five or ten. By the end of May, she was earning almost three hundred dollars a week.

Belle was making money, but it was Benita who knew what to do with it She opened up a savings account, thought briefly about finding better accommodation but abandoned the idea when she figured out how much more it would cost her in rent. She was set on saving money, not spending it. She had a plan in place, and it was working. So what if it took a stiff drink or two each night for Benita to become Belle?

Once her street clothes were off and her body was on display, once the doll had been wound up and the music was driving her, she felt nothing at all, found it easy to pivot and sway and gyrate as if she were all alone on the tiny stage, sealed off from the gaze of the men who crowded the bar each night, deaf to their suggestions and invitations.

"It's you who's bringing them in, Belle," Clive told her before the show one night. "I'm thinking of letting the other two girls go. Making you a solo act. Pay you more, of course. Whadda ya say?"

"How *much* more?" she asked.

When she got back to the dressing room there was no sign of Miranda and Rosita, just a folded sheet of paper and an empty bottle on top of her beer-sodden clothes. She opened the note, glanced at the single word scrawled across the page, and ripped the paper to shreds. Then she put on her stinking clothes and left through the back door.

Out on the street she was Benita again, and for a moment she felt bad that by agreeing to go solo she had cost the other girls their jobs. Then she thought about the wage she would be earning, three times as much as when she was part of a trio, and felt just fine. Anyway, those two would have no trouble finding other work. They were white.

"Hey, Benita!"

She was on her way down Kingsway when she heard her name, her real name. She looked across the street and saw Amelia teetering along the sidewalk in a tight skirt and impossibly high heels. She was waving wildly and laughing her familiar raucous laugh.

"C'mon over here! I can't walk too far in these stupid shoes I got on me."

At this time of night, cars were few and far between, and those that were out were cruising. Men on the prowl, Benita thought. Men looking for girls on street corners, girls like Amelia.

She crossed the street and got a big hug from her old neighbour, Amelia. With her broken tooth fixed and wearing false eyelashes, she looked like a different person.

"You look real good, Amelia," she said. "Things must be going okay for you, huh?"

"I been doing great. I'm making a whole lotta money now. And I don't gotta do that stupid dancing no more. Pretty soon, I guess, I'll be getting my car, just like I told you that one time."

"Well, I'm glad for you," Benita said. "Where are you living these days? You sure left our place in a big hurry. You never even said goodbye. I miss having you next door."

Amelia's small brown eyes flickered, shifted sideways, and gazed down the empty street.

"I'm over on Powell Street now, me and a couple other girls. Got my own room and all. Free groceries too. I don't even got to pay rent."

"How come?" Benita asked.

"The guy we work for takes care of all that stuff." Amelia looked defiant. "It's easy money, so don't you start giving me a hard time now. I know what I'm doing. Phil takes care of us real good. I don't gotta worry no more about anything, just turn a few tricks for him six nights a week is all. He gives us Sunday off so we can go to church."

Amelia said this with a straight face. Unsure whether it was intended as a joke or not, Benita ignored it. Instead, she said that she had finally found a job herself and was making good money. When she added that she was working at the Blue Flamingo, Amelia started to laugh, and after a moment Benita joined in, and then they clung to each other, laughing hysterically, until a car pulled up beside them, and Amelia let go of Benita and straightened up.

"Looks like here comes business," she said, fluttering her false eyelashes in an exaggerated wink that set Benita off laughing again.

The driver of the brown Pontiac leaned across the passenger seat and rolled the window down. He was middle-aged, pasty-faced, in need of a shave.

"How much?" The voice was raspy. *A smoker for sure*, Benita thought, and imagined his breath on Amelia.

"Depends what you're looking for," Amelia said.

Benita bent down and said, "I'm off, now. Sure you'll be okay on your own?"

She felt the guy's eyes slither over her as she straightened up to leave.

"Hey, not so fast there, Miss," he said. "You're the one I'm interested in."

Benita recoiled. "I'm not for sale," she snapped and heard Amelia laugh again shrilly.

"Hoity-toity, huh?" He sniggered. "That's okay. I can handle that, no problem. Tell you what, ladies. How's about fifty bucks for a threesome? That's fifty *each*. You got a place we can go to?"

When Benita got back to her lodgings it was already morning. She was exhausted but could not sleep, could not still her racing mind nor ease the coiled tension in her body. It kept her tossing and turning in the narrow bed until she abandoned it to sit by the window and watch flames of red and gold ripple across the sky, flooding the darkness with waves of colour, emptying her mind of all thought and bringing some kind of peace at last.

She did not go back to bed. Instead she walked through Chinatown and along Cordova to Gas Town, the oldest quarter of a still young city. She was only a street away from Woodwards Store where she had first met Larry. She remembered their first meeting, how he had pretended not to be looking at her when she came into the cafeteria, how she had pretended to be reading French poetry. She had become somebody different since that time, and no doubt so had he. If she were to meet him now, they would be strangers to each other. And yet he was the father of her daughter Miriam, the daughter he had never seen.

Despite her lack of sleep, Benita was charged with energy. She quickened her pace and strode through the financial district of West Hastings, barely noticing the ornate banks and office buildings, marching on until she found herself in the quiet, secluded streets of the West End where the air was fragrant with the scent of magnolias, and roses bloomed in tiny gardens.

She found a diner at the foot of Denman Street and ordered a burger and milkshake. From her table by the window, she could see the sweep of English Bay with the blue sea glinting in the sun and the sandy beach cluttered with people, kids, and dogs, all of them idling away this perfect afternoon at the start of summer.

When she left the diner, she made her way down to the bay and sat on one of the huge logs that had washed up on the beach and now served as seats for the weary or backrests for picnickers. The ocean spread itself out before her, and the rhythmic shush and swoosh of the peaceful little waves was hypnotic. The sun grew hot, and for a long while Benita thought of nothing, felt nothing, just sat watching the sea until the light began to change and shadows fell upon the beach. Only then did she stand and command her tired legs to take her as far as the nearest bus stop. She had walked far enough for one day. Besides, she did not want to risk being late on her first night as a solo performer.

CHAPTER THIRTY-ONE

When Jericho George delivered Benita's postcard to Miriam, she was sitting at the kitchen table busily colouring a map of the British Commonwealth. She had no idea where Ghana was, and anyway she had grown bored with red. She was contemplating a switch to yellow just to liven things up when the postcard was placed in front of her. She put the red crayon back in the box and waited until Hepzibah and Clara came and sat down beside her before she picked it up. She scrutinized the picture of English Bay and then passed it around the table for the others to examine.

"I'd sure like to see the ocean," Clara said to no one in particular before handing it on to Jericho George. When it came back around the table to Miriam again, she flipped it over and read the message aloud.

"Dear Miriam. I am very sorry I missed your First Communion. I am working on a plan for us. With love from your mother."

"Huh," said Jericho George.

Then Clara said, "Guess she must be feeling real bad about not showing up for your First Communion, eh?"

Hepzibah looked over at Miriam. "But she says she's working on a plan."

Miriam closed her face and said nothing. She was nine years old, a solitary child surrounded by three older, surrogate parents. She worked at being inscrutable.

The school year came to an end and the lake ran clear again. The forest floor turned green and in the sudden warmth of the sun, wild flowers showed their timid faces on the slopes of Mount Cardinal.

In late July, Jericho George was bumping along the track from Blanchette with a pile of groceries for three different families in LaPierre and a whole month's worth of mail. He was whistling tunelessly and had the windows rolled down so that he could breathe in the summer-scented air. About a mile from the village he spotted a small, hunched figure trudging along the rutted road followed by a large red dog. He braked and a cloud of dust rose up behind the truck. He stuck his head out the window.

"Looks like you got a long walk ahead of you, Miriam," he said.

"Uh-huh," answered Miriam, keeping her eyes fixed on the path.

"Need a ride some place? That bag of your looks mighty heavy."

"Nope," she said. "It's okay, but thanks anyways."

"So where you headed exactly?" he asked.

"Can't tell you."

She looked up at him and he saw that her face was flushed from the heat and from the weight of the stuffed canvas bag she was hauling. Miriam kicked viciously at a clod of dried mud and sent it flying. Then she sighed.

"Okay then, but promise not to tell Clara and Hepzibah?"

Jericho George said nothing, waited patiently for her to continue.

"I'm *trying* to run away, only stupid Berry won't go home! He keeps on following me, and dogs can't go where I'm going."

"Okay," said Jericho George. He waited awhile, then asked cautiously, "Where's that?"

"Vancouver." Miriam's tone was mutinous, but he saw that she was not far from tears.

"Huh," he said. "Pretty long ways to go then. I guess you're wanting to see Benita, eh?"

"Yep."

"She know you're on your way?"

Miriam shot him a scornful look. "Course not. It's a surprise. Remember how she said she's working on a plan? She said it on that one card she sent me, the one with the picture of the sea."

"Yeah, I remember she said that."

"Well, nothing's happened, so I'm thinking that her plan's not working too good. I'm going down there to help her along a bit. Only I got a problem."

"What's that?" Jericho George asked her.

"Told you already! Dumb Berry's my problem. He just keeps on following me and following me."

Jericho George did not want to see the first tear fall, and he figured it was well on its way. He hopped down from the truck and hoisted the heavy bag off the ground.

"Dog's just doing his job is all, Mirri. He figures he has to protect you. I don't reckon he's ever gonna leave you, so then what'll happen when you have to get on that bus for Vancouver? You're gonna have to leave him behind, that's what. Then you're gonna feel pretty bad, eh?"

Miriam nodded, rubbed at her eyes, and looked up at Jericho George.

"Uh-huh. So what d'you reckon I should do then?"

Jericho George pondered awhile.

"Well, first thing is maybe we should make sure Berry gets home safe. Then we can sit down and figure out a new plan. Maybe talk it over with Clara and Hepzibah even. What do you say?"

Miriam tried not to look relieved.

"Maybe," she said. Then, "Okay. He's kind of tired anyways. I guess he needs a drink."

Back at the house, Berry lapped up a gallon of water before flopping down in a patch of shade next to Hepzibah's plant shack, duty done for the day. Clara mixed a jug of Koolaid and Miriam finished most of it before it reached the table. Then they all sat down and listened to her tell her running away story.

When Clara erupted in laughter, Miriam faltered in the telling, and Hepzibah fixed her steady gaze upon her daughter until she was silent and serious again. Jericho George listened passively; it was not his story to tell. At the end of the account Clara said, "That Berry's a pretty good dog, huh?"

"Yup," said Jericho George.

Miriam said, "Well I'm sure not happy with him right now." But only because it seemed like she pretty much had to say it. Then she turned to her great-grandmother.

"So what should I do now?" she said.

Hepzibah ignored the question. Instead, she told Miriam to fetch the writing pad and pen from the kitchen drawer. Then she spent some time writing two letters. When she had finished, she handed them to Miriam. "Okay?" she asked.

Miriam read them and smiled. Then she read them aloud to Clara and Jericho George. Finally she answered her great-grandmother.

"Okay," she said. "That'll work."

When Kathleen Kinsella saw the little girl climb down from the Greyhound bus, followed by Clara, her other grandmother, she felt tears well up from the hidden place where they were stored and had to fight with herself to staunch them before stepping forward to welcome her visitors.

Clara smiled her broken-toothed smile, but did not speak. Kathleen could not take her eyes off Miriam and wanted nothing but to fold her in her arms and keep her there. Instead, she shook her hand and asked questions about the long trip from Prince George, and after they got through all of that Miriam said, "But where's my mother?"

Then the three of them stood in the terminal, a little island of silent, awkward strangers. For a while they watched buses disgorging passengers from Kamloops and Kelowna, others departing for Cranbrook and Trail. Thirty minutes crept by, each one of them counted off by Miriam who was watching the station clock. Then Kathleen excused herself and went in search of the Ladies' washroom where she spent a great deal of time washing her hands and fixing her hair and wondering what on earth she should do if Benita did not show up at all. She wished that Larry was with her to offer a few suggestions, but of course she hadn't told him about the letter that had come from Hepzibah, nor about the plan that had been made so that Miriam could visit her mother. It might have unsettled him, and she did not want that. His life was on track now. He was a priest of God and could not be a parent to the child he had not known about for so long. She, on the other hand, was more than ready to do anything at all for this cherished little granddaughter.

When she got back to the main concourse, she found Miriam, Clara, and Benita gathered together in a cluster of smiles, but not talking, she noticed, finding that strange. After all that time apart, wouldn't you think they'd be clucking away to each other like a clutch of hens? But maybe the three of them were just lost for words, she told herself.

Outside the station, Kathleen found a taxi and bundled the lot of them inside. Once on the move, though, she developed a new worry. She had readied Larry's old room for Miriam and outfitted the spare bedroom for Clara with newly purchased sheets and towels from Woodwards. But what if Benita wanted to stay with them, too? Would she be willing to share the double bed with Clara? If not, where was she going to put her?

When she had first caught sight of Benita at the bus depot she hardly recognized her. She looked so much harder and older than the way she had remembered her. *Not a good way to change*, Kathleen thought, and wondered what had happened to bring about that tough, defensive, closed-up attitude that permeated her being. The clothes Benita wore were stylish, but cheaply made, and although Kathleen was loath to even think it, maybe a little on the sluttish side. No, that was surely the wrong word. Benita looked shop-worn; that was the word for it. Shop-worn and worn out.

When they got to the house, Kathleen showed them the rooms she had prepared for them. Miriam looked first at the bookshelves that still held Larry's old yearbooks and annuals and his collection of Hardy Boy paperbacks, and then out the window at the laden peach tree and leafy maple. Kathleen stood in the doorway watching her.

"Was this my father's room?"

"It was. Yes, Pet."

"Huh," said Miriam. And that was all.

Downstairs, Benita was also standing by the window, but she was not looking out at the splashy display of roses and dahlias in the garden, she was staring at the large framed picture of Father Larry Kinsella that had pride of place on top of the glass-fronted cherry wood china cabinet. When Kathleen came in with a laden tray of tea things she said, without turning her head,

"Is *that* why you didn't tell him?"

Kathleen deposited the tray on the coffee table and sat down on the sofa.

"Sit down, Dear," she said, pointing to the easy chair across from her.

Benita hesitated, then shrugged and sat.

"Charlie and I did the wrong thing, Benita. And we both regretted it deeply. I think the guilt might have even have led to the stroke that killed him, although he never did take care of himself so I can't really say for sure. When Larry found out about Miriam, he was already a priest. It's been hard on him, too. Can you forgive us, do you think? For the sake of Miriam?"

For a moment Benita did not respond at all.

"Put the picture away for a while. I have to figure out how to explain all of this to Miriam."

When Clara and Miriam came downstairs, the photo of Larry was gone, and Benita was alone in the room. The three of them sat looking at each other until Miriam began to giggle.

"What's so funny?" Clara asked her.

"Don't know" said Miriam. "I just can't stop laughing."

"Maybe it's 'cause you're planning to grab one of those fancy little cakes off that tray, huh?" Benita teased her.

A fresh fit of laughter overtook Miriam and shook her whole scrawny little body.

"Okay, better hush up now, Miriam." Clara spoke anxiously. "This house is pretty damn fancy. I'm kinda scared we might drop something."

"Like one of those little cakes Miriam has her eye on, you mean?" Benita said.

"Uh-huh," said Clara.

And Benita started to laugh and so did Clara, and when Kathleen came into the room with the teapot and a bottle of orange Fanta for Miriam, all three of them were laughing uncontrollably.

Thank God for that. At least they're laughing, she thought. She busied herself pouring tea and handing out plates and napkins until they managed to settle down a bit, although when she used her cake tongs to serve the petit fours they all burst into howls of laughter again and for a moment she felt excluded, an alien in her own home.

Benita was the first to recover.

"Sorry, Mrs. Kinsella," she said. "It's just that all of this is pretty different from the way things are in LaPierre, and I guess it's making us feel a little nervous. Right, Ma?" she asked Clara who nodded in reply. "Right, Miriam?"

"Yeah. I got a real bad laugh attack, and then I got the others going. I'm okay now, though."

Kathleen beamed at Miriam in relief.

"Well, Sweetheart, you know what they say, don't you? Laughter is the best medicine. Now go ahead and eat up every one of these cakes. You must be half starved from that long bus trip. And don't anyone be worrying about crumbs and spills. This old house needs a bit of life put back into it. Besides, Trice will help with the clean-up. He'll be in seventh heaven if he finds a bit of cake on the floor."

The little dog had been confined to the kitchen, but now Kathleen let him into the front room to meet the visitors. He scuttled around busily sniffing any hands on offer for inspection, his stump of a tail wagging wildly, pointed ears pricked, bright little eyes peering out from under his white forelock. Miriam was enchanted.

"He's so little," she said.

"Not like Berry, eh?" said Clara. "And this guy's real clean, too."

"That's because he gets a good bath once a month," Kathleen said. And Miriam said, "My dog just gets washed by the rain and the snow. He's pretty much of an outside dog. He only comes indoors when it gets *real* cold."

Miriam watched the little white dog hunt down cake crumbs, and Clara watched Miriam, while Kathleen kept an eye on Benita who had gone silent again. Kathleen blamed it on the photo of Larry, now hidden away in her bedroom upstairs. She should have removed it earlier, she thought, although, really, it had served to explain things better than she could have done with words.

She glanced at the clock. Soon it would be time to start preparing the evening meal. She had a nice lamb casserole all set to go, just needed to pop it into the oven to heat up. But there was still the problem of the sleeping arrangements.

"Will you be staying here tonight, dear?" The question had to be asked. Might as well get it over and done with.

Miriam stopped playing with the dog and snapped to attention. Benita darted a quick glance at Clara who gazed into her cup as if it contained the elixir of eternal life instead of Red Rose tea.

"No thanks. I work nights, so I'll be staying at my own place while Miriam and Clara are in town."

"But me and Clara came all the way here to see you," Miriam said. "I thought you'd be staying right here with us."

Suddenly there was tension in the room, and Kathleen did her best to dispel it.

"How about another bottle of Fanta for you, Miriam?" she asked brightly.

"No, thank you," Miriam answered politely, then turned her steady gaze back to her mother, waiting for her response as if there had been no interruption.

"I told you already, Miriam. I work at night, and I get back very, very late. You'd all be in bed and I'd wake everyone up."

"You can wake me up all you want. I won't care," said Miriam. "I bet Clara and Granny won't care either."

Clara got up and began to gather up the used cups and plates. "You just hush up now, Miriam. Don't be bugging your mother. She's gonna come back to see us tomorrow for sure."

There was a sudden flurry of activity while the tea things were removed to the kitchen and Clara set about washing them. After a few minutes of sitting in the spotlight of Miriam's angry glare, Benita stood up and prepared to leave. She stuck her head around the kitchen door, thanked Kathleen for tea, said goodbye to her mother, and when she returned to the living-room to make peace with Miriam she found the room empty except for Trice who was curled up in ball on Kathleen's chair by the window. She went back to the kitchen.

"Where did Miriam go?" she asked.

"Bathroom," said Clara.

"Hmm. More likely sulking," Benita said with a half-smile. "She can be pretty stubborn."

Like someone else I know, thought Kathleen, but said, "I'll tell her goodbye from you if you have to rush off, Benita. Don't worry about her, she'll be fine. We'll take Trice over to the park for his evening walk, and that'll keep her busy."

Benita was thinking of Trice as she closed the gate carefully behind her, although it crossed her mind that he was small enough to slither underneath if he were so inclined. She turned right and headed up Winchester Avenue towards the bus stop. She wasn't expected at the Blue Flamingo until nine but her mind was in turmoil and she hadn't been able to stay in the house a moment longer, had needed to be on the move so that she could process what she had learned about Larry. A priest! He had run for cover then, run away from her and from the responsibility of dealing with a child on the way. He hadn't been able to face up to life, had taken flight and run straight into the arms of Holy Mother Church.

Coward! she thought, and quickened her pace. *Chickenshit coward!* He'd thrown money at her for an abortion and then run for the hills. Wasn't Rome said to be built on seven hills? He'd run to the right place then. All those hills...

The bus stop was in sight, and she was reaching for her change purse when she heard footsteps behind her, coming at a fast run. She spun around at the last minute and was almost knocked off her feet by Miriam in full flight.

"Hey, hey, hey! Slow down! What the heck are you *doing* here, Miriam?"

"Trying to catch up to you." Miriam was flushed and panting from the heat of the day and from the exertion of her run. "You left without me."

"I'm on my way to work like I told you. I told your granny to say goodbye to you."

"Uh-uh. You're not gonna say goodbye to me." Miriam stood ramrod straight, prepared for battle.

"You can't come with me right now, Miriam."

"Why can't I?"

"Because kids aren't allowed at the place I work."

"Why not?"

"'Cause it's a place for adults only; that's why."

"What kind of a place is it then?"

"A bar."

"Hah! You mean you're selling liquor to white guys? That's pretty funny, huh?"

Benita's bus was coming. She could see it in the distance. "Miriam, you get back to the house right now," she said. "I mean it. Your granny will be worried sick when she finds out you're gone. That's not right and you know it."

"Okay, but she's my granny and you're my mom, and I'm sticking with you. You can go to work tonight. I'm not gonna stop you. I'll just wait for you at your place till you get home."

The bus arrived and went away again without them. In silence Benita and Miriam marched back to the Kinsella house where Benita announced a change of plan. Miriam would be spending the night with her, and they'd both be back the next day in time for lunch.

"Good," said Clara. She smiled her broken smile and went upstairs with Miriam to pack pyjamas and a change of clothes for the next day.

CHAPTER THIRTY-TWO

I had not heard from my mother for some time, and in the lull between council sessions I found myself thinking about her, and about Renzo and Molly who had just had their third child. When Renzo phoned with the news of Marco's safe arrival, he told me how sorry he and Molly were that Cannon Law prevented me from being the baby's godfather.

"Doesn't make much sense to me, Larry. Who better than a priest to serve as a child's spiritual parent? Let's hope they have a real good reason for preventing us from choosing our best friend for the job."

"It would have been a real honour, Renzo, but, as they say, them's the rules."

The call from home reminded me that my mother, unlike Renzo's, was alone in an empty house with only a little dog for company, and I wondered again why she had not written recently. Could it be that she was still grieving for my father, or worse, that she had become depressed? On an impulse, I went to a travel agency on the Via Veneto and booked myself onto the next flight to Canada. I would not announce my arrival, I decided, just show up on the doorstep and surprise everyone, first my mother and then the Rosetti family up in Kamloops.

Unlike the rest of Canada, the West Coast is blessed with mild winters and summers that are warm, but rarely hot. Rome, when I left it, was sweltering, and had been abandoned by all Romans lucky enough to be able to head for the hills or the seashore in the hottest month of the year. In August, Rome is full of noisy, sweating, sometimes cranky tourists who slog their dutiful way through their "must see" lists and seek refuge from the relentless sun in any cafe or trattoria in their path. I was glad to escape the crowds and the heat for a while, and I looked forward to the relative cool of British Columbia.

To my surprise, when I arrived in Vancouver, I found it embroiled in a heatwave of its own with the temperature in the mid-eighties. The international airport, built on a deltaic island in the mouth of the Fraser River, is a long way from downtown, but with the exception of Oak Street, where the synagogues were open for Sabbath services, I did not see a single person wearing a jacket. It was warm, no doubt about it.

When the cab reached Winchester Avenue, I told the driver to drop me off a block from the house and I walked the rest of the way, hoping that Trice would not sound the alarm and alert my mother. If I found her busy fixing her evening meal, I would talk her into abandoning it and letting me treat her to dinner at the White Spot. Then I would do my best to persuade her to drive up to Kamloops with me the following day. We'd find a decent motel for the night and show up the next morning at Renzo's parish church in time for Marco's baptism.

Mum had certainly done a great job with the roses this year, I thought, and this spell of hot weather seemed to suit them. Each bush was weighed down with huge velvety blooms, and their fragrance hung over the little garden like a perfumed cloud. I knocked at the front door and heard Trice give a shrill warning bark, knocked again, and heard him scurrying along the hallway with my mother shushing him crossly. I stood on the doorstep anticipating her astonishment, followed by delight at seeing me again after the long period of absence. Instead, I saw shock and consternation.

"Oh, Larry," she said faintly, a hand over her mouth. "Why on earth didn't you tell me you were coming?"

"Well, I thought I'd give you a surprise. What's wrong, Ma? Don't tell me you didn't get a chance to hoover today and the house is a mess? Come on now, it's not the Queen of England come to call on you. It's me, your only son! So are you going to let me the door in or do you need time to think about it?"

"Of course not, Pet. Come in, come in. It's just that I had a letter from—"

I cut her off with a hug and kiss, put my bag down on the floor and closed the door behind me. Trice was jumping around my feet like a Mexican bean as my mother launched into some kind of explanation, but I stopped listening to her the moment I looked through the open doorway at the end of the passage and saw three people busy at work in the kitchen.

When one of them looked up from the table, I found myself face to face with Benita Pigeon for the first time in nine years. She stared at me, her face devoid of expression, her eyes unreadable, as they had always been to me.

My mother began to babble. "He really caught me by surprise, Benita. I had no idea at all he was coming. I would have told you, of course, if I'd had even an inkling of this, but I didn't."

"Told her what, Granny?"

My daughter came out of the kitchen and stood next to her mother. Benita put a hand on her shoulder.

"Here's someone you've always wanted to meet, Miriam."

And Miriam said, "But I already met him. He's the guy who took my picture when I made my first communion."

Benita said sharply. "No, you've never seen him before in your life. He lives in Italy. And now here he is, so finally you get to meet your father."

But Miriam had gone flying into the front room and had come back with a framed photograph. She held it up defiantly, so that all of us could see her in her long white dress on the day of her First Communion in LaPierre.

Standing before me now in the hallway of my mother's house in Mount Pleasant, Vancouver, the house where I had grown up and where her own mother had spent so many hours, Miriam looked nothing at all like the sad little seven year-old in the photograph. She had grown taller, of course, but there was also a self-assuredness about her which had not been there the first time I laid eyes on her.

On this hot day she was wearing a bright yellow sundress. I noticed that she was graceful in her movements and wondered fleetingly if she was athletic. I tried not to stare at her, this little person who had occupied my thoughts ever since I had first learned of her existence.

"It was you, right?" she said. "You took this picture of me, didn't you?"

I nodded mutely. Then Clara came out of the kitchen drying her hands on a dishtowel. She said, "Yup, I seen this guy before, Benny. He was up at LaPierre that one time."

And Benita said, "Is that right, huh? Well, Ma, I knew this guy a long, long time ago, so I guess I better introduce you to Father Larry Kinsella." Then she turned to me and said, "Nice to meet you again, Father."

Anger rippled through her words, and I saw the flash of fury in her eyes before she turned away in disgust. Miriam, still holding her photo, stared at me.

"I don't get it. How can you be my father if you're a priest?"

I didn't answer, and my poor, flustered mother stepped into the breach.

"Why don't we all sit down now and have a nice cup of tea? The dinner can wait a while, sure it can. You come and help your Granny, Miriam, and we'll let the grown-ups talk for a bit, shall we?"

She shunted Miriam off to the kitchen and propelled the rest of us into the front room where, for the next few minutes, Benita maintained a hostile silence and I did my best to engage Clara in conversation. It was tough going, even though, after years of living among sophisticated and gregarious Romans, I had acquired much of their social ease and expertise.

All my attempts to launch some kind of dialogue came to nothing, and I was relieved when my mother finally trundled the tea trolley into the room, followed by Miriam carrying a plate of sandwiches.

My mother stretched out the tea pouring operation for as long as possible, fussing about with sugar tongs and milk and plates and paper serviettes, but finally everyone was seated and we all busily swallowed and chewed and waited for someone to say something. It certainly wasn't going to be me, I decided. Besides, I was fully occupied in trying to prevent Trice from humping my left ankle. I uncrossed my legs and discreetly moved my foot out of reach. As I did so, I glanced up and saw that Clara was watching my antics and laughing silently behind her serviette. I leaned over and dangled half a sandwich in front of the dog's nose and he removed himself from my ankle and took himself off to the rug to see if what I had given him was worth eating. I hoped the investigative process would take him a good long while.

Benita stood up and made a show of checking her watch.

"Sorry, Mrs. Kinsella, but it's time for us to go. If we stay for dinner I'll be late for work. Come on Miriam. We gotta go."

Miriam looked at her mother and then at me. "Uh, d'you think maybe I should stay here tonight? Just this one time?"

When Benita did not answer, she ploughed on hopefully. "Granny Kathleen might need me to help her with dinner. Seeing as we got extra company now and everything."

Miriam looked at me as she spoke. I felt my throat tighten and had to look away from her to regain my composure. I was thinking that she had just met her father for the first time and knew nothing about him other than that he had come to LaPierre for her First Communion and that he was a priest. She was thinking that, if she left now, I might go away again and then she'd be right back again to being a little girl with no father.

Those were her thoughts. I could read what she was thinking, and I was certain I was not wrong.

Benita's expression softened and for a moment she hesitated, but when she spoke it was decisively.

"You can't stay here tonight, Miriam, because Father Kinsella needs his bedroom back. Run upstairs now and get the rest of your stuff out of there.

The look on my mother's face made me realize that, far from bringing joy, my unannounced arrival had ruined all her plans. I should have known, though, that she would think of the child rather than herself.

"Oh, sweetheart," she said, getting up and putting her arms around Miriam. "Your mother wants you with her. We *all* want you. We just have to figure out a way to share you between us."

Miriam trudged upstairs disconsolately, and when she was out of the room I stood up, careful not to step on Trice who was now exploring my other ankle.

"Listen, Benita, I'm leaving in the morning, and I'll be gone for the next couple of days. Ma, I didn't have a chance to tell you yet but I'm driving up to Kamloops tomorrow. Renzo and Molly have a new baby, and I want to get there in time for his baptism on Sunday."

For a moment it looked as if Benita wanted to ask about Renzo and Molly, but then she tightened her lips and said nothing, and when Miriam came downstairs carrying her little bag the two of them left for the bus stop. It was hard to sit there and watch them leave, because, having found her, I didn't want to let her out of my sight.

"Does Benita take Miriam to work with her then, Ma?" I asked when Clara had taken herself off to the kitchen to start on the washing up. My mother looked up from collecting cups and saucers.

"She can't, Larry. She works at some kind of a night club."

"So who looks after Miriam while she's working?"

"That I couldn't tell you, Pet. Clara and Miriam only arrived yesterday, and last night was their first night in town. I'm sure Benita will have someone in to sit with the child while she's at work though, she's a great little mother altogether."

But I wasn't so sure. What if Miriam had to stay by herself for most of the night? How safe would she be? She was eight years old and this was her first time in a city.

I spent a restless night in my old bed and was up at dawn. I said my prayers out in the back yard where the laden peach tree and the scent of a perfect summer morning brought back memories of childhood and made me glad to be home again. I prayed for my mother, and for Renzo and Molly and their growing family, and then for Miriam and Benita, but the person who was perhaps the most in need of God's help I did not pray for at all.

Later that morning I rented a Buick Riviera from a place on Georgia Street and headed up the Fraser Canyon to exchange the muggy swelter of the coast for the dry, searing heat of the inland semi-desert. Kamloops baked in the August sun, and as I approached it, having followed the Thompson River all the way from Lytton, the temperature according to the local radio station stood at 106 degrees. This was Shuswap territory, scorched now by the sun, barren and treeless. Sagebrush stirred and drifted aimlessly, and I figured the only things that could thrive out here were cactus and rattlesnakes. For much of the year, though, these were prosperous ranch lands and only in the dry summer months were the cattle moved up to higher ground where there was still grazing to be found. The burnt grasslands reminded me of my last trip north, and I guessed that much of the province must be in a state of high alert for forest fires.

Renzo and Molly were delighted to see me and touched that I had turned up in person for the baptism of their little son, who looked angelic in his white christening robe. Danny and Mirella were on their best behaviour during the ceremony, but at the post-christening dinner back at the house they grew fractious from the heat, and as soon as the meal was over and the rest of the guests had left, Molly took them upstairs to give them their bath and put them to bed. While she was busy with the children, I filled Renzo in on the latest episode of my life. He was clearly shocked.

"Jeez, Larry, this all sounds like a bit of a mess. You need to be careful."

"Careful about what?" Molly had come back with Marco, fast asleep in his little rocking cradle. She put it on the floor between herself and Renzo and sat down to listen to an abbreviated version of recent events. There were beads of sweat on her forehead and when she pushed her hair back from her face, it fell to her shoulders in waves, as bright and luxuriant as ever.

"You know, Larry," she said when she was settled, "it must have been a real shock for Benita to see you like this, I mean as a priest. And then think about that poor little girl. She must be so confused right now. It would almost have been easier for her if you hadn't shown up on the doorstep like that. She would have had a nice visit with your mom and then gone back to her normal life."

"Normal? Aren't you forgetting something, Molly? She'd still be going back without Benita. How normal is it for a kid to live eight hundred miles away from her mother and be brought up by a grandmother and great-grandmother? How normal is it for a kid to have a mother who chooses to leave her behind so that she can work in some sleazy joint on Kingsway?"

When I saw the look of outrage on Molly's face, I wanted to run for cover, but it was too late.

"I don't believe I'm hearing this." She all but hissed at me. "All that time, while you were engaged in arcane discussions with a bunch of old fogies in red hats and enjoying a life free of responsibilities, Benita was raising your child as best she could. You have absolutely *no* right to sit in judgment of her or her parenting skills!"

Molly had never been softly spoken, but now her voice rose to a near shriek, and Marco stirred and snuffled in his cradle. Renzo shot out a practiced foot and set it rocking vigorously but when the baby's snuffles turned to squawks of protest, his father reached over, plucked him out, and held him aloft. Not the right thing to do, according to Molly.

"Oh, for pity's sake, Renzo! Why do you have to pick him up every time he utters so much as a peep? You're teaching him that all he has to do is yell and we'll come running. Didn't you learn anything at all from the other two?"

I saw that she was overtired and on edge. With a sigh, she took the baby from Renzo, unbuttoned her blouse and put him to the breast. When he had latched on and was sucking away busily Molly turned back to me.

"Sorry for that little outburst, Larry. Blame it on my hormones if you like. You know I love you."

Of course I did. They were my oldest friends and were able to see beyond the dog collar to the kid they had gone to school with. I knew that I would always hear the truth from them, even though I might not like it.

CHAPTER THIRTY-THREE

I left Kamloops well before the sun rose to scorch and burn its way through another August day and was back in Vancouver by early afternoon. The heat was still oppressive, but there were thunderclouds gathering over the North Shore mountains, a sure sign that the weather was about to break. There had been plenty of time to think during the long drive through the Fraser Canyon, and I had decided that it would best for everyone if I stayed at the Cathedral rectory until my return to Rome. It was a huge old place on Richards Street, built to accommodate visiting clergy as well as the resident priests at Holy Rosary. If I were in residence, I'd be able to say Mass at the cathedral each morning and spend the rest of the day with Miriam whilst staying out of Benita's way altogether.

As it turned out, however, there was no need for me to relocate. My mother and Clara were both home when I got there, but of Miriam and Benita there was no sign.

"We haven't seen them since you left for Kamloops, Larry. I'm starting to get anxious about them."

When I saw how drawn and tired my mother looked, I regretted my unannounced visit yet again. All I had brought her was worry, and now I was worried too.

Clara was sitting at the kitchen table sorting through a box of letters. From the large printing and brightly coloured illustrations, I guessed that they had all come from Miriam. Trice was snuffling around the bag I had dropped by the door, and I took out the box of chocolates I had bought in Kamloops.

"Don't worry, Ma. I'll find them. Where does Benita work? I'll start by trying there."

She looked at me blankly.

"I don't know, Larry. She never said."

Clara had not acknowledged me at all. She seemed to occupy some distant zone I could not reach, and I wondered how my mother, given as she was to inconsequential chatter, coped with the silence and lack of communication.

Then Clara surprised us both.

"Blue Flamingo. Place she works at is called the Blue Flamingo. That's what she told Miriam, anyways."

Who had not heard of the notorious Blue Flamingo? It called itself a cabaret and occupied a seedy stretch of Kingsway. Renzo and I had gone there ourselves once as teenagers in the hope of hearing the Viscounts, although truth to tell we were really more interested in the exotic dancers who performed during the breaks. Not that we ever got to see them. The guy at the door eyed us up and down and gave us on our marching orders.

"Get lost kids. Come back in a couple of years and I *might* let you in."

Well, I was going back now, but not for the music or the dancing girls.

It was fully dark by the time I arrived. I was not dressed in clerical garb, of course. It would have been scandalous for a Catholic priest to be seen entering the Blue Flamingo Cabaret, but since I had never served in the Vancouver Archdiocese of Vancouver I felt secure in my anonymity. As it was, nobody even looked at me. The place was dark and smoky and half empty. There was a band playing on the small stage: a lanky guitarist strumming chords, a wailing tenor sax, and a spaced-out drummer lethargically beating a snare drum. A cocktail waitress walked by with a tray of drinks for a raucous group who looked like loggers just released from the bush, or maybe long-distance truck drivers who had been on the road too long. The waitress wore a skimpy black pinafore and a little white apron. She was tall and skinny with white-blonde hair out of a bottle, and she certainly wasn't Benita. I ordered rye whiskey and ginger ale and sipped it as the music ground to a merciful halt. There was some half-hearted applause, and then a middle-aged man climbed onto the stage and thanked the Kingsway Kings for their mighty fine music. The band shuffled off, and the guy with the microphone stepped forward again.

"Alright, gentlemen, here comes what you've all been waiting for. Before we welcome our next band, Vancouver's very own Gassy Jacks, let's say hello once again to our talented and lovely go-go dancer, the incomparable, the one and only Miss Belle!"

And suddenly there she was - Benita, in thigh-high black leather boots and a tightly laced corset that barely covered her breasts. She wore what looked like a chainmail belt around her waist and a metal-studded choker round her neck. There was a loud cheer from the loggers and appreciative wolf whistles from solitary drinkers scattered around the room. The jukebox in the corner blasted out Acker Bilk's "Midnight in Moscow" and Benita began a series of sinuous movements that had nothing to do with dancing and everything to do with titillation.

Italian women can be flamboyantly provocative, and after years of living among them I was impervious to such an overtly sexual display. I was shocked only because it was Benita I was watching now, Benita who was encouraging every man in that sleazy dive to lust after her, to mentally strip and make use of her. I felt disgusted. If this was how she earned a living, she was no better than a common hooker. I stood up abruptly, momentarily blocking the view of the guys at the next table as I made my way to the exit.

"Hey, sit down, asshole," one them grouched as I stumbled past. "The act isn't over yet. Show some respect, why don't you?"

I ignored him, kept going till I reached the door and pushed through it onto the street. Outside it was still hot and sticky, and I found that I was sweating heavily. Thunder rumbled from somewhere up the Fraser Valley, and from time to time sheet lighting swept across the dark sky like northern lights bleached of their shifting bands of colour. There was an all-night diner across the street and with a cup of bitter, over-brewed coffee in front of me, I sat by the window and let the waves of anger surge through me, pushing aside all rational thought.

Intermittently I would tell myself that Benita's life was her own and that I should concern myself only with trying to live my life as Christ taught us. As a servant of God I should be seeking the higher path, the path of mercy, justice, and peace. But then I would think of Miriam, my daughter, and the higher path would disappear, leaving me once again overcome by outrage.

When I could sit no more I went outside and paced the street until I saw the doors of the Blue Flamingo swing open to release the first cluster of drinkers. I crossed the street and walked down the alley looking for the side door and then back up to the street again, repeating the short trip over and over like a bear in a cage. When Benita finally emerged, I was standing so close to the door that I could smell the alcohol on her breath. Her face was flushed, her eyes glassy, and she barely reacted to my presence.

"Dancing while under the influence is highly dangerous, 'Belle'. You might fall off the stage."

Not at all what I had planned to say, but those were the words that came out of my mouth.

Benita smiled. She had changed into street clothes and had removed all traces of the makeup she had worn on stage.

"What's this? A sermon from the saintly Father Kinsella? I'm surprised that Holy Mother Church would allow a priest to frequent a joint like this. Or are you here as an evangelist, out to save the souls of us weaker mortals?"

Her words were cutting, her tone contemptuous, and there was no hint of double negatives or faulty participles, no "Indian talk" at all. I knew she was baiting me, and I obliged her by reacting.

"Maybe somebody needs to remind you that you have a daughter, Benita. Does Miriam know what you do for a living? What kind of a mother she has? And where is that daughter of yours right now?

Who's taking care of her while you strut around on a stage and let a bunch of drunks drool over your half-naked body?"

"At least they're normal men, *Father*, not repressed freaks like you. Now get out of my way and go home to your mother. I've got nothing to say to you."

"I'm going nowhere until I know that Miriam is safe. Where is she, Benita?"

She pushed past me almost violently and when I reached out to stop her she turned on me like a feral cat, hissing and clawing.

"Don't you *touch* me, you creep! You lay as much as a finger on me, and I'll scream so loud all the drunks in the neighbourhood will come running. So will the police. I can't wait to hear you explain to them what a Catholic priest is doing after midnight in a back alley outside the Blue Flamingo."

I let go of her arm, not because of her threat, but because I was suddenly sickened by my own behaviour. We were both of us acting like out of control kids, and I was ashamed of myself.

"Benita, please listen to me for a moment. I just want to know that Miriam is being looked after, that she's not on her own in a strange city. She's only eight years old for God's sake."

The storm had broken and the rain was coming down in torrents. A siren wailed its approach, and an ambulance raced by followed by a police car with its lights flashing. Benita had begun to move away, but when she turned to face me again I saw that her rage, like mine, was subsiding and had gone from boiling point to a steady simmer.

"Miriam is no concern of yours. You might be her biological father, but you will never be more to her than that. Now I'm going home. Please don't try to follow me."

I drove home in the rain aware that I had accomplished nothing at all and had probably jeopardized not only my own relationship with Miriam, but maybe even my mother's. I tried to pray to a God I could not reach and felt useless, both as a man and as a priest. I slept poorly, wondering how best to explain to my mother and Clara why Miriam would not be back, at least not until after I had returned to Europe.

At some point during the night the rain had stopped, and morning brought cooler air and new life to parched trees and fading flowers. To my great astonishment it also brought Benita, with Miriam in tow. I knew how hard it must have been for her to show up, knew too that she had done it for her mother and my mother and Miriam. I put *Belle* entirely out of my mind for a while and felt a degree of admiration for Benita.

We ate lunch outdoors, a summer meal of cold chicken with potato salad and fresh tomatoes from a neighbour's garden. Miriam drank Orange Fanta and the rest of us had iced tea followed by strawberry shortcake. Trice scuttled around the lawn, and my mother filled his bowl with scraps from the picnic. The worry was gone from her face, and happiness lit her up from within, but I saw that Clara was keeping a watchful eye on her daughter. Then Benita announced that she was leaving Miriam with us for the rest of the afternoon and took herself off without further explanation. She had not so much as glanced in my direction, and the two of us had not exchanged a single word. I knew that Clara had noticed, knew too that my mother had refused to see it, not wanting to let anything spoil what was to her a perfect afternoon.

When the dishes had been put away, Miriam went and fetched her sketchbook and pencil and sat down on an old tartan rug that I remembered from summers long past. Trice, full of leftover chicken, had flopped down in a patch of shade, and Miriam started to draw him. She was busy for a few moments, then she heaved a sigh of frustration and ripped out the page.

"He won't lift his head up. When I try to draw him he just looks like a rug or something. I can't make him look like a dog."

"Hey, Trice!" I whistled and snapped my fingers and his curly white head shot up.

"How about right now, Miriam?"

Her pencil flew in a race against time before Trice figured out that there was no more food on offer. He was clearly still in snooze mode and not at all keen to stir himself.

"Yup, I think I got him that time," Miriam said, and closed her sketchbook. I'm gonna send his picture to Hepzibah."

I tried to remember what it was like to be eight years old with a long afternoon stretching ahead and nobody to play with except a dog who was more interested in sleeping. An idea came to me.

"Hey, Miriam, how would you like to go to the zoo?"

"Where's the zoo at?" she said.

"Stanley Park."

"How many bus rides to get there?"

"None. We'll go by car."

"You got a car?"

"I'm renting one while I'm here in Canada."

"Has it got room for Clara and Kathleen?"

"Lots of room."

"Okay, I'll go get them."

She sprang up and ran into the kitchen to round up her two grandmothers, and pretty soon the four of us were on our way to the park. Miriam sat up front with me and I drove through Chinatown with the windows rolled down so that we could hear the hubbub of the street and smell the chicken and garlic and ginger and fish and all the other aromas that wafted out of already busy restaurants.

From Pender I turned onto Georgia Street and headed straight for the park. Occupying one thousand acres of forest and shoreline, yet still very close to the heart of downtown, Stanley Park has long been the pride of Vancouver and the envy of cities the world over. The park had first opened in 1888 and its familiar landmarks, Lost Lagoon, Siwash Rock, the Nine-o'clock Gun, and world-famous totem poles, are dear to Vancouverites. In addition to tennis courts, a lawn bowling club, and a cricket pitch, it has several playgrounds and two waterparks. Lumberman's Arch, once the site of a Squamish Nation village with a name so full of 'x' s and 'y' s that no white person is able to pronounce it, is now home to a large picnic area with the zoo tucked away in the far corner. Small and cramped though it is by world standards, it had enough penguins, wolves, emus, buffalo, kangaroos, monkeys, bears, dolphins, and Beluga whales to ensure a steady stream of visitors, and I figured that an active eight-year-old would zip around the place in thirty minutes at most. Miriam, though, was enraptured, first by the polar bears and then by the monkeys. Clara laughed at their antics, but Miriam focused on one young capuchin as he swung effortlessly from bar to bar in a cage that was far too small.

"I gotta to try to remember how long and skinny his arms are and how small and round his head is," she said when I came and stood beside her. "I forgot to bring my drawing book."

"Maybe you forgot, but, see, I didn't."

Clara opened her canvas shoulder bag and brought out Miriam's sketchbook and pencils and after that we were stuck with the monkeys until Miriam was satisfied that she had captured them 'like they really are'.

My mother watched her with a smile. "You were just like that when you were little, Larry. Not that you were much good at drawing, but you were every bit as focused as your daughter when something captured your interest."

"Stubborn you mean," Clara said. "Miriam's stubborn like her mother."

And my mother said, "Like her mother *and* father then."

When we finally reached their compound, one of the polar bears was pacing back and forth but the other one lay listlessly on a cement rock with nowhere to cool off other than a moat full of tepid water.

"Are there polar bears up where you are, Miriam?" my mother asked.

"Uh-uh. No white ones like these guys, but we got plenty black ones. Some grizzlies too."

"How about monkeys then? Do you have any of those at all?"

My mother was teasing her now, and Clara laughed, but Miriam pretended to ponder the question.

"No monkeys, but we got moose. You guys got moose down here?"

"You've got us there, Miriam," I said. "No moose in Vancouver."

She smiled complacently. "I guess I'm just gonna have to make a picture for you then."

We got back to the house minutes before Benita arrived, and she allowed me to drive the two of them back to her lodgings on Carrall Street only because Miriam was clearly exhausted after her day at the zoo. I was shocked when I saw where she was living. The three-storey brick rooming house was derelict and the neighbourhood itself home to a wandering tribe of down and outs, panhandlers, drunks, and hookers.

"I know what you're thinking," Benita said as I pulled up to let them out. "But she's as safe here as anywhere else in this city."

I had my doubts, but this time, for the sake of Miriam, I said nothing more than goodnight to the two of them.

When Benita showed up with Miriam the following morning I proposed a return trip to the zoo so that she could ride the miniature railway that ran around the forested wolf enclosure. Clara, however, had a different idea.

"I wanna go see them people you stayed with when you went to school down here that one time."

"The O'Carrolls?" Benita looked mystified. "I never kept in touch with them except to let them know when Miriam was born."

"Well, they were real good to you, Benny. I feel kinda bad about those guys. We never even thanked them. We gotta do that before me and Miriam go back home, okay?"

On the way over to Shaughnessy Miriam chattered away to my mother, but both Benita and Clara were silent. I wondered about the welcome I would receive from the O'Carrolls and wished I could just drop the lot of them off at the house and pick them up again after their visit. But I needn't have worried. Surprised as they must have been by the unlikely gathering on their front doorstep, the O'Carrolls were as gracious and hospitable as ever. They were genuinely delighted to see Benita and welcomed Clara and Miriam with real warmth. We drank tea in their elegant living room, and while my mother and Peggy O'Carroll chatted about the Catholic Women's League, Cormac engaged me in conversation about the future of Vatican Two under the leadership of the newly elected Pope Paul VI.

After a while Benita took Miriam on a tour of the house and garden, leaving Clara to sit and watch and listen. As usual she said very little, but when we were leaving the house she thanked the O'Carrolls for giving a home to her daughter, and when she smiled her broken smile at them I saw that they were moved. Both of them clung to Benita with tears in their eyes, hugged Miriam, and begged them all to come back soon. They were good and generous people, and I could tell from watching Benita that she knew, as I did, that it had been right to have come. After that, I began to see Clara in a new light.

I was aware that time was passing and taking me where I did not want to go. One night, I dreamt of being swept along by the black and rushing water of a mighty river to a sudden precipice, and then plunging through cascades of silence into nowhere. For the first time in my life, I felt threatened by the future, unsure of everything except that I had a daughter and that I loved her.

The weekend before my return to Rome marked the end of Miriam and Clara's stay in Vancouver. It was also Labour Day weekend, and I suggested that we celebrate with a trip to the PNE. It was a big year in the history of the fair because the Agrodome had just opened, providing more space for the agricultural displays. Its real purpose though, at least as most Vancouverites saw it, was to house the city's fledgling hockey team, the Vancouver Canucks, and when I saw the size of the crowd gathered outside the main gates on Hastings Street, I figured that many of them had come to the Exhibition just so that they could check out the new arena.

We had arranged to meet Miriam at noon, and my mother fussed and fretted while I scanned the surging throng for a glimpse of her. Benita had agreed to drop her off at the entrance to the fairgrounds rather than waste precious time by bringing her to the house, and now, too late, I questioned the wisdom of the plan. My mother too was pessimistic.

"For God's sake, we'll never find her in this mob, Larry. Not unless Benita has her up on stilts waving a giant flag with her name on it."

But Clara only smiled. "Don't you worry about it, Kathleen. Benny'll find us. We just gotta wait a while."

So that's what we did. We stood in the sunshine and watched people line up for tickets and shuffle through the turnstiles to disappear into Hastings Park. It was an ideal day to stand and wait. The sky was blue, the sun hot, and an obliging little breeze rippled through from time to time to keep things pleasant. My mother relaxed and stopped looking at her watch and it wasn't long at all before we were joined by Benita, with Miriam in a yellow sundress with her hair in two long braids.

"I'm so excited," she said. "And guess what? My mom's gonna stay too!"

If any day can be said to be perfect, that one was. We saw everything the Exhibition had to offer: farm animals, flower displays, quilts, home baking, household gadgets, show jumping, and then more animals. When I saw that my mother and Clara were tiring, I sat them down at a picnic table and lined up for hamburgers and fries and milkshakes for all of us. We ate within sight of the Coast mountains standing tall on the far side of the Burrard Inlet, cloaked in summer green now and without their winter caps of snow. Later on we stopped for bear-claw donuts and then for ice cream, and after that Miriam wanted cotton candy on a stick.

"You're gonna throw up, girl," Clara warned her.

"No, I won't," Miriam said. "I promise I won't, I just wanna try it."

And Benita said, "Oh, let her have it then."

And Miriam walked around proudly with her sticky pink trophy, just like every other kid at the fair. An ordinary kid with an ordinary family, that's what she was that day, an ordinary, happy little kid. And just like other families, we ended up at the funfair where we packed as many rides as we could into the time that remained before Benita had to leave. She had made it clear that she wouldn't be leaving Miriam behind, not even for the fair, although it could have been that Miriam didn't want to be left. I didn't ask, not wanting to risk spoiling things in any way.

After Miriam, Benita, and I had ridden the new wooden roller coaster for the third time, and I was starting to feel queasy, we wandered back down the hill to try our luck at the sideshows. My mother and Clara trailed behind, tired out from a day of sun and activity. When we reached the ring toss, I bought a handful of tickets and we each took a turn. I was proud to see that Miriam's aim was excellent. Her mother, however, was every bit as hopeless as she had been as a teenager, and the sudden rush of memories made me smile. A lot of years had gone by since then, but I hadn't lost any of my skill, and Miriam was thrilled when I won one of the giant stuffed animals on display.

"How about that tiger?" I asked her, still thinking of the past.

"Nope, we already got one of those guys at home. His name's Horace. I used to play with him all the time when I was a baby, so he's all beat up"

Benita laughed. "Did you know it was your father who won that tiger for me a long time ago, Mirri?"

"No, you never told me that!"

"Well I'm telling you now."

After much deliberation, Miriam chose a hideous chimpanzee for her prize. When we got back to the car we had a hard time fitting him into the back seat and I got exasperated with the chimp which made Clara laugh all the way home.

On Sunday morning, my last day in Vancouver, I concelebrated High Mass at Holy Rosary Cathedral. I figured that Clara must have done a bit of negotiating because Benita was already there with Miriam when we arrived at the entrance on Dunsmuir Street.

"Here she is then, Ma," she said to Clara. Miriam, wearing a blue cotton dress and white cardigan, looked subdued and downcast, and I wondered if she had been coerced into attending Mass, or if it was the grandeur of the cathedral, such a far cry from the simple little white chapel at La Pierre, that overwhelmed her. The bells began to ring out their Sunday call to prayer and the organ struck a mighty chord from within.

"Let's go and find good seats up front before the place fills up," my mother said, putting a protective arm around Miriam.

Benita was already moving towards the steps down to the street.

"I'll see you later, then," she said.

"Oh, but will you not stay for Mass, Dear?" My mother looked disappointed.

"No. Those days are over for me, Mrs. Kinsella. I'm way too much of a sinner to be going to Mass. But Miriam's going to pray for me, right, Miriam?"

Miriam nodded and turned to follow my mother and Clara into the church. I waited until they had disappeared.

"We're all sinners, Benita, and God loves us in all of our imperfection. Why not stay, now that you're here? It would make Miriam happy, too."

"No" she said, dismissively. "I don't believe in any of that Catholic stuff any more. Save your sermon for the faithful, Father. I'm going for coffee."

Archbishop O'Leary said Mass, and I was one of the two concelebrants. It was a solemn high Mass accompanied by what was known as the "bells and smells" of Roman Catholic ritual. Incense swirled while the organ thundered; the choir sang the Kyrie, and we three vested priests led the congregation in the formal worship of our unseen God. There was a moment, just before the consecration of the bread and wine, when it struck me that here, on the high altar, robed in liturgical vestments and standing with outstretched arms before a large gathering of the faithful, I ceased to be Larry Kinsella and became instead the ageless, timeless, universal priest. And I thought that maybe it was not too different from the way in which Benita, when she removed her street clothes and appeared on stage in stripper's garb, became Belle. The problem was that I was no longer sure which was my assumed role and which my real identity. Was I Father Kinsella or Larry Kinsella, the deeply confused and alienated lover of Benita Pigeon, and father of her child, Miriam? And who was she now? Benita or Belle?

The archbishop delivered a sermon that was dull and rambling. The old fellow loved the sound of his own voice, I thought, and hoped that my mother wouldn't ask me to comment on his homily because I had stopped listening after the first long minute. Instead I thought about Miriam, sitting quietly between my mother and Clara in the third pew from the front. She wasn't listening either; I could tell from the way her eyes wandered from one stained window to the next, no doubt in the hope of finding something interesting that would stave off the boredom of the homily. I wondered if all I had managed to give her was a week of frenzied activity in a futile attempt to make up for my previous absence from her life. Had I made her happy, or just added to her confusion? What was I to her now? What would I be in the future? What could I be?

The sermon finally came to an end and the congregation rose from its collective slumber and stood for the credo, then sat again for the collection and the preparation of the gifts. At the end of Mass, when I stood with my fellow priests to give the final blessing, I saw the door at the back of the cathedral open and close briefly as Benita slipped inside, accompanied by a fleeting shaft of sunlight.

"In nomine patris et filio, et spiritui sancto," I intoned with the Archbishop. I lifted my right hand, and as I made the sign of the cross, I prayed that God would bless all those present, but especially this woman, Benita, that He would guard and protect her all the days of her life, that His Face would shine upon her, and that she would not be alone.

CHAPTER THIRTY-FOUR

For the first time since Larry had left home to enter the seminary, Kathleen was able to say goodbye to him without shedding a tear. In fact she was relieved to see him go. His visit had been a tense affair from start to finish, and she hadn't known quite what to do with him, how to help him through what seemed to be a perilous patch in his life's journey. Much of the poise and confidence he had acquired in his adult years, what she referred to as *polish*, seemed to have deserted him, leaving him confused and vulnerable.

Benita had been smart to stay away while Larry had been there, she thought, because the house could not have contained all that anger, his as well as hers. And then of course there was Miriam. It was Miriam who had caused him to lose his footing and to flounder. Kathleen had gone out to the airport with him on the Sunday evening. They had said their goodbyes, and today he was safely back in Rome, for which she thanked God.

Now she was preparing herself for another goodbye, and this one would be more painful. Early the next morning, Clara and Miriam would be taking the bus back up to Prince George where they would be met by Jericho George for the rest of the journey home. Kathleen experienced a sharp pang of resentment that she had been cheated of her precious time with Miriam, followed by remorse.

You selfish old woman, she thought. *Stop feeling sorry for yourself, and think about the little girl.* Because it was clear to her that, by herself, she could never have given Miriam the joy—no other word for it—that Larry had provided, nor the fun. He had given her a whole week of new experiences and adventures and laughter that she would never forget. She only hoped that his sudden arrival into that little life, and now his abrupt departure from it, would not leave Miriam feeling confused and abandoned. And yet, for a sensitive eight-year-old, how could it be otherwise?

Kathleen snapped out of her reverie and turned her attention to the day ahead. She and Clara had already made a cake for Miriam's last day, "a Vancouver cake" Clara called It, because they had decorated it with ocean waves of blue frosting and mountain peaks and tall green trees and a couple of white blobs that were supposed to be seagulls. Maybe they would have a picnic in the garden, Kathleen thought. Miriam would like that. She went to ask Clara what she thought of the idea.

Benita and Miriam arrived late, bringing with them mutinous expressions and no luggage.

"Trouble," said Clara when she saw them at the gate, and Kathleen's heart sank.

"Where's your stuff, Miriam?" she asked. I thought you'd have everything ready for your trip home tomorrow."

Miriam looked at Kathleen, then at Clara. "I'm not going," she said defiantly.

"What do you mean, Sweetie? You have to go back. School starts this week, and you're going to be in Grade Three. You don't want to miss your first day back."

"I've told her all that," Benita said.

Clara said, "How about Hepzibah? She's gonna be waiting for you up in LaPierre. And ol' Jericho George coming all the way down to Prince George in his truck to pick us up?"

"Yeah, I feel kinda bad about that. But you can explain to them, can't you, Gran?"

"Explain what?" Clara asked.

"That I'm not going anywhere without Benita. I'm staying with her till she's ready to take me home. I already told her."

"You have to go back, Miriam," Benita said. "This is not your place."

"But this is where you are."

"Only for a while. Then I'm coming home."

"Okay, same with me. I'm staying till we can both go home. Together."

It was a standoff, with neither Benita nor Miriam showing any sign of yielding. Clara attempted to bring about a truce.

"Hey, me and Kathleen, we made a special cake for you, Miriam. Come and see." Miriam stared mutinously at the cake with blue water and snow-capped mountains and tall trees, the Vancouver cake.

"Is it a *goodbye* cake?" she asked. "If it's a goodbye cake, I'm not gonna eat it 'cos I'm not saying goodbye."

Then she began to cry, huge wailing sobs that welled up from within and shook her whole skinny little frame. Trice ran around in circles for a while and then planted himself beside Miriam and howled along with her until Benita put her arms around Miriam.

"Hush up now, baby, you're upsetting the poor dog."

Miriam stopped bawling and peered at Trice through her fingers. Then she knelt down on the floor next to him and stroked the little dog.

"You're such a big baby, Trice. Quit your bawling now. There's nothing the matter. I'm just sad is all."

Clara went over to the table and cut the cake and they all sat down to eat it. When Miriam's plate was empty she looked up at Clara and Kathleen and then at Benita.

"That was good cake, but I'm still not going." Her eyes were red and puffy from all the crying and there was a wobble in her voice.

Kathleen said, "Here's an idea for you, Pet. How about you write a letter to your great-grandmother and tell her about your problem?"

Miriam looked suspicious. "Where are you three going?"

"Nowhere, Sweetheart. We'll be right here, but we're going to do a grown-up thing. We're going to try to work out what to do. First we'll clear the table and then we'll have a, what do you people call it? A pow-wow."

Benita rolled her eyes. "You've been watching too many westerns."

Still, she was smiling as she gathered up the used dishes. Clara followed her daughter into the kitchen while Miriam went up to

Larry's room to work on her letter to Hepzibah. Kathleen sat by the phone in the hallway and talked to Larry in Rome. When the call ended, she told Clara and Benita what he had suggested.

"Hmm," said Benita. "I gotta think about that for a while."

"No," said Clara. "Miriam's gotta think about it first. Ask her."

So after Miriam finished writing her letter, they went into another huddle around the kitchen table and told her about Larry's idea. She covered her eyes with her hands to shut out all distraction while she thought. After a while she took away her hands.

"That plan's about me, but what about Benita? It's gotta be both of us or no deal. I already told you."

Kathleen smiled at her. "You're a great little girl altogether, Miriam. I'll have to bring you with me next time I need to buy a new car. You'll get me the best deal in town for sure."

Then she and Clara and Miriam waited while Benita held a debate with herself. Nobody spoke while she pondered, but Miriam started to swing her feet, and Kathleen knew she was not as calm as she appeared to be. Minutes passed

"Okay," said Benita. "But on one condition."

And even though Kathleen protested vigorously when she heard it, Benita proved to be every bit as stubborn as her daughter. When Kathleen finally yielded, there was a loud cheer from everybody which brought Trice from his basket in a state of high hopes and excitement.

Miriam went to add a postscript to her letter to Hepzibah. Then she fetched Trice's leash from its hook by the door and they all walked down to the mailbox on the corner to post the letter. Then Miriam and Benita and Clara got on the bus and went back to the rooming house on Carrall Street to pack up Benita's stuff. While they were gone, Kathleen called Cormac O'Carroll and enlisted his help with Miriam's immediate registration at St. Bridget's School, and when *that* was done she went upstairs to prepare a bedroom for Benita.

CHAPTER THIRTY-FIVE

At first things went smoothly enough. Miriam settled in quickly at her new school. She was athletic, friendly, and cheerful and had no trouble making friends or keeping up academically with the rest of her class. Every morning, Benita walked her to school, and at the end of the day she was there to meet her and to help her with her homework before she left for her shift at the Blue Flamingo. Kathleen told the two of them that, even though she missed Clara's company, especially during the day, she had never been happier, despite being forced to accept rent money from Benita.

"Yeah, well that's the deal, Kathleen. I'm not letting you keep the two of us. I get paid plenty and you just have your old-age pension, so that's the end of it."

When Kathleen told Larry about the unwanted rent money, he advised her to put it straight into the account he had set up for Miriam, and after that she was content. Miriam was happy too, and so was Trice with all the extra company. It was Benita who eventually began to come adrift.

The first sign of unrest appeared shortly after Hepzibah's letter arrived from LaPierre. Clara had added a post-script and so too had Jericho George. He told them that the first snow had already fallen and that he had gone into the bush with Isaac King and brought down a young bull moose that would provide plenty meat for the winter. Benita read the letter aloud to Miriam and Kathleen and noticed that Miriam was inattentive, showing little interest in the news from home. Already, it seemed, her daughter was moving away from her old life and getting caught up in the world of white people. Later that evening, Benita became lost in her own thoughts and snapped to attention only when Miriam's cross voice intruded .

"You're not listening to me, Ma. I keep trying to tell you I need stuff for the bake sale at school tomorrow. Can we make cupcakes before you go to work?"

Kathleen, sitting by the window with the late edition of the Vancouver Sun, looked up. "What's the bake sale for, Sweetheart?"

"It's to raise money for the Indian Missions."

"Is that right? And here was me thinking the missions were all in Africa and South America. I thought that India was a lost cause altogether. Isn't the whole place full of Hindus?"

"Not those Indians! Our kind of Indians! Sister Martha said the bake sale money is to help Indians like me get a Catholic education."

Benita was sitting with Hepzibah's letter still open in front of her. She folded it carefully and put it back in its envelope.

"Indians like you, huh? Is that what your teacher said?"

"Yup. She said that I was one of the lucky ones, but there are other little girls and boys stuck on reservations up north who are very poor and their parents can't look after them so they have to go away to school."

"And what did you say?"

"I said I didn't know any kids like that. I said that she should come up to LaPierre some day and see *our* school, and Sister said did we learn about Jesus at school, and I said no, but we learned all about Jesus at home and from the priest when he came to the village. Then she said, 'Well, we need to raise money for children less fortunate than you, Miriam.' So *now* can we make cupcakes?"

Benita said nothing more, but Kathleen knew from her silence and tension that she was angry. She folded her newspaper and stood up.

"Why don't you and I make a batch of cupcakes right now, Miriam? Your mother has to leave for work pretty soon. Here,

Benita, have a read of the paper for a few minutes. We'll get those cupcakes in the oven, and then we'll have dinner, okay?"

Indians like you—the words had hit her like a hammer blow and left their mark. She still felt it hours later when she stepped onto the stage and unhooked the black leather corset to reveal her breasts. The skirt would come off next. It was a weeknight and the place was only half full. Nobody showed any interest in her, and wouldn't until she was half naked. Right now she faced a scattering of solitary drinkers who were trying to shut out the world and its troubles for a while.

Usually Benita welcomed an indifferent crowd, saw it as easy money, but tonight she had brought with her her own troubles, as well as a whole lot of anger. While the Kingsway Kings were playing, she had knocked back her usual two stiff shots of rum and coke and now she waited for the buzz of numbed-out euphoria to turn her into Belle. Tonight though, for the first time, it did not come, and without it she was filled with self-loathing, and contempt for those who ogled her.

"You seemed a bit wooden tonight, Belle." Clive intercepted her on her way to the changing room. "Make sure you shake it up a bit tomorrow night, know what I'm saying?"

The following night, she downed three drinks in quick succession, and the sudden rush of alcohol made her dizzy and clumsy. When she was up on stage a wave of nausea swept over her, and she stumbled awkwardly and fell. There were a couple of boos from the floor, and a loud catcall, but also some sympathy.

"Shut up, asshole!" somebody yelled, and to her embarrassment a man climbed up onto the stage and helped her to her feet.

"You okay, Miss?"

"Yeah, I'm fine. Thanks."

Then Clive hustled out to introduce Jimmy and the Jumping Beans, and Benita limped off the stage to a faint round of applause.

The next morning she overslept, and it was Kathleen who walked Miriam to school instead of Benita.

"I'm sorry," she told Miriam when she met her from school that afternoon. It won't happen again."

But it did. And Kathleen was worried.

In November, Kathleen and Benita both attended the parent-teacher interviews at St. Bridget's School. Sister Martha told them what a fine little student Miriam was, how popular she was with her classmates.

"Miriam is a natural leader," the elderly nun said, smiling at Kathleen whom she knew well. "But she's also kind-hearted, truthful, and independent. I'd say that somebody must be setting her a wonderful example at home."

Benita stared at her blankly.

"Yeah, well it sure ain't me, Sister. I'm just a dumb Indian."

For a moment, Sister Martha was stunned into silence and then she snapped, "Now why in heaven's name would you want to say something like that, Mrs. Pigeon?"

Benita all but spat back. "*Miss*! It's *Miss* Pigeon. I'm what you call an unmarried mother. Why don't you check that out with Mrs Kinsella here?"

"Well, I thought that went pretty well," Kathleen said brightly, when they were on their way home again. She felt proud of her granddaughter, but, it had to be said, ashamed of Benita's outburst. Like Sister Martha, she just hadn't been able to see the point of it at all.

Benita stomped along beside her splashing through the puddles on the sidewalk. The rain was coming down hard, and her face was hidden by her umbrella.

"Uh-huh. Kind of depends on whether you're thinking about the white half of Miriam or the Indian half, though, doesn't it?"

"Now that's just *nonsense*." Kathleen's voice was uncharacteristically sharp. "Why on earth would anyone think of her as half of anything? I think of her as Miriam, and I love her to bits."

Benita was silent for a moment. Then she stuck her face beneath Kathleen's umbrella, startling her.

"I know you do," she said. "I do know that."

That night she did not drink at all, and as she stripped and strutted around the stage, she told herself that at least it was better than turning tricks in a back alley like Amelia Joe, or the hookers who sidled into the Blue Flamingo each night to look for customers. Clive was taking a hell of a chance to allow soliciting, she thought. Just a couple of months earlier, the police had raided the Brass Balls Cabaret Club down on Cordova Street and closed the place down for operating as a common bawdy house. It surely wouldn't be long before they hit the Blue Flamingo.

For a couple of days things returned to normal at 56 Winchester Avenue, but then came the incident of the scissors. When Benita was sober she was fully aware of the danger she faced when she was alone on the street, not just as a woman, but a native woman. Months ago, on the advice of Amelia Joe and others, she had taken to carrying a tiny pair of nail scissors whenever she walked alone. They travelled in her jacket pocket where they lay dormant, their vicious little pointed tip nestled in the folds of the fabric. It was not much of a weapon, but Benita felt safer knowing it was there - right up to the time when she had put it to use.

That night, after her shift at the Blue Flamingo, she had decided to swing by the Clarissa Hotel where Amelia Joe now plied her trade. Ever since finding out that Amelia was only sixteen years old rather than the twenty she had claimed to be, Benita had taken to checking up on her from time to time. She was half way down Powell Street when she heard a man cursing, followed by the unmistakable sound of a woman moaning. For a moment she was tempted to keep walking, but when she glanced into the alley she saw that the woman was Amelia.

The man, his fly still gaping open and pants undone, had her by the hair and was swinging his belt at her. The buckle had already done its damage to one side of her face where blood welled from a gash over her right eye and streamed down her cheek.

"You lousy piece of Indian shit!" He lunged at her again, his belt lashing her neck and shoulders. "Five bucks is all you're worth, you ugly whore."

Amelia cowered against the wall in a futile attempt to protect her head from his blows, and he tightened his grip on her hair and swung her around to face him. The guy's back was to Benita and she did not hesitate. She reached into her coat pocket, drew out the scissors, gripped them tightly, and drove their pointed end into his white, larded, fleshy buttocks.

He roared in pain and let go of Amelia. When he turned to face Benita, she saw not a fat, white slob, but a wounded bull moose, maddened by pain and deadly dangerous. Screaming curses, she stabbed blindly with the scissors again and again, neither knowing nor caring what damage she was inflicting, until he took off down the alley and she was stabbing at nothing at all. Not until she heard Amelia yelling her name over and over did she stop her attack, stop screaming, and finally stand in silence, trembling and shaking and staring at the bloodied scissors in her hand.

That night she did not go home at all. Clinging to each other, she and Amelia made their way to the room Amelia rented by the week. There was a full bottle of cheap wine on the window ledge, and they emptied half of it before Benita could stop shaking enough to be able to set to work on Amelia's face.

"Might need some stitches," she said, surveying the damage. The bleeding had slowed, but continued to seep through the damp wash cloth she had used to clean the wounds and soothe the welts left by the belt buckle.

"Nah, I'll be okay," said Amelia. "I can see fine, and my mouth's not swollen up too bad."

But the wine was working on Benita, making her loud and aggressive.

"You know what? That animal got away too easy. He needs to be hunted down and put in a cage. The cops should go after him before he kills somebody."

"Yeah, as if that would ever happen." Amelia sniggered. "The police don't give a damn about us Indians. We're for arresting, not protecting. There was this one girl, eh? She had a room right down the hall from me. A couple months ago she took a guy there and he stabbed her over and over and then took off. She crawled out into the passage way and another girl found her there. She ran and got somebody to call the cops and an ambulance, but soon as she gave the address of this place they weren't interested. It took five phone calls before they showed up and by that time she'd bled to death. If they'd've phoned from a rich white neighbourhood they'd've come running, you can bet. Another girl, she got stabbed right outside of a strip joint over on Wall Street. They never even tried to find out who killed her. To them, all she was is just another native hooker. Them's the kind'a murders that don't get written up in the newspapers. Everybody knows that."

Amelia had never spoken at such length before. Benita let her ramble on until the bottle was empty and the bleeding had slowed to a trickle. Then she stretched out on the bed, still fully clothed.

"Stay here with me, Benita, okay?" she said, closing her eyes. "Just till I fall asleep, eh?"

In the morning, when there was no response to Kathleen's persistent knocking, Miriam went into her mother's room and found that the bed had not been slept in. She said nothing, just got her stuff ready for school and walked in silence beside her grandmother, the two of them bundled up against the driving rain and the skittery wind that gusted around them.

When they reached St. Bridget's, Miriam finally spoke.

"Do you think she's okay, Granny? I'm kind of worried about her these days, and I don't know what to do about it.

When she had disappeared through the school doors, the same doors that Larry and Renzo and Molly had gone through all those years before, Kathleen went into the church next door and lit three candles, one for Larry, one for Miriam, and one for Benita.

"Help her, Lord," she prayed. "We're losing her, and I don't know how to get her back." Then she prayed to the Blessed Virgin. "Mary, Mother of us all, protect Benita from darkness and despair. Give her the strength to turn back to the light and be a good mother to our precious Miriam."

Then she went home to wait for Benita. For a while she sat by the window and stared out at the skeletal trees that lined the street, their bare branches shuddering in a wind that swirled among them before rising up to push the grey clouds into billowing mounds. She felt as bleak as the wintry scene outside. It was almost December, but Christmas seemed too far away to think about, as if this year it might not happen at all. But happen it would, and she would do her best to make it special, if only for Miriam. The thought of Miriam snapped her out of her gloomy mood. She got up and filled the kettle, and while she was waiting for the water to boil, she went and got a pen and note pad from the drawer. Then she made herself a cup of tea and sat down to write a long letter to Larry.

November slunk off with the fog, and dark December crept in, damp and chilly. Miriam came home from school elated because she had been chosen by her classmates to be Mary in the Christmas Pageant.

"I'm *so* happy," she told Benita. "I thought for sure I'd end up as a stupid angel or something and just have to stand around with a halo on my head, singing carols."

"Could have been worse, though," Benita said. "You could have been the donkey."

"No, that's a fat kid called Phillip. He volunteered for it."

"Well, that's wonderful news, Miriam," said her grandmother. "I can't think of a more perfect Mary than you."

Miriam flipped her long braids back. "I dunno about *that*. I wish I was a bit shorter. Joseph only comes up to my shoulder."

Kathleen laughed. "Poor little Joseph. Maybe he'll get a bit of a growth spurt before Christmas. Not that it matters to us, right Benita? We'll only be looking at Mary anyway."

Caught up in the excitement of the pageant and all the pre-Christmas activities at school, Miriam seemed not to notice that Benita no longer woke up in time to walk her to St. Bridget's. If she was aware that sometimes her mother arrived home in the early hours of the morning in a drunken stupor, she did not comment on it, either to Benita or to Kathleen. And if Benita ever noticed the dark circles under Miriam's eyes, she made no mention of it.

On the afternoon of the pageant, with not a sign still of Benita, Kathleen grew alarmed. Had she come home at all the night before? She rapped again at the bedroom door, and when she pushed it open, she was hit by the vaporous fumes of alcohol that filled the room like a deadly miasma. Pushing aside the thick curtains she opened the window wide letting in gusts of cold, clean air. Then she crossed the room and shook Benita, gently at first, then harder.

"Come on now, Benita. It's Miriam's pageant today. This is no day to be sleeping in. Time to wake up!"

Benita opened her eyes and gazed up at her blearily. She looked dreadful. Her skin had a yellowish tinge, her eyes were swollen and bloodshot, and last night's mascara had streaked and run down her cheeks.

"What time is it?" she croaked. "I feel really sick. I must be coming down with the flu or something."

The flu me eye, thought Kathleen. *I'd say it's more of the "or something"*.

Out loud, though, she said, "Let's see if we can do something about that, shall we? We don't want you missing the pageant."

She went downstairs and, a few minutes later, returned with a tray. Benita had managed to prop herself up in bed but her eyes were closed against the bright wintry light that flooded the room. She moaned softly.

"Headache bad?" Kathleen asked. Benita nodded mutely.

"Here, swallow these and drink this down with them."

She handed Benita two aspirins and a glass of fizzy Alka-Seltzer, and when the glass was empty, she gave her strong black coffee and waited until the cup was empty.

"That should do the trick. It's what I used to give to Charlie, God rest his soul. He used to get the flu every Christmas and Easter, regular as clockwork—sometimes on his birthday too. Now get out of bed and go and take a nice hot bath. After that you'll feel as right as rain."

For the Christmas pageant, Miriam wore a blue veil that covered her long dark hair and framed her oval face. When she appeared on stage accompanied by the diminutive Joseph, Kathleen nudged Benita, and they both smiled when the holy couple reached the stable and Miriam sank to her knees beside the manger.

"She's a good little problem solver, isn't she?" Kathleen whispered. "Now he's taller than her."

It had been Miriam's own idea, the kneeling thing. She had suggested it to Mr. Carswell who taught PE and drama and was in charge of this year's Primary Pageant.

"Your knees will get sore, Miriam. It's a long time to be kneeling."

"I don't care. If I don't kneel, Baby Jesus gets stuck with a giant mother and a midget dad. I'm gonna kneel."

But she soon discovered that Mr. Carswell was right. Her knees were sore already and they still hadn't got to the part where the Wise Men arrived with the gold, frankincense, and myrrh. Maybe she should have stayed standing after all. Baby Jesus wouldn't have cared. At least he had two parents when he was born. And at least they had stuck around when he was growing up. Hers sure hadn't. Okay, so she did have a father now. Sort of. But really, what use was a father who was a priest in Rome? No, when it came right down to it, and not counting her three grandmothers, she only had Benita, and it was a big relief to know that her mother was out there in the audience right now watching her and not off somewhere getting drunk. Miriam had seen plenty of drunk people in Blanchette, women as well as men, and Jericho George had told her over and over again how much trouble alcohol caused. Her mother was a good person, and she loved her alright, but she was a big headache to Miriam these days, and she didn't know what to do about it. When she had talked it over with her teacher, Sister Martha had reached out and put her arms around her.

"I know, Miriam. Your poor mother's going through a bit of a rough time right now, and all we can do is pray for her."

Which was fine, but Miriam had already been doing that for weeks and, as far as she could see, it wasn't doing a darn bit of good. So she had done the next best thing. She'd written a long letter to Father Larry. He might be able to give her some ideas.

After the pageant, Kathleen took Miriam to the Dairy Queen for a burger and a strawberry milkshake. Benita, with nothing but two aspirin in her stomach, was still feeling weak and nauseous and ate nothing at all.

"I'll get something later on," she told Kathleen. Miriam, working her way through a mound of French fries, looked up.

"So was I a good Mary?" she asked.

"You were just beautiful, darling," Kathleen reached over and stroked her cheek. "Wait till you see the photos I took of you. We'll have to get copies made and send them up to LaPierre. Wasn't she great, Benita?"

"The best Mary there ever was, that's for sure."

Kathleen laughed nervously. "Apart from the real one, of course."

"Well, *she's* been gone for almost two thousand years, so for me Miriam's the real thing."

God help us all, Kathleen thought, and went to order a banana split for Miriam.

Benita stood up too. "Time for me to get going. No rush for you, though. Your granny will take you home. Hey, I'm real proud of you, Mirri."

Miriam looked up at her mother. "Good, but do you think you'll be able to take me to school in the morning?"

"Sure I will. I promise."

And Kathleen, back with Miriam's banana split, thought, *Oh dear.*

Benita stepped out into a cold, clear night. It was the kind of night when you could expect to see a star blanket in the sky above LaPierre. Here in the city, though, the smog and the street lights shut out the stars, and only the moon was visible. All the way to the Blue Flamingo she fought with herself, determined not to drink at all so as to arrive home sober, but when she got there she could not bring herself to take off her clothes without a rum and coke.

She waited for the alcohol to release her from herself, and when it did not happen, she downed a second shot, and then another. She was drunk by the time she reached the stage and while the jukebox pumped out its noise she fumbled with the hooks of her leather bustier.

"Want some help, little lady? Hell, you're drunk as a skunk. Let me give you a hand."

A white guy jumped onto the stage and Benita felt his hands on her body. In a haze of rage and wild panic her nails clawed and slashed at his face, and when she drew blood he let go of her and swore viciously. The crowd on the floor roared its approval, and Clive had half a mind to let them fight it out for a while longer, let the crowd have its fun—might be good for business. Then he saw that Belle looked about ready to pass out so he strong-armed the guy down to the floor and set him up with a couple of free drinks. He half carried, half dragged Benita to the changing room at the back of the nightclub and tossed her clothes at her.

"You're drunk, and you're fired, Belle. The only job you'll ever get now is down on the corner of Hastings and Main with the rest of your kind. You'll find lots of your friends already down there. Now get dressed and get lost."

The rest of the night passed in a blur. Benita had no memory of getting into her street clothes, nor of leaving the Blue Flamingo, and when she found herself out on the street and felt the bitter sting of the cold, she discovered that she had left her jacket behind. There was a liquor store still open on the corner and she went in and bought a screw-top bottle of California Red. Out on the street again she opened the bag, unscrewed the cap and drank deeply. *Just need to warm up a bit*, she thought.

She was so cold; shaky, too, from lack of food and from the alcohol already in her system.

"You're drunk and you're fired. You're drunk and you're fired." She heard herself mumbling the phrase out loud and it scared her.

"You're drunk and you're fired and you're prob'ly crazy too."

She crossed Main Street and started to laugh. *Guess Larry's old man was right about you from the get-go.* She stopped on East Pender and drank from the bottle again, and after that she stopped feeling cold, stopped feeling anything at all. She knew where she was going.

She was going to hang out with her friend, a friend who wouldn't look down on somebody who was drunk and fired and half-crazy.

When she got to Powell Street she saw Amelia standing outside the Clarissa Hotel, but when she tried to call out to her she couldn't get her tongue to move, couldn't get the name out. She stepped off the curb to cross the street and found that her legs had turned to rubber and wouldn't carry her in a straight line. She teetered into the middle of the road and stopped there, mesmerized by the lights of a car coming straight at her.

"Go 'way." She held up her brown bag like a traffic baton. "I was here first. Scram!"

Somebody screamed her name, and she heard the screech of tires followed by violent cursing. Then she felt herself being half-carried, half dragged to the sidewalk.

"What the hell are you up to, Benita? You damn near got hit by that car. Are you trying to get yourself killed?"

"Maybe. Who are you? An angel?"

Benita giggled and handed the almost empty bottle to Amelia.

"Here," I got you a present," she said, and then she was violently sick.

Amelia took off her coat, wrapped it around Benita and managed to get her off the street and up to her room. She cleaned her up and made her drink black coffee before she spoke again.

"This is no good, Benita. You gotta smarten up, or you're not gonna be able to take care of your kid."

"I got fired tonight," Benita said. She started to shiver even though the room was hot and stuffy. "I'm drunk, and I'm fired and I can't even walk Miriam to school in the morning. I'm good for nothing, Amelia."

"Bullshit. You're the best person I know. Now quit your snivelling and go to sleep. I'm gonna wake you up in a couple hours and put you in a taxi. You need to get home. Take my coat when you go. There's ten bucks in the pocket for the fare."

But it turned out that getting a cab to stop and pick up a fare from the Clarissa Hotel was a challenge in itself.

"I don't stop for hookers," one driver yelled out the window when Amelia tried to flag him down. Most slowed to a crawl, glanced out the window at them, and kept right on going.

"It's because there's two of us," Amelia said. "How 'bout I disappear and you try on your own?"

"Take your coat then, said Benita. You're gonna freeze your ass off in this weather."

"Nah, you need it more than I do." She grinned. "Besides, it's covered in puke. How'm I gonna pick up guys with that stink on me?"

It was already daylight when the taxi pulled up at 56, Winchester Avenue, and Benita thought she might be too late. The door opened while she was still fumbling with the key, and Kathleen did not comment on her pallor and shakiness, nor on the smell of stale vomit that emanated from her.

"Come in, Pet," she said instead. "There's a little girl here who's going to be very happy to see you. She said she wasn't going to go to school this morning without you."

Miriam was sitting at the kitchen table in front of her untouched breakfast, and Benita's heart turned over when she saw that she had been crying. Miriam almost never cried.

"I'm kinda wrecked, Miriam," she said, "But I made it. Let's go shall we?"

Miriam sniffed and wiped her eyes.

"Huh," she said. "I knew all the time you'd come. I kept telling Granny you'd take me to school today for sure because you promised. My stuff's right there by the door. We're gonna be late, but I don't care."

CHAPTER THIRTY-SIX

The newly elected pontiff, Pope Paul VI, opened the second session of Vatican Two at the end of September, almost a month after my return to Rome. In those early days of his papacy, he had confounded all expectations, first by continuing with the Council, and then by inviting many additional lay observers, both Catholic and non-Catholic, to attend. The aims of the session were far-reaching and ambitious, and I was happy to devote myself to my role as adviser. It was a relief to be able to focus my mind on matters of the Church again instead of the perplexing situation I had left behind me in Vancouver, and I was determined to shut out all distraction and concentrate on the task at hand.

After the session ended on December 4th. I carried on with the work of producing statements of fundamental propositions in preparation for their approval during the third session.

I had made plans to spend Christmas in Assisi, at the shrine of the beloved Saint Francis. But then had come the letter from my mother followed not long afterward by a worrisome letter from Miriam which compelled me to revise my plans and fly home. I got into Vancouver a few days before Christmas, and this time I went straight to the Cathedral and booked myself into the rectory for the holiday period. They were only too glad to have me there at one of the busiest times in the church year, and I knew I would be putting in long hours in the confessional. Those were still the days when no practicing Catholic would dream of receiving holy communion on Christmas Day unshriven.

When I got to the house, things seemed tranquil enough. Miriam gave me a rapturous welcome and my mother was clearly relieved to see me.

"Thank you for coming, Pet," she said as she put on the kettle for my first cup of tea. "I'm afraid I'm out of my depth here."

Benita was nowhere to be seen and neither was Trice.

"She took him out for a walk," my mother told me. "I think she wanted to be out of the house when you got here."

It was dark by four o'clock, and Miriam switched on the lights of the Christmas tree she had helped decorate the day before. The three of us sat in the semi-dark with the coloured lights casting a soft glow over the room, and Miriam said it made her feel Christmassy. She and my mother had set up the nativity scene on the coffee table, and the little grey donkey with the chipped ear stood at Mary's side in the same spot he had stood every Christmas of my life. I told Miriam about the time I had dropped one of the kings and his hand had snapped off and he'd lost his pot of gold.

"Were you sad about it?"

"Very sad. But then your grandfather went and got his crazy glue and fixed him up as good as new."

Miriam wanted to inspect Dad's repair job, but my mother told her she was not to disturb the manger scene until after the twelfth day.

"Why?" she asked.

"Because it's bad luck," said my mother in exactly the same *don't-argue-with-me* voice she had used on me when I was a child.

"Okay then," said Miriam, and when she caught my eye I winked at her.

I waited with the two of them until it was time to leave for evening Mass at the cathedral, but I did not see Benita until the following day. When I did, I was shocked. She had lost weight and her eyes were sunken in her face, her skin sallow and oily. It wasn't her appearance that disturbed me though as much as the air of defeat that hung over her like a cloud, and the submissive, almost apologetic manner with which she greeted me. She looked as if her spirit had given up and left her, and I could see why my mother and Miriam were worried. She was in a bad state, that much was clear, and I asked myself what, if anything, I could do to help her. She said little during lunch and turned me down flat when I suggested a trip downtown to show Miriam the Woodwards Christmas windows.

"You guys go. I'm kinda tired. Think I'll take a nap."

But later, when I dropped off Miriam and my mother before heading back to the cathedral, we found Trice alone in the house, yapping with indignation at having been deprived of his afternoon walk.

"Don't worry," my mother told Miriam. "She's probably doing a bit of Christmas shopping."

Miriam thought about that for a moment and shook her head. "Doubt it," she said.

And I did too.

When I arrived at Holy Rosary, people were already lined up outside the confessionals and only one was still unoccupied. I went in and switched on the red light, and while I waited for the first penitent, I checked the time on my watch. With all four confessionals in use, I figured we'd be able to clear the line-up well before the start of evening Mass, and I said a quick prayer that through this sacrament I was about to administer, people would receive the grace to be open to God's infinite love and mercy.

For the next twenty-five minutes I listened to the usual litany of misdemeanours: pride, selfishness, dishonesty, impatience, overindulgence in alcohol or food, bad language, impure thoughts; and a few that were more serious such as fraud, theft, assault, and adultery. In short, people were up to their same old tricks and there was nothing new under heaven.

As always, I waited an extra couple of minutes to allow for a last-minute rush, and I was just about to make my getaway when the penitent's door opened once again. I administered the blessing and bent my ear to listen, but this time I heard something quite different from the usual "Bless me, Father" lead-in to the sacrament.

"Don't bother with any of that priest stuff, Larry. I just need you to sit there and let me talk for a while. If I say it out loud, it might help me to make some sense of things. I seem to have ended up in the gutter and I'm really scared."

I shut my mouth and let her talk, and she began with the incident outside the beer parlour up in Prince George and continued right up to the night she got fired from the Blue Flamingo. At some point I switched the red light off to show that confessions were no longer being heard. At some point Mass began on the main altar, but Benita kept on talking, and I kept on listening.

"So I guess I'm my father's daughter after all. I'm a violent drunk. When I stabbed that guy in the alley, I wanted to hurt him. Hell, I wanted to kill him, and I know I would have done it too if I'd been holding a knife instead of a pair of scissors. And when I stood in the street the night I was drunk and saw that car coming at me, I wanted it to hit me. See, I really don't care any more if I live or die. The only thing that's holding me together is Miriam, but whenever I think of her, the innocence of her, the goodness, I tell myself that I'm not worthy to be her mother. In other words, I'm pretty much fucked, Larry. I guess your dad was right about me after all. You should have listened to him right from the start."

The bitter monologue came to an abrupt halt, and I thought for a moment that she might cry. She did not.

"I don't believe in God's forgiveness any more," she said. "So no Latin mumbo-jumbo from you now, okay?"

"Okay, but will you at least let me give you a blessing, Benita?"

I spoke in barely a whisper, so it is possible that she did not hear me. She had been kneeling in the dark, her face hidden. Now there was a brief flicker of light on the other side of the grille as the door opened and closed, and then she was gone.

Perhaps it would have been wiser to stay right where I was, just to sit there in silence and collect my thoughts for a while, but I didn't. Instead, I removed my stole, pushed open the door of the confessional and left the cathedral through the side door, still wearing my long black cassock. I saw Benita trudging along Dunsmuir Street, shoulders hunched, head down, and it didn't look as if confession had done anything to lighten the enormous burden she was carrying. And yet she had chosen to share it with me. That was what I had taken to heart. I caught up with her, put my hand on her elbow so as not to alarm her, spoke her name. She spun around, saw that it was me, and shook off my hand.

"I'm all talked out, Larry. I don't want your blessing or your advice. Thank you for letting me say what I had to say. I know who I am, and now so do you. All we need to talk about is Miriam. But not right now."

I heard a spark of life in her voice that had not been there before and it gave me hope.

"I know all that, Benita. I only chased you down to see what you think about about an idea I've just had."

"What's that? Join Alcoholics Anonymous? Sorry. Not interested."

We had reached the Hudson Bay department store on Georgia Street and we were surrounded by throngs of Christmas shoppers.."

I stopped walking, grabbed her arm, and edged her over to the side of the road to avoid getting bumped by people in a rush to get somewhere fast.

"You know, Benita, I listened to you while you said your piece. Now it's your turn to shut up and listen. It will take less than a minute of your time. Do you think you can give me that much?"

When I told her about my plan for Christmas Day she stared at me in disbelief.

"You know what? That has to be the craziest suggestion I ever heard."

I said nothing more; let her think about it for a while. By that time we were getting a few odd looks from passers-by and it dawned on me that I wasn't in Rome any more. In Vancouver, as in the rest of North America, a priest wearing a cassock outside the church had already become a rare sight. I turned to leave and felt Benita grab my arm.

"Hey, Larry, know what I'm thinking right now? I'm thinking that you might be a little bit crazy, but you're really not such a bad guy." Then she smiled. "For a white man that is."

On the morning of Christmas Eve, my mother and Benita took Miriam to the Hudson Bay to do some last minute shopping and I went over to see the Rosettis. Renzo and Molly had driven down from Kamloops to spend Christmas with his parents and now their little house was filled with the noise of children and the enticing aromas of a traditional Italian kitchen. It was great to see all of them again but the visit was short and I spent the rest of the day at the cathedral preparing for midnight Mass and hearing last-minute confessions.

That night, as I followed the Archbishop down the aisle in solemn procession to the accompaniment of "Adeste Fideles," I saw my mother up front with Miriam beside her, and next to her, Benita, Renzo, and Molly. It was the sight of all the people I loved standing together in front of the altar that made me feel again the promise of Christmas, season of hope, when goodness seems possible and sadness is displaced by joy.

I was less sure about that the following day, however, when not even the spirit of Christmas was enough to disguise the bleakness and squalor of the Clarissa Hotel.

"Looks kind of run-down, huh? Just like the place my mom used to stay at before we moved in with Granny."

It was early afternoon on Christmas Day, and Miriam and I were sitting in my rental car looking out at the grim streetscape that surrounded us. *No Christmas joy to be had here*, I thought, and wondered what on earth had prompted me to come up with such a crazy suggestion. What had I been thinking? Then we saw Benita emerge from the hotel, and with her a young woman teetering along the sidewalk in a short tight dress and outrageously high heels. Miriam hopped out of the car and opened the back door for them.

Benita said, "Hi, guys. This is my friend, Amelia Joe."

I could only guess at the thoughts that went through my mother's head later that afternoon as we sat down to eat our Christmas dinner. And had my father lived to witness the sight of a native hooker from the Downtown Eastside seated at his dining table, I think he might have chosen that very moment to keel over and enter the next life. But maybe not. It was possible that even Dad might have been able to recall that Christ had befriended prostitutes and sinners and had embraced those who were outcast from mainstream society.

Possible, I thought, *although highly unlikely.*

Mom had taken precautionary measures and discreetly hidden away all the alcohol in the house. Instead of wine there was a bottle of grape juice on the table and Benita laughed when she saw it.

"No need for the rest of you to drink that stuff at Christmas, Kathleen. Leave it for me and Miriam. When we got back from Mass last night, I made her a promise that I'm all through with drinking. She's never gonna see me drunk again."

"She'll stick to it too," said Miriam. "My mom always keeps her promises."

"That's for sure," Amelia said. "And I'm gonna have some of that there grape juice too. I don't need no wine today."

The rest of us had exchanged gifts earlier in the day, but after dinner, Amelia opened the big box that had been set aside for her under the tree and took out the stylish black wool coat that Benita and my mother had found for her at the Bay the day before.

"Oh my God!" she said when she saw it. "I never had a brand-new coat before. This is beautiful!"

Benita made her try it on for size and she strutted up and down the room like a model.

"You look real pretty," Miriam told her, and it was true. Dressed in her new coat and flattered by the soft lights of Christmas, Amelia did look pretty, and I saw too that she looked like the child she still was. My mother asked her to spend the rest of the night at our place, but she said no, that she had to work later, so I told her I would drop her off downtown.

"Okay then," she said. "But better bring Benita along too, Father, or the cops might think you're a customer."

Benita smirked and I saw my mother blanch and make a discreet sign of the cross, but Miriam wanted to know what kind of store would be open even on Christmas Day.

"Just the one I work at, Honey," Amelia told her. "It stays open real late every day of the year, so I gotta get back on the job."

Miriam pouted. "But don't you want to play 'Sorry' with us? I'm allowed to stay up as late as I want tonight. You *can't* go now! I'll even let you sleep in my bed if you want."

Amelia glanced at the Christmas tree in the corner and then at the little crib scene on the coffee table, and for a moment, it looked as if she might change her mind.

"I'd sure like to stay here with you guys. This has been the best Christmas of my whole life. But I gotta work. I'm trying to make lots of money so's I can go back home one day. Then you can all come visit me at my house."

She gave Miriam a goodbye kiss and thanked my mother for inviting her. When she was halfway out the door she turned back.

"Hey, Miriam, when you come to my new house, you can show me how to play that Sorry game, okay?"

We dropped her off at the Clarissa Hotel, and when we were driving back through the desolate streets of the Downtown Eastside Benita said, "You know something, Larry? She's only sixteen years old but that kid did her best to turn me in my tracks and stop my slide down to hell. She's like my little sister, and I feel like I have to take care of her somehow."

"You mean get her off the street?"

Benita looked over at me.

"Where would she go? She's got this idea about making a pile of money and going back to the reserve in Cranbrook, but life there wasn't too great for her either. Plenty of women get beat up on the reserves. Most of them just put up with it."

It struck me that she might be thinking about her own mother and about her abusive father, Johnny Pigeon.

"I figure the street's really all that Amelia knows, Larry. She's used to getting beat up. Once she even laughed about it, told me that guys pay her extra to do stuff their wives won't put up with."

"But that's monstrous!" I said. "Normal men don't beat their wives."

"You think? And how would you know anything about normal men, Father Kinsella?"

I turned off Hastings onto Main Street and followed it past the old clock that stood at the entrance to Mount Pleasant. For a while neither of us spoke.

"I'm sorry, Larry. I shouldn't have said that. You did a good thing for Amelia today. But you can't change other people, you can only change yourself."

"Okay," I said. "But can we talk about the future for a bit, Benita? Yours, I mean. And Miriam's. Next week it will be 1964, a new year and a new start to things. Have you thought about what you're going to do?"

"What I want to do is go home, Larry, but not like this, a failure. I want to be someone that Miriam can be proud of. I want to help my own people up in LaPierre but I just don't know how to do it. I'm kinda lost, and I'm still scared I could end up on the street like Amelia. What it comes down to, I guess, is that I'm real afraid of the future."

It was my turn to say nothing, and that was just fine with Benita. She had always been comfortable with silence, just like her mother, Clara, so when we reached Winchester Avenue, I drew up in front of the house, parked, and pondered for a while. It was almost nine o'clock, and I knew that Miriam would be waiting for us, knew too that I might not get another chance to be alone with Benita. Every house in the street was lit up, with Christmas trees on display in front windows and wreaths on most of the doors. With all of its letdowns and disappointments, its surfeits and over-indulgences, its petty squabbles and fractiousness, this was still the most hopeful day of the year and nobody wanted to turn out the lights and bring it to an end. Perhaps because of that, I decided to take a chance.

"I know," I said into the silence.

Benita turned to face me. "Know what?"

"What you could do."

"Is this another crazy idea of yours?"

"Maybe," I said, and told her what I had come up with.

"No," she said when I stopped talking. "No way."

When I did not respond, did not argue with her or attempt to persuade her, she said, "What's behind this plan of yours, Larry? Is it because of Miriam? Or is it because you want to control my life?"

She was scared and confused, but at the same time hopeful. I wanted to take her hand and tell her not to worry, that everything would be alright, but I was afraid to touch her. I had touched her long ago and that touch had brought only turmoil and disruption into both of our lives. I still blamed myself for everything bad that had happened to her, so now I kept my distance and tried to speak to her as if she were just another troubled soul seeking guidance from a priest.

"Only you have control over your life, Benita."

But even to my *own* ears the words sounded pompous and condescending, and I saw from her expression that I was losing her. So I told her the truth. I told her I had been thinking about when both of us were still at school and she had been studying literature and had come across a saying of Oscar Wilde's that had stuck with her.

"You told me about it one day in the lunch room at Woodwards. You had the book with you. Do you remember?"

I could see her searching her memory, trying to retrieve words stored there long ago, and then her eyes lit up.

"'All of us are in the gutter but some of us are looking at the stars.' Wasn't it Oscar Wilde who said that? I thought it was beautiful, but you said it was just sentimental."

"I was young and conceited then. I guess that life has made me a bit humbler. These days I'm not so sure about a lot of things, Benita. But I *am* sure about this: what I'm trying to do right now is to get you to look at the stars."

CHAPTER THIRTY-SEVEN

I did not go home again for almost three years. Air travel from Rome was expensive, and even though Cormac O'Carroll had been able to secure a full scholarship to cover Benita's studies at UBC, I was still making hefty monthly contributions to Miriam's trust fund. Besides, I did not want Benita to think I was checking up on her or trying to direct her life in any way. So by the time I got back in Vancouver again, Benita had already graduated with a Bachelor's degree in Social Work. The first few letters I had received from her had been about her studies, her fellow-students, and how hard she had found it to adjust to being back in the classroom.

"My classmates are all so young!" she had written. "and so full of life. They make me feel like an old lady!"

But old lady or not, she had outshone them all and had earned her degree with distinction.

Miriam's letters were more frequent, and from them I learned about her teachers, her sports teams, her many friends, and Trice who, she said, seemed to think he was her dog now, a notion seconded by my mother.

"The two of them have energy to burn," she had written in one of her early letters. "I'd say they were made for each other."

So it was a forlorn little dog I found when I returned to Vancouver at the end of July. He still waited hopefully by the front door each evening, fully expecting Benita and Miriam to return, but they were long gone and wouldn't be coming back. Shortly after their arrival in Blanchette. Benita had written,

I don't want Miriam to forget where she comes from, Larry. Not that she'll be here forever. She couldn't stay even if she wanted to. I don't need to remind you that she was born out of wedlock to an Indian mother and a white father, which means she has no Indian status. But she's very bright, and she has her grandmother down in Vancouver, so I figure she'll probably go back there when it's time for university. As for me, the Department of Indian Affairs has given me a job as a social worker. Pretty ironic, huh? Benita Pigeon working for the government!

Eventually she hoped to get involved with the Dena'dzlie Tribal Council and, with their support, launch a campaign to establish an alcohol-free reserve as some of the Ojibway people in Ontario were trying to do.

Up here on our reserves, there was no access to alcohol before 1940, and many of our people's problems began when it was first introduced. We know now that alcoholism contributes to neglect of children, violent assault, and domestic abuse, as well as serious health problems like diabetes and liver disease. I figure that in the future our people are going to have way more control over the land, so we need to be ready to take that on and to be responsible for our own welfare. I still have a lot of anger inside of me, Larry, but now I'm going to use it to fight domestic violence, not white people!

It was hard to know what Miriam thought about her mother's decision. In September, she would have entered Grade Seven at St. Bridget's. The move north had meant losing her friends, her home, her grandmother, and her dog. But Miriam had faced big changes before and had proved herself resilient and adaptable. I had faith in her ability to cope with the move and I was happy she was with her mother. It was my own mother I worried about now, although when I broached the subject she deftly redirected my concern back to the dog.

"Poor old Trice. He misses the pair of them terribly," she said. "And he's lost altogether without Miriam to take him for walks and throw the ball for him."

Mom had lost weight since the last time I'd seen her, but when I mentioned it she shrugged it off impatiently.

"Give me some credit now, Larry, would you? I'm not some shrinking violet that's going to fade away altogether. I just have to get used to being on my own again, and you can rest assured that I'll be fine. I still have my friends, I have the Church, and I have Trice for company. And I'll tell you something else, Larry. I think what Benita has decided to do with her life is splendid, and that's the truth. It's just the child I'm worried about. I'm thinking that life on the reserve is going to be hard on her. It would have been different maybe if they'd gone back to LaPierre, but my guess is that Blanchette is a rough old place altogether."

She might be worried about Miriam, I thought, but she would surely hit the roof when I told her about my own plans for the future. As we headed across town at noon the next day I felt as if I was on my way to a dental appointment instead of lunch at the White Spot. Before setting out, she had insisted that I change back into the clerical suit and Roman collar I had abandoned in favour of the stylish summer clothes I had brought with me from Rome.

"But, Ma, it's not required of priests any more, at least not for casual family occasions like today."

The look she gave me was withering.

"Don't you be telling me that, Larry. Another brick torn out of the foundation of Holy Mother Church, thanks to Vatican Two. That new Pope of ours has a lot to answer for, letting himself be pushed into all sorts of new-fangled liberal ways. Well, I still believe that a priest should stand out in a crowd and be proud of the collar he wears to show the rest of the world that he was called by God. So put it on now, Pet. I'll not be having any of this modern malarkey. God bless us, the next thing you'll be doing is growing your hair long and wearing sandals like those hippies down in San Francisco."

We found a table by the window overlooking the wide sweep of Georgia Street. Traffic was heavy, with cars heading to Stanley Park or over the Lions Gate Bridge to the North Shore, and on this glittering day in high summer, Vancouver was at its glorious best. I waited until we had finished our burgers before I broke the news that I had signed on for a year in the Diocese of Prince George and would be replacing Father Hines up in Blanchette.

My mother wiped her mouth with her napkin and sat up straight—an ominous sign, I thought—as I prepared for battle.

"Now why in God's name would you do a thing like that, when you have a great future ahead of you in the Church?"

"I also have a daughter, Ma, in case you've forgotten."

"How could I? No, I'm afraid it's *you* who has forgotten something, Larry. You seem to have forgotten that you're a priest, not a family man. Your vocation is to serve the Catholic Church, not to follow Miriam through life trying to be something you can never be without breaking your vows."

It was foolish of me to plead my case, but I did my best. I tried to explain that I was not interested in climbing the hierarchical ladder, had no desire at all to be a bishop, and believed that my future might lay in serving the needs of the Carrier Nation by living and working among them.

"You're not cut out for missionary work, Larry. And this plan of yours is foolhardy and reckless. Have you given any thought at all to the consequences? Have you thought about what this will do to Benita and Miriam?"

Right up to the moment I said goodbye to her on my last morning in Vancouver, my mother pleaded with me to change my mind about the move north.

"Listen, Larry, go on up to Kamloops and have a nice visit with Molly and Renzo and the children. Go and do a bit of hiking or fishing by yourself and put in some time in prayer. Then listen to Our Lord. Let Him tell you what you should do."

I put my arms around her.

"And what do think Our Lord will tell me to do, Ma?"

"I don't *think* anything, Larry. I already *know*. He'll say, 'Turn around now, son, and get yourself back down to Vancouver. I have you in mind for Archbishop.'"

Then she gave it her final shot. "Maybe even a cardinal one day."

CHAPTER THIRTY-EIGHT

I had bought a two-year old Pontiac Laurentian from a dealership on Kingsway, and the day before I left I drove over to Morice House in Kitsilano to visit Father Hines. He told me that the Lakes region up around Blanchette was prime hunting and fishing territory and that it would be a sin not to take advantage of it. I hadn't fished for years, hadn't fired a rifle since I was a teenager, but when I went home I dug out my fishing rod and Dad's old Winchester from the attic and packed them both in the trunk. Father Hines hadn't offered much in the way of advice but his parting words stayed with me:

"A year won't be enough, Larry, unless it's just a holiday you're after. To do any good up there you have to win the trust of the people, and you won't do that in twelve months. No, I'd say you'd need to give it five years at least." He put a hand on my shoulder and gave me a wink. "And after *that* you won't want to leave at all."

Other than Bishop McFadden, Father Hines was the only person to offer me any encouragement. I certainly didn't get it from Renzo and Molly, both of whom were of the same mind as my mother and appalled by my decision. We managed to avoid the topic entirely until the end of my visit to Kamloops, but their disapproval had been there from the start, lurking in the background much like the tension that existed between the two of them, felt, but suppressed until the time came for me to continue my journey north.

Renzo came out to the car with me and begged me to change my mind. He began by suggesting that I was putting my vows in jeopardy. Then he told me that Benita might not want me in Blanchette and that the people up there would not respect a priest with a child. He talked about Miriam, and the confusion she would be forced to suffer about my role in her life. I listened patiently until Molly came running out to give me a hug and say goodbye. Then I switched on the ignition and put the car in gear. Even then Renzo persisted.

"Larry, listen to me. Go up to Prince George and tell the Bishop you've had second thoughts about your assignment. Tell him you've changed your mind. Then get into the car and drive hell for leather back to Vancouver."

In those days you could smell Prince George long before you reached it. The stink from two major pulp mills drifted across town and into the valleys, and on hot summer days it hung above the city in a noxious haze, especially pungent when combined with the smoke from forest fires. On my way to the Chancery Office the city struck me as insubstantial and flimsy, a frontier town, peopled mainly with loggers, truckers, and Indians.

Bishop Felix McFadden was something of an old-style crusader, full of zeal for the Catholic faith and determined to keep it alive among the indigenous communities of the region. His was the spirit of Father Morice, I thought, the French Oblate missionary in Fort St. James who had created a writing system for the Carrier people and had produced *The Carrier Language: A Grammar and Dictionary*, a major linguistic work. But Father Morice, despite the legacy he left, was said to have been difficult to work with, unfriendly even, something that could never be said of Felix McFadden. He wore a perpetual smile, laughed frequently, and had no time at all for ceremony and formality. I felt cheered by his warm welcome and words of encouragement.

"Larry, if I didn't have complete faith in you as a man and as a priest, I would never send you up to Blanchette. I care far too much about the people to send them someone who might not be able to handle the job. Don't think it's an easy one, though. Poor old Fred Hines was worn out by the time he retired, but he wouldn't let me move him because he loved those people. My guess is that you will too, once you've spent some time with them."

So after an early dinner at the Oblate rectory and a quick prayer in the chapel, I got into my car and turned east onto the gravel road that would take me to Blanchette. The harsh glare of day was veiled in mauve as dusk descended on Prince George, and the few small farms I passed sat serenely in the soft light of evening. For much of the year it was hard to wrest a living from the soil in this bleak region of sub-boreal forest. Now though, in the fading of the summer light, in that brief interlude between the going of the sun and the coming of the stars, it was beautiful.

Then the farms were behind me, and on either side of the road fir trees stood like sentinels as far as the eye could see. Beyond them were the lakes, Kluskis, Trembleur, Babine, Takla, Stuart, Fraser, none of them within sight of this lonely highway with its potholes and flying rocks. Here there were no houses, no lights, no other cars, nothing to distract me but hope and uncertainty.

I am not so clear any more about the right and the wrong of things but I pray that the road I am now taking will lead me to a good place. I have given my life to God in atonement for the sin of my youth, but I have not yet made reparation to Benita for the harm I did to her, and Miriam, my daughter, will be part of my life forever. I can let neither of them go.

Is that wrong? Is it wrong to love them? I do not believe so. As for the native people of Blanchette, I know already that many of them will not trust my whiteness and for that I cannot blame them. It will be difficult to replace Father Hines, even if I were to take his advice and stay for five years or longer. And although I know, despite my mother's forebodings, that Miriam will welcome me and find a place for me in her life, I am less certain about Benita. Will she perhaps see me as an intruder, a violator even, of her sacred space? I hope not, but if she tells me to go, I will leave at the end of a year. I used to be so sure of the road ahead of me but I am no longer certain of anything, least of all the future.

A holy man once told me that that we all need to be humbled by some kind of failure or suffering before God can reach down and lead us from darkness into the light. Oscar Wilde had it right. We are all in the gutter, but some of us are looking at the stars. The way down is also the way up, and the way back is sometimes the only way forward. That seems to have been true for Benita. I hope it will be true for me, too.

DEIRDRE SANTESSO

Deirdre Santesso has lived and worked in Northern B.C., the Chilcotin-Cariboo, and the West Kootenays. She currently lives with her husband in Nanoose Bay on Vancouver Island.

CPSIA information can be obtained at www.ICGtesting.com
Printed in the USA
LVOW10s0927290815

452044LV00001B/243/P